THE EPIC OF KINGS
SHAHNAMEH

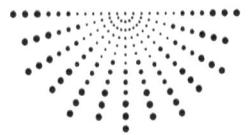

FERDOWSI

Translated by
HELEN ZIMMERN

"The houses that are the dwelling of today will sink beneath shower and sunshine to decay but storm and rain shall never mar the palace that I have built with my poetry."

— FERDOWKI

CONTENTS

The Shahs of Old	7
Feridoun	15
Zal	26
Zal and Rudabeh	31
Rustem	46
The March into Mazinderan	56
Kai Kaous Committeth More Follies	73
Rustem and Sohrab	80
Saiawush	104
The Return of Kai Khosrau	119
Firoud	131
The Vengeance of Kai Khosrau	143
Byzun and Manijeh	150
The Defeat of Afrasiyab	162
The Passing of Kai Khosrau	167
Isfendiyar	178
Rustem and Isfendiyar	185
The Death of Rustem	198

THE SHAHS OF OLD

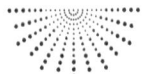

Kaiumers first sat upon the throne of Persia, and was master of the world. He took up his abode in the mountains, and clad himself and his people in tiger-skins, and from him sprang all kindly nurture and the arts of clothing, till then unknown. Men and beasts from all parts of the earth came to do him homage and receive laws at his hands, and his glory was like to the sun. Then Ahriman the Evil, when he saw how the Shah's honour was increased, waxed envious, and sought to usurp the diadem of the world. So he bade his son, a mighty Deev, gather together an army to go out against Kaiumers and his beloved son Saiamuk and destroy them utterly.

Now the Serosch, the angel who defendeth men from the snares of the Deevs, and who each night flieth seven times around the earth that he may watch over the children of Ormuzd, when he learned this, appeared like unto a Peri and warned Kaiumers. So when Saiamuk set forth at the head of his warriors to meet the army of Ahriman, he knew that he was contending against a Deev, and he put forth all his strength. But the Deev was mightier than he, and overcame him, and crushed him under his hands.

When Kaiumers heard the news of mourning, he was bowed to the ground. For a year did he weep without ceasing, and his army wept with him; yea, even the savage beasts and the birds of the air joined in the wailing. And sorrow reigned in the land, and all the world was darkened until the Serosch bade the Shah lift his head and think on vengeance. And

Kaiumers obeyed, and commanded Husheng, the son of Saiamuk, "Take the lead of the army, and march against the Deevs." And the King, by reason of his great age, went in the rear. Now there were in the host Peris; also tigers, lions, wolves, and other fierce creatures, and when the black Deev heard their roaring he trembled for very fear. Neither could he hold himself against them, and Husheng routed him utterly. Then when Kaiumers saw that his well-beloved son was revenged he laid him down to die, and the world was void of him, and Husheng reigned in his stead.

Now Husheng was a wise man and just, and the heavens revolved over his throne forty years. Justice did he spread over the land, and the world was better for his reign. For he first gave to men fire, and showed them how to draw it from out the stone; and he taught them how they might lead the rivers, that they should water the land and make it fertile; and he bade them till and reap. And he divided the beasts and paired them and gave them names. And when he passed to a brighter life he left the world empty of a throne of power. But Tahumers, his son, was not unworthy of his sire. He too opened the eyes of men, and they learned to spin and to weave; and he reigned over the land long and mightily. But of him also were the Deevs right envious, and sought to destroy him. Yet Tahumers overcame them and cast them to earth. Then some craved mercy at his hands, and sware how they would show him an art if he would spare them, and Tahumers listened to their voice. And they taught him the art of writing, and thus from the evil Deevs came a boon upon mankind.

Howbeit when Tahumers had sat upon the golden throne for the space of thirty years he passed away, but his works endured; and Jemshid, his glorious son, whose heart was filled with the counsels of his father, came after him. Now Jemshid reigned over the land seven hundred years girt with might, and Deevs, birds, and Peris obeyed him. And the world was happier for his sake, and he too was glad, and death was unknown among men, neither did they wot of pain or sorrow. And he first parcelled out men into classes; priests, warriors, artificers, and husbandmen did he name them. And the year also he divided into periods. And by aid of the Deevs he raised mighty works, and Persepolis was built by him, that to this day is called Tukht-e-Jemsheed, which being interpreted meaneth the throne of Jemshid. Then, when these things were accomplished, men flocked from all corners of the earth around his throne to do him homage and pour gifts before his face. And Jemshid prepared a feast, and bade them keep it, and called it Neurouz, which is the New Day, and the people of Persia keep it to this hour. And Jemshid's power increased, and the world was at peace, and men beheld in him nought but what was good.

Then it came about that the heart of Jemshid was uplifted in pride, and he forgot whence came his weal and the source of his blessings. He beheld only himself upon the earth, and he named himself God, and sent forth his image to be worshipped. But when he had spoken thus, the Mubids, which are astrologers and wise men, hung their heads in sorrow, and no man knew how he should answer the Shah. And God withdrew his hand from Jemshid, and the kings and the nobles rose up against him, and removed their warriors from his court, and Ahriman had power over the land.

Now there dwelt in the deserts of Arabia a king named Mirtas, generous and just, and he had a son, Zohak, whom he loved. And it came about that Ahriman visited the palace disguised as a noble, and tempted Zohak that he should depart from the paths of virtue. And he spake unto him and said-

"If thou wilt listen to me, and enter into a covenant, I will raise thy head above the sun."

Now the young man was guileless and simple of heart, and he sware unto the Deev that he would obey him in all things. Then Ahriman bade him slay his father, "for this old man," he said, "cumbereth the ground, and while he liveth thou wilt remain unknown." When Zohak heard this he was filled with grief, and would have broken his oath, but Ahriman suffered him not, but made him set a trap for Mirtas. And Zohak and the evil Ahriman held their peace and Mirtas fell into the snare and was killed. Then Zohak placed the crown of Thasis upon his head, and Ahriman taught him the arts of magic, and he ruled over his people in good and evil, for he was not yet wholly given up to guile.

Then Ahriman imagined a device in his black heart. He took upon himself the form of a youth, and craved that he might serve the King as cook. And Zohak, who knew him not, received him well and granted his request, and the keys of the kitchen were given unto him. Now hitherto men had been nourished with herbs, but Ahriman prepared flesh for Zohak. New dishes did he put before him, and the royal favour was accorded to his savory meats. And the flesh gave the King courage and strength like to that of a lion, and he commanded that his cook should be brought before him and ask a boon at his hands. And the cook said-

"If the King take pleasure in his servant, grant that he may kiss his shoulders."

Now Zohak, who feared no evil, granted the request, and Ahriman kissed him on his shoulders. And when he had done so, the ground opened beneath his feet and covered the cook, so that all men present were amazed thereat. But from his kiss sprang hissing serpents, venomous and black; and the King was afraid, and desired that they should be cut off from the root. But as often as the snakes were cut down did they grow again, and in vain the wise men and physicians cast about for a remedy. Then Ahriman came once again disguised as a learned man, and was led before Zohak, and he spake, saying-

"This ill cannot be healed, neither can the serpents be uprooted. Prepare food for them, therefore, that they may be fed, and give unto them for nourishment the brains of men, for perchance this may destroy them."

But in his secret heart Ahriman desired that the world might thus be made desolate; and daily were the serpents fed, and the fear of the King was great in the land. The world withered in his thrall, the customs of good men were forgotten, and the desires of the wicked were accomplished.

Now it was spread abroad in Iran that in the land of Thasis there reigned a man who was mighty and terrible to his foes. Then the kings and nobles who had withdrawn from Jemshid because he had rebelled against God, turned to Zohak and besought him that he would be their ruler, and they proclaimed him Shah. And the armies of Arabia and Persia marched against Jemshid, and he fled before their face. For the space of twice fifty years no man knew whither he was gone, for he hid from the wrath of the Serpent-King. But in the fulness of time he could no longer escape the fury of Zohak, whose servants found him as he wandered on the sea-shore of Cathay, and they sawed him in twain, and sent tidings thereof to their lord. And thus perished the throne and power of Jemshid like unto the grass that withereth, because that he was grown proud, and would have lifted himself above his Maker.

So the beloved of Ahriman, Zohak the Serpent, sat upon the throne of Iran, the kingdom of Light. And he continued to pile evil upon evil till the measure thereof was full to overflowing, and all the land cried out against him. But Zohak and his councillors, the Deevs, shut ear unto this cry, and the Shah reigned thus for the space of a thousand years, and vice stalked in daylight, but virtue was hidden. And despair filled all hearts, for it was as though mankind must perish to still the appetite of those snakes sprung from Evil, for daily were two men slaughtered to satisfy their desire. Neither had Zohak mercy upon any man. And darkness was spread over the land because of his wickedness.

But Ormuzd saw it and was moved with compassion for his people, and he declared they should no longer suffer for the sin of Jemshid. And he caused a grandson to be born to Jemshid, and his parents called him Feridoun.

Now it befell that when he was born, Zohak dreamed he beheld a youth slender like to a cypress, and he came towards him bearing a cow-headed mace, and with it he struck Zohak to the ground. Then the tyrant awoke and trembled, and called for his Mubids, that they should interpret to him this dream. And they were troubled, for they foresaw danger, and he menaced them if they foretold him evil. And they were silent for fear three days, but on the fourth one who had courage spake and said-

"There will arise one named Feridoun, who shall inherit thy throne and reverse thy fortunes, and strike thee down with a cow-headed mace."

When Zohak heard these words he swooned, and the Mubids fled before his wrath. But when he had recovered he bade the world be scoured for Feridoun. And henceforth Zohak was consumed for bitterness of spirit, and he knew neither rest nor joy.

Now it came about that the mother of Feridoun feared lest the Shah should destroy the child if he learned that he was sprung from Jemshid's race. So she hid him in the thick forest where dwelt the wondrous cow Purmaieh, whose hairs were like unto the plumes of a peacock for beauty. And she prayed the guardian of Purmaieh to have a care of her son, and for three years he was reared in the wood, and Purmaieh was his nurse. But when the time was accomplished the mother knew that news of Purmaieh had reached the ears of Zohak, and she feared he would find her son. Therefore she took him far into Ind, to a pious hermit who dwelt on the Mount Alberz. And she prayed the hermit to guard her boy, who was destined for mighty deeds. And the hermit granted her request. And it befell that while she sojourned with him Zohak had found the beauteous Purmaieh and learned of Feridoun, and when he heard that the boy was fled he was like unto a mad elephant in his fury. He slew the wondrous cow and all the living things round about, and made the forest a desert. Then he continued his search, but neither tidings nor sight could he get of Feridoun, and his heart was filled with anguish.

In this year Zohak caused his army to be strengthened, and he demanded of his people that they should certify that he had ever been to them a just and noble king. And they obeyed for very fear. But while they sware there arose without the doorway of the Shah the cry of one who demanded justice. And Zohak commanded that he should be brought in, and the man stood before the assembly of the nobles.

Then Zohak opened his mouth and said, "I charge thee give a name unto him who hath done thee wrong."

And the man, when he saw it was the Shah who questioned him, smote his head with his hands. But he answered and said-

"I am Kawah, a blacksmith and a blameless man, and I sue for justice, and it is against thee, O King, that I cry out. Seventeen fair sons have I called mine, yet only one remaineth to me, for that his brethren were slain to still the hunger of thy serpents, and now they have taken from me this last child also. I pray thee spare him unto me, nor heap thy cruelties upon the land past bearing."

And the Shah feared Kawah's wrath, beholding that it was great, and he granted him the life of his son and sought to win him with soft words. Then he prayed him that he would also sign the testimony that Zohak was a just and noble king.

But Kawah cried, "Not so, thou wicked and ignoble man, ally of Deevs, I will not lend my hand unto this lie," and he seized the declaration and tore it into fragments and scattered them into the air. And when he had done so he strode forth from the palace, and all the nobles and people were astonished, so that none dared uplift a finger to restrain him. Then Kawah went to the market-place and related to the people all that which he had seen, and recalled to them the evil deeds of Zohak and the wrongs they had suffered at his hands. And he provoked them to shake off the yoke of Ahriman. And taking off the leathern apron wherewith blacksmiths cover their knees when they strike with the hammer, he raised it aloft upon the point of a lance and cried-

"Be this our banner to march forth and seek out Feridoun and entreat him that he deliver us from out the hands of the Serpent-King."

Then the people set up a shout of joy and gathered themselves round Kawah, and he led them out of the city bearing aloft his standard. And they marched thus for many days unto the palace of Feridoun.

Now these things came about in the land of Iran after twice eight years were passed over the head of Feridoun. And when that time was accomplished, he descended from the Mount Alberz and sought out his mother, questioning her of his lineage. And she told him how that he was sprung from the race of Jemshid, and also of Zohak and of his evil deeds.

Then said Feridoun, "I will uproot this monster from the earth, and his palace will I raze to the dust."

But his mother spake, and said, "Not so, my son, let not thine youthful anger betray thee; for how canst thou stand against all the world?"

Yet not long did she suffer the hard task to hinder him, for soon a mighty crowd came towards the palace led by one who bare an apron uplifted upon a lance. Then Feridoun knew that succour was come unto him. And when he had listened to Kawah, he came into the presence of his mother with the helmet of kings upon his head, and he said unto her-

"Mother, I go to the wars, and it remaineth for thee to pray God for my safety."

Then he caused a mighty club to be made for him, and he traced the pattern thereof upon the ground, and the top thereof was the head of a cow, in memory of Purmaieh, his nurse. Then he cased the standard of Kawah in rich brocades of Roum, and hung jewels upon it. And when all was made ready, they set forth towards the West to seek out Zohak, for, they knew not that he was gone to Ind in search of Feridoun. Now when they were come to Bagdad, which is upon the banks of the Tigris, they halted, and Feridoun bade the guardians of the flood convey them across. But these refused, saying, the King bade that none should pass save only those who bore the royal seal. When Feridoun heard these words he was wroth, and he regarded not the rushing river nor the dangers hidden within its floods. He girded his loins and plunged with his steed into the waters, and all the army followed after him. Now they struggled sore with the rushing stream, and it seemed as though the waves would bear them down. But their brave horses overcame all dangers, and they stepped in safety upon the shore. Then they turned their faces towards the city which is now called Jerusalem, for here stood the glorious house that Zohak had builded. And when they had entered the city all the people rallied round Feridoun, for they hated Zohak and looked to Feridoun to deliver them. And he slew the Deevs that held the palace, and cast down the evil talisman that was graven upon the walls. Then he mounted the throne of the idolater and placed the crown of Iran upon his head, and all the people bowed down before him and called him Shah.

Now when Zohak returned from his search after Feridoun and learned that he was seated upon his throne, he encompassed the city with his host. But the army of Feridoun marched against him, and the desires of the people went with them. And all that day bricks fell from the walls and stones from the terraces, and it rained arrows and spears like to hail falling from a dark cloud, until Feridoun had overcome the might of Zohak. Then Feridoun raised his cow-headed mace to slay the Serpent-King. But the blessed Serosch swooped down, and cried-

"Not so, strike not, for Zohak's hour is not yet come."

Then the Serosch bade the Shah bind the usurper and carry him far from the haunts of men, and there fasten him to a rock. And Feridoun did as he was bidden, and led forth Zohak to the Mount Demawend. And he bound him to the rock with mighty chains and nails driven into his hands, and left him to perish in agony. And the hot sun shone down upon the barren cliffs, and there was neither tree nor shrub to shelter him, and the chains entered into his flesh, and his tongue was consumed with thirst. Thus after a while the earth was delivered of Zohak the evil one, and Feridoun reigned in his stead.

FERIDOUN

Five hundred years did Feridoun rule the world, and might and virtue increased in the land, and all his days he did that which was good. And he roamed throughout the kingdom to seek out that which was open and that which was hid, and wrong was righted at his hands. With kindness did he curb the sway of evil. He ordered the world like to a paradise, he planted the cypress and the rose where the wild herb had sprouted.

Now after many years were passed there were born to him three sons, whose mother was of the house of Jemshid. And the sons were fair of mien, tall and strong, yet their names were not known to men, for Feridoun had not tested their hearts. But when he beheld that they were come to years of strength he called them about his throne and bade them search out the King of Yemen, who had three daughters, fair as the moon, that they should woo them unto themselves. And the sons of Feridoun did according to the command of their father. They set forth unto Yemen, and there went with them a host countless as the stars. And when they were come to Yemen, the King came forth to greet them, and his train was like to the plumage of a pheasant. Then the sons of Feridoun gained the hands of the daughters of Serv, King of Yemen, and departed with them to their own land. And Serv gave to his new sons much treasure laid upon the backs of camels, and umbrellas too did he give unto them in sign of kingship.

Now it came about that when Feridoun learned that his sons were

FERDOWSI

returning, he went forth to meet them and prove their hearts. So he took upon him the form of a dragon that foamed at the mouth with fury, and from whose jaws sprang mighty flames. And when his sons were come near unto the mountain pass, he came upon them suddenly, like to a whirlwind, and raised a cloud of dust about the place with his writhings, and his roaring filled the air with noise. Then he threw himself upon the eldest born, and the prince laid down his spear and said, "A wise and prudent man striveth not with dragons." And he turned his back and fled before the monster, and left him to fall upon his brothers. Then the dragon sprang upon the second, and he said, "An it be that I must fight, what matter if it be a furious lion or a knight full of valour?" So he took his bow and stretched it. But the youngest came towards him, and seeing the dragon, said, "Thou reptile, flee from our presence, and strut not in the path of lions. For if thou hast heard the name of Feridoun, beware how thou doest thus, for we are his sons, armed with spears and ready for the fight. Quit therefore, I counsel thee, thine evil path, lest I plant upon thy head the crown of enmity."

Then the glorious Feridoun, when he had thus made trial of their hearts, vanished from their sight. But presently he came again with the face of their father, and many warriors, elephants, and cymbals were in his train. And Feridoun bore in his hand the cow-headed mace, and the Kawanee, the apron of Kawah, the kingly standard, was waved above his head. Now when the sons saw their father, they alighted from their steeds and ran to greet him, and kissed the ground before his feet. And the cymbals were clashed, and the trumpets brayed, and sounds of rejoicing were heard around. Then Feridoun raised his sons and kissed their foreheads, and gave unto them honour according to their due. And when they were come to the royal house he prayed to God that He would bless his offspring, and calling them about him, he seated them upon thrones of splendour. Then he opened his mouth and said unto them-

"O my sons, listen unto the words that I shall speak. The raging dragon whose breath was danger was but your father, who sought to test your hearts, and having learned them gave way with joy. But now will I give to you names such as are fitting unto men. The first-born shall be called Silim (may thy desires be accomplished in the world!) for thou soughtest to save thyself from the clutches of the dragon, nor didst thou hesitate in the hour of flight. A man who fleeth neither before an elephant nor a lion, call him rather foolhardy than brave. And the second, who from the beginning showed his courage, which was ardent as a flame, I will call him Tur, the courageous, whom even a mad elephant cannot daunt. But the youngest is a man prudent and brave, who knoweth both how to haste and how to tarry; he chose the midway between the flame and the ground, as it beseemeth a man of counsel, and he hath proven himself brave, prudent, and bold. Irij shall he be called, that the gate of power may be his goal, for first did he show gentleness, but his bravery sprang forth at the hour of danger."

When Feridoun had thus opened his lips he called for the book wherein are written the stars, and he searched for the planets of his sons. And he found that Jupiter reigned in the sign of the Archer in the house of Silim, and the sun in the Lion in that of Tur, but in the house of Irij there reigned the moon in the Scorpion. And when he saw this he was sorrowful, for he knew that for Irij were grief and bale held in store. Then having read the secrets of Fate, Feridoun parted the world and gave the three parts unto his sons in suzerainty. Roum and Khaver, which are the lands of the setting sun, did he give unto Silim. Turan and Turkestan did he give unto Tur, and made him master of the Turks and of China, but unto Irij he gave Iran, with the throne of might and the crown of supremacy.

For many years had the sons of Feridoun sat upon their golden thrones in happiness and peace, but evil was hidden in the bosom of Fate. For Feridoun had grown old, and his strength inclined to the grave. And as his life waned, the evil passions of his sons waxed stronger. The heart of Silim was changed, and his desires turned towards evil; his soul also was steeped in greed. And he pondered in his spirit the parting of the lands, and he revolted thereat in his thoughts, because that the youngest bore the crown of supremacy. Then he bade a messenger mount him upon a dromedary swift of foot, and bear this saying unto Tur-

"O King of Turan, thy brother greeteth thee, and may thy days be long in the land. Tell unto me, I pray thee, for thou hast might and wisdom, should we remain thus ever satisfied, for surely unto us, not unto Irij, pertaineth the throne of Iran, but now is our brother set above our heads, and should we not strive against the injustice of our father?"

Now. when Tur had listened to these words, his head was filled with wind, and he spake unto the messenger and said-

"Say unto your master, O my brother, full of courage, since our father deceived us when we were young and void of guile, with his own hands hath he planted a tree whence must issue fruit of blood and leaves that are poison. Let us therefore meet and take counsel together how we may rid us of our evil fate."

When Silim heard this he set forth from Roum, and Tur also quitted China, and they met to counsel together how they should act. Then they sent a messenger unto Feridoun the glorious, and they said-

"O King, aged and great, fearest thou not to go home unto thy God? for evil hast thou done, and injustice dost thou leave behind thee. Thy realm hast thou allotted with iniquity, and thine eldest born hast thou treated with disfavour. But we thy sons entreat thee that ere it be too late thou listen to our voice. Command thou Irij to step down from the throne of Iran, and hide him in some corner of the earth, that he be weak and forgotten like ourselves. Yet if thou doest not our bidding, we will bring forth riders from Turkestan and Khaver filled with vengeance, and will utterly destroy Irij and the land of Iran."

When Feridoun had listened to these hard words he was angered, and straightway said-

"Speak unto these men, senseless and impure, these sons of Ahriman, perverse of heart, and say unto them, Feridoun rejoiceth that ye have laid bare before him your hearts, for now he knoweth what manner of men ye are. And he answereth unto you that he hath parted his realm with equity. Many counsellors did he seek, and night and day did they ponder it, and gave unto each that which seemed best in their sight. And he now speaketh unto you a word that he doth bid you treasure in your hearts, As ye sow, so also shall ye reap, for there is for us another, an eternal home. And this is the rede sent unto you by an aged man, that he who betrayeth his brother for greed is not worthy to be sprung from a noble race. So pray unto God that He turn your hearts from evil."

When the messenger had heard these words he departed. Then Feridoun called Irij before him and warned him against the craft of his brethren, and bade him prepare an army and go forth to meet them. But Irij, when he had heard of the evil thoughts of his brothers, was moved, and said-

"Not so, O my father, suffer that I go forth alone and speak unto my brethren, that I may still the anger that they feel against me. And I will entreat them that they put not their trust in the glory of this world, and will recall unto them the name of Jemshid, and how that his end was evil because that he was uplifted in his heart."

Then Feridoun answered and said, "Go forth, my son, if such be thy desire. The wish of thy brethren is even unto war, but thou seekest the paths of peace. Yet I pray thee take with thee worthy knights, and return unto me with speed, for my life is rooted in thy happiness."

And he gave him a letter signed with his royal seal that he should bear it unto the kings of Roum and China. And Feridoun wrote how that he was old, and desired neither gold nor treasures, save only that his sons should be united. And he commended unto them his youngest born, who was descended from his throne and come forth to meet them with peace in his heart.

Now when Irij was come to the spot where his brethren were encamped, the army saw him and was filled with wonder at his beauty and at his kingly form, and they murmured among themselves, saying, "Surely this one alone is worthy to bear the sceptre." But when Silim and Tur heard this murmur their anger was deepened, and they retreated into their tents, and all night long did they hold counsel how they might do hurt unto their brother.

Now when the curtain that hid the sun was lifted, the brethren went forth unto the tents of Irij. And Irij would have greeted them, but they suffered him not, but straightway began to question him, and heap reproaches upon his head. And Tur said-

"Why hast thou uplifted thyself above us, and is it meet that thy elders bow down before thee?"

When Irij heard their words, he answered, "O Kings greedy of power, I say unto you, if ye desire happiness, strive after peace. I covet neither the royal crown nor the hosts of Iran; power that endeth in discord is an honour that leadeth to tears. And I will step down from the throne of Iran if it shall foster peace between us, for I crave not the possession of the world if ye are afflicted by the sight. For I am humble of heart, and my faith bids me be kind."

Now Tur heard these words, but they softened not his spirit, for he knew only that which is evil, and wist not that Irij spoke truly. And he took up the chair whereon he sat and threw it at his brother in his anger. Then Irij called for mercy at his hands, saying-

"O King, hast thou no fear of God, no pity for thy father? I pray thee destroy me not, lest God ask vengeance for my blood. Let it not be spoken that thou who hast life takest that gift from others. Do not this evil. Crush not even the tiny ant that beareth a grain of corn, for she hath life, and sweet life is a boon. I will vanish from thy sight, I will live in solitude and secrecy, so thou grant that I may yet behold the sun."

But these words angered Tur only the more, and he drew from his boot a dagger that was poisoned and sharp, and he thrust it into the breast of Irij, the kingly cedar. And the young lord of the world paled and was dead. Then Tur cut the head from the trunk, and filled it with musk and ambergris, and sent it unto the old man his father, who had parted the world, saying-

"Behold the head of thy darling, give unto him now the crown and the throne."

And when they had done this evil deed the brethren furled their tents, and turned them back again unto the lands of Roum and Cathay.

Now Feridoun held his eyes fastened upon the road whither Irij was gone, and his heart yearned after him. And when he heard that the time of his return was come, he bade a host go forth to meet him, and he himself went in the wake. Now when they were gone but a little way they beheld a mighty cloud of dust upon the sky. And the cloud neared, and there came thence a dromedary whereon was seated a knight clad in the garb of woe. And he bare in his arms a casket of gold, and in the casket were rich stuffs of silk, and in the stuffs was wrapped the head of Irij. And when Feridoun beheld the face of the messenger his heart was smote with fear, but when he saw the head of his son he fell from his horse with sorrow. Then a cry of wailing rent the air, and the army shouted for grief, and the flags were torn, and the drums broken, and the elephants and cymbals hung with the colours of mourning, because that Irij was gone from the world. And Feridoun returned on foot unto the city, and all the nobles went with him, and they retraced their steps in the dust. Now when they were come to the garden of Irij, Feridoun faltered in his sorrow, and he pressed the head of the young King, his son, unto his breast. And he cast black earth upon his throne, and tore his hair, and shed tears, and his cries mounted even unto the seventh sphere. And he spake in his grief and said-

"O Master of the world, that metest out justice, look down, I pray thee, upon this innocent whom his brethren have foully murdered! Sear their hearts that joy cannot enter, and grant unto me my prayer. Suffer that I may live until a hero, a warrior mighty to avenge, be sprung from the seed of Irij. Then when I shall have beheld his face I will go hence as it beseemeth me and the earth shall cover my body."

Thus wept Feridoun in the bitterness of his soul, neither would he take comfort day and night, nor quit the garden of his son. And the earth was his couch and the dust his bed, and he watered the ground with his tears.

And he rested in this spot till that the grass was grown above his bosom, and his eyes were blinded with weeping. Yet his tongue did not cease from plaining and his heart from sorrow. And he cried continually-

"O Irij, O my son, my son, never prince died a death like thine! Thy head was severed by Ahriman, thy body torn by lions."

Thus mourned Feridoun, and the voice of lamentation was abroad.

Then it came about that after many years had passed Feridoun bethought him of the daughter of Irij, and how that men said she was fair. And he sought for her in the house of the women; and when he learned that she was fair indeed, he desired that a husband be found for her, and he wedded her unto Pescheng, who was a hero of the race of Jemshid. And there was born unto them a son fair and strong, worthy the throne. And when he was yet but a tender babe they brought him to Feridoun and cried-

"O Lord of earth, let thy soul rejoice, behold this Irij!"

Then the lips of Feridoun were wreathed with smiles, and he took up the infant in his arms and cried unto God, saying-

"O God, grant that my sight be restored unto me, that I may behold the face of this babe."

And as he prayed his eyes were opened, and his sight rested upon his son. Then Feridoun gave thanks unto God. And he called down blessings upon the child, and prayed that the day might be blessed also, and the heart of his enemies be torn with anguish. And he named him Minuchihr, saying, "A branch worthy of a noble stock hath borne fruit." And the child was reared in the house of Feridoun, and he suffered not that ill came near unto him, and though the years passed above his head the stars brought him no evil. And when he was of a ripe age Feridoun gave to Minuchihr a throne of gold, and a mace, and a crown of jewels, and the key to all his treasures. Then he commanded his nobles that they should do him reverence and salute him king. And there were gathered about the throne Karun, the son of Kawah, and Serv, King of Yemen, and Guerschasp the victorious, and many other mighty princes more than tongue can name. But the young Shah outshone them in strength and beauty, and joy was once more in the land.

But tidings of the splendour that surrounded Feridoun pierced even unto the lands of Roum and China, and the kings thereof were troubled and downcast in their hearts. Then they conferred how they should regain the favour of the Shah, for they feared Minuchihr when he should be come unto years of might. So they sent a messenger unto Feridoun bearing rich gifts, and bade him speak unto their father and say-

"O Shah, live for ever I bear a message from the humblest of thy slaves, who are bowed unto the earth with contrition, wherefore they have not ventured into thy presence. And they pray that thou pardon their evil deed, for their hearts are good, and they did it not of themselves, but because it was written that they should do this wrong, and that which is written in the stars surely it is accomplished. And therefore, O King, their eyes are filled with tears, and they pray thee incline unto them thine ear. And as a sign of thy grace send unto them Minuchihr thy son, for their hearts yearn to look upon his face and do him homage."

Now when Feridoun had listened to the words of his sons, he knitted his brows in anger, for he knew that they sought only to beguile him. And he said unto the messenger-

"Go, say unto your masters that their false-hearted words shall avail them nothing. And ask them if they be not shamed to utter white words with tongues of blackness. I have heard their message, hear now the answer that I send. Ye say unto me that ye desire the love of Minuchihr, and I ask of you, What did ye for Irij? And now that ye are delivered of him ye seek the blood of his son. Verily I say unto you, never shall ye look upon his face save when he leadeth a mighty army. Then shall be watered with blood the leaves and fruits of the tree sprung from the vengeance that is due. For unto this day hath vengeance slumbered, since it became me not to stretch forth mine hand in battle upon my sons; but now is there sprung a branch from the tree which the enemy uprooted, and he shall come as a raging lion, girt with the vengeance of his sire. And I say unto you, take back the treasures ye have sent me, for think ye that for coloured toys I will abandon my vengeance, and efface for baubles the blood that ye have spilled, or sell for gold the head of mine offspring? And say yet again that while the father of Irij lives he will not abandon his intent. And now that thou hast listened unto my message, lay it up in thy heart and make haste from hence."

When the messenger had heard these words he departed with speed. And when he was come unto Silim and Tur he told them thereof, and how he had seen Minuchihr sitting upon a throne of gold, and how for strength he was like unto Tahumers, who had bound the Deevs. And he told how heroes bearing names that filled the world with wonder stood round about him, Kawah the smith, and Karun his son, and Serv, the King of Yemen, and next in might unto the Shah was Saum, the son of Neriman, the unvanquished in fight, and Guerschasp the victorious, his treasurer. Then he spake of the treasures that filled the house of Feridoun, and of the army great in number, so that the men of Roum and China could not stand against them. And he told how their hearts were filled with hatred of the Kings because of Irij.

The Kings, when they heard this and the message of their father, trembled for fear. And Tur said unto Silim-

"Henceforth we must forego pleasure, for it behoveth us to hasten, and not tarry till the teeth of this young lion be sharpened, and he be waxed tall and strong."

Then they made ready their armies, and the number of their men was past the counting. Helmet was joined to helmet, and spear to spear, and jewels, baggage, and elephants without number went with them, and you would have said it was a host that none could understand. And they marched from Turan into Iran, and the two Kings rode before them, their hearts filled with hate. But the star of these evil ones was sinking. For Feridoun, when he learned that an army had crossed the Jihun, called unto him Minuchihr his son, and bade him place himself at the head of the warriors. And the host of the Shah was mighty to behold, great and strong, and it covered the land like unto a cloud of locusts. And they marched from Temmische unto the desert, and Minuchihr commanded them with might. And on his right rode Karun the Avenger, and on his left Saum, the son of Neriman, and above their heads waved the flag of Kawah, and their armour glistened in the sun. Like as a lion breaketh forth from the jungle to seize upon his prey, so did this army rush forth to avenge the death of Irij. And the head of Minuchihr rose above the rest like to the moon or the sun when it shineth above the mountains. And he exhorted them in words of fire that they rest not, neither weary, until they should have broken the power of these sons of Ahriman.

Now Tur and Silim, when they saw that the Iranians were come out against them, set in order their army. And when the day had torn asunder the folds of night, the two armies met in battle, and the fight waged strong until the setting of the sun. And the earth was a sea of blood, and the feet of the elephants were like to pillars of coral. And when the sun was sunk to his rest, Tur and Silim consulted how they might seize upon Minuchihr by fraud, for they saw that his arm was strong and his courage undaunted. So Tur set forth at the head of a small band to surprise him in his tents. But Minuchihr was aware of his evil plans, and sprang upon him. And when Tur would have fled Minuchihr followed after him and struck a lance into his back. And when he had killed him he cut his head from his trunk, and the body did he give unto the wild beasts, but the head he sent to Feridoun. And he wrote to him and sent him greeting, and told him all that was come about, and how he should neither rest nor tarry until the death of Irij be avenged.

Now Silim, when he learned the fate of his brother, was sore afraid, and cast about him for an ally. And there came unto him Kakoui, of the seed of Zohak. But Minuchihr wrestled with him for a morning's space and overcame him also, though the Deev was strong and powerful in fight. Then Silim was cast down yet more, and he sought to hide him by the seashore. But Minuchihr cut off his path and overtook him, and with his own hand he slew him, and cut his head from his trunk. And he raised the head upon his lance. And when the army of Silim saw this they fled into the hills, and vanished like cattle whom the snow hath driven from their pasture. Then they took counsel and chose out a man from among their midst, one that was prudent and gentle of speech. And they bade him go before the Shah and say-

"Have mercy upon us, O Shah, for neither hate nor vengeance drove us forth against thee, but only this, that we obeyed the wills of our lords. But we ourselves are peaceful men, tillers of the earth and keepers of cattle, and we pray thee that thou let us return in safety whence we are come. And we acknowledge thee our Shah, and we pray thee make thy servants acquainted with thy desires."

When Minuchihr had heard these words he spake and said-

"My desire is not after these men, neither is my longing after blood but mercy. Let every man lay down his arms and go his ways, and let peace be in the land, and joy wait upon your feet."

When the men heard this they praised the Shah, and called down blessings upon his head. And they came before him, every man bearing his armour and the weapons of battle. And they laid them at his feet, and of weapons there was reared a mighty mountain, and the blue steel glistened in the sun. Then Minuchihr dismissed them graciously. And when the army was dispersed he sent a messenger unto Feridoun bearing the head of Silim and a writing. And when he had ordered all things he set out at the head of his warriors unto the city of Feridoun. And his grandsire came forth to meet him, and there came with him many elephants swathed in gold, and warriors arrayed in rich attire, and a large multitude clad in garments of bright hue. And flags waved above them, and trumpets brayed, and cymbals clashed, and sounds of rejoicing filled the air. But when Minuchihr saw that his grandsire came towards him, he got from his horse and ran to meet him, and fell at his feet and craved his blessing. And Feridoun blessed Minuchihr and raised him from the dust. And he bade him sit again upon his horse and took his hand, and they entered the city in triumph. And when they were come to the King's house, Feridoun seated Minuchihr upon a throne of gold. Then he called unto him Saum, the son of Neriman, and said-

"I pray thee bring up this youth and nourish him for the kingdom, and aid him with thy might and mind."

And he took the hand of Minuchihr and put it into that of Saum, and said-

"Thanks be unto God the merciful, who hath listened unto my voice, and granted the desires of His servant. For now shall I go hence, and the world will I cumber no more."

Then when he had given gifts unto his servants he withdrew into solitude, and gazed without cease upon the heads of his sons, neither refrained he from bewailing their evil fate, and the sorrow they had brought upon him. And daily he grew fainter, and at last the light of his life expired, and Feridoun vanished from the earth, but his name remained behind him. And Minuchihr mourned for his grandsire with weeping and lamentation, and raised above him a stately tomb. But when the seven days of mourning were ended, he put upon his head the crown of the Kaianides, and girt his loins with a red sash of might. And the nation called him Shah, and he was beloved in the land.

ZAL

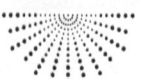

Seistan, which is to the south of Iran, was ruled by Saum, the Pehliva, girt with might and glory, and, but for the grief that he was childless, his days were happy. Then it came to pass that a son was born unto him, beautiful of face and limb, who had neither fault nor blemish save that his hair was like unto that of an aged man. Now the women were afraid to tell Saum, lest he be wroth when he should learn that his child was thus set apart from his fellow-men. So the infant had gazed upon the light eight days ere he knew thereof. Then a woman, brave above the rest, ventured into his presence. She bowed herself unto the dust and craved of Saum the boon of speech. And he suffered her, and she spake, saying-

"May the Lord keep and guard thee. May thine enemies be utterly destroyed. May the days of Saum the hero be happy. For the Almighty hath accomplished his desire. He hath given to him an heir, a son is born unto the mighty warrior behind the curtains of his house, a moon-faced boy, beautiful of face and limb, in whom there is neither fault nor blemish, save that his hair is like unto that of an aged man. I beseech thee, O my master, bethink thee that this gift is from God, nor give place in thine heart to ingratitude."

When Saum had listened to her words he arose and went unto the house of the women. And he beheld the babe that was beautiful of face and limb, but whose head was like unto that of an aged man. Then Saum, fearing the jeers of his enemies, quitted the paths of wisdom. He lifted his head unto heaven and murmured against the Lord of Destiny, and cried, saying-

"O thou eternally just and good, O source of happiness, incline thine ear unto me and listen to my voice. If I have sinned, if I have strayed in the paths of Ahriman, behold my repentance and pardon me. My soul is ashamed, my heart is angered for reason of this child, for will not the nobles say this boy presageth evil? They will hold me up to shame, and what can I reply to their questions? It behoveth me to remove this stain, that the land of Iran be not accursed."

Thus spake Saum in his anger, railing against fate, and he commanded his servants to take the child and cast it forth out of the land.

Now there standeth far from the haunts of men the Mount Alberz, whose head toucheth the stars, and never had mortal foot been planted upon its crest. And upon it had the Simurgh, the bird of marvel, builded her nest. Of ebony and of sandal-wood did she build it, and twined it with aloes, so that it was like unto a king's house, and the evil sway of Saturn could not reach thereto. And at the foot of this mount was laid the child of Saum. Then the Simurgh, when she spied the infant lying upon the ground, bereft of clothes and wherewithal to nourish it, sucking its fingers for very hunger, darted to earth and raised him in her talons. And she bare him unto her nest, that her young might devour him. But when she had brought him her heart was stirred within her for compassion. Therefore she bade her young ones spare the babe and treat him like to a brother. Then she chose out tender flesh to feed her guest, and tended the infant forsaken of his sire. And thus did the Simurgh, nor ever wearied till that moons and years had rolled above their heads, and the babe was grown to be a youth full of strength and beauty. And his renown filled the land, for neither good nor evil can be hidden for ever. And his fame spread even unto the ears of Saum, the son of Neriman.

Then it came to pass that Saum dreamed a dream, wherein he beheld a man riding towards him mounted upon an Arab steed. And the man gave him tidings of his son, and taunted him, saying-

"O thou who hast offended against every duty, who disownest thy son because that his hair is white, though thine own resembleth the silver poplar, and to whom a bird seemeth fit nurse for thine offspring, wilt thou abjure all kinship with him for ever?"

Now when Saum awoke he remembered his dream, and fear came upon him for his sin. And he called unto him his Mubids, and questioned them concerning the stripling of the Mount Alberz, and whether this could be indeed his son, for surely frosts and heat must long since have destroyed him. Then the Mubids answered and said—

"Not so, thou most ungrateful unto God, thou more cruel than the lion, the tiger, and the crocodile, for even savage beasts tend their young, whilst thou didst reject thine own, because thou heldest the white hair given unto him by his Creator for a reproach in the sight of men. O faint of heart, arise and seek thy child, for surely one whom God hath blessed can never perish. And turn thou unto him and pray that he forgive thee."

When Saum had heard these words he was contrite, and called about him his army and set forth unto the mountains. And when they were come unto the mount that is raised up to the Pleiades, Saum beheld the Simurgh and the nest, and a stripling that was like unto himself walking around it. And his desire to get unto him was great, but he strove in vain to scale the crest. Then Saum called upon God in his humility. And God heard him, and put it into the heart of the Simurgh to look down and behold the warrior and the army that was with him. And when she had seen Saum she knew wherefore the chief was come, and she spake and said—

"O thou who hast shared this nest, I have reared thee and been to thee a mother, for thy father cast thee out; the hour is come to part us, and I must give thee again unto thy people. For thy father is Saum the hero, the Pehliva of the world, greatest among the great, and he is come hither to seek his son, and splendour awaiteth thee beside him."

When the youth had heard her words his eyes were filled with tears and his heart with sorrow, for he had never gazed upon men, though he had learned their speech. And he said—

"Art thou then weary of me, or am I no longer fit to be thy housefellow? See, thy nest is unto me a throne, thy sheltering wings a parent. To thee I owe all that I am, for thou wast my friend in need."

And the Simurgh answered him saying, "I do not send thee away for enmity, O my son; nay, I would keep thee beside me for ever, but another destiny is better for thee. When thou shalt have seen the throne and its pomp my nest will sink in thine esteem. Go forth, therefore, my son, and try thy fortune in the world. But that thou mayst remember thy nurse who shielded thee, and reared thee amid her little ones, that thou mayst remain under the shadow of her wings, bear with thee this feather from her breast. And in the day of thy need cast it into the fire, and I will come like unto a cloud and deliver thee from danger."

Thus she spake, and raised him in her talons and bore him to the spot where Saum was bowed to the dust in penitence. Now when Saum beheld his son, whose body was like unto an elephant's for strength and beauty, he bent low before the Simurgh and covered her with benison. And he cried out and said-

"O Shah of birds, O bird of God, who confoundest the wicked, mayst thou be great for ever."

But while he yet spake the Simurgh flew upwards, and the gaze of Saum was fixed upon his son. And as he looked he saw that he was worthy of the throne, and that there was neither fault nor blemish in him, save only his silvery locks. Then his heart rejoiced within him, and he blessed him, and entreated his forgiveness. And he said-

"O my son, open thine heart unto the meanest of God's servants, and I swear unto thee, in the presence of Him that made us, that never again will I harden my heart towards thee, and that I will grant unto thee all thy desires."

Then he clothed him in rich robes and named him Zal, which being interpreted meaneth the aged. And he showed him unto the army. And when they had looked on the youth they saw that he was goodly of visage and of limb, and they shouted for very joy. Then the host made them ready to return unto Seistan. And the kettle-drummers rode at their head, mounted upon mighty elephants whose feet raised a cloud of dust that rose unto the sky. And the tabors were beat, and the trumpets brayed, and the cymbals clashed, and sounds of rejoicing filled the land because that Saum had found his son, and that Zal was a hero among men.

Now the news spread even unto Minuchihr that Saum was returning from the mountains with great pomp and joy. And when he had heard it he bade Nuder go forth to meet the Pehliva and bid him bring Zal unto the court. And when Saum heard the desires of his master he obeyed and came within his gates. Then he beheld the Shah seated upon the throne of the Kaianides, bearing his crown upon his head, and on his right hand sat Karun the Pehliva, and he bade Saum be seated on his left. And the Shah commanded Saum that he should speak. Then Saum unbosomed himself before the Shah and spake concerning his son, neither did he hide his evil deed. And Minuchihr commanded that Zal be brought before him. So the chamberlains brought him into the presence of the King, and he was clad in robes of splendour, and the King was amazed at his aspect. And he turned and said unto Saum-

"O Pehliva of the world, the Shah enjoineth you have a care of this noble youth, and guard him for the land of Iran. And teach him forthwith the arts of war, and the pleasures and customs of the banquet, for how should one that hath been reared in a nest be familiar with our ways?

Then the Shah bade the Mubids cast Zal's horoscope, and they read that he would be a brave and prudent knight. Now when he had heard this the Pehliva was relieved of all his fears, and the Shah rejoiced and covered Saum with gifts. Arab horses did he give unto him with golden saddles, Indian swords in scabbards of gold, brocades of Roum, skins of beasts, and carpets of Ind, and the rubies and pearls were past the numbering. And slaves poured musk and amber before him. And Minuchihr also granted to Saum a throne, and a crown and a girdle of gold, and he named him ruler of all the lands that stretch from the Sea of China to that of Sind, from Zaboulistan to the Caspian. Then he bade that the Pehliva's horse be led forth, and sent him away from his presence. And Saum called down blessings upon the Shah, and turned his face towards home. And his train followed after him, and the sound of music went before them.

Then when the tidings came to Seistan that the great hero was drawing nigh, the city decked itself in festive garbs, and every man called down the blessings of Heaven upon Zal, the son of Saum, and poured gifts at his feet. And there was joy in all the land for that Saum had taken back his son.

Now Saum forthwith called about him his Mubids, and bade them instruct the youth in all the virtues of a king.

And daily Zal increased in wisdom and strength, and his fame filled the land. And when Saum went forth to fight the battles of the Shah, he left the kingdom under his hands, and Zal administered it with judgment and virtue.

ZAL AND RUDABEH

*A*non it came about that Zal desired to see the kingdom. And he set forth, and there followed after him a goodly train, and when they had journeyed a while they marched with pomp into Cabul. Now Mihrab, who was descended from Zohak the Serpent, reigned in Cabul, yet he was worthy, prudent, and wise. When he heard that the son of Saum, to whom he paid tribute, drew nigh unto the city, he went out to meet him, and his nobles went with him, and slaves bearing costly gifts. And Zal, hearing that Mihrab was at hand, prepared a feast in his tents, and Mihrab and his train feasted with him until the night was far spent. Now, after the King was gone, Zal praised his beauty. Then a noble rose up and said unto him-

"O Zal, thou knowest not beauty since thou hast not beheld the daughter of this man. For she is like unto the slender cypress, her face is brighter than the sun, her mouth is a pomegranate flower."

When Zal heard these words he was filled with longing, and sleep would not visit his eyelids for thinking of her beauty.

Now, when the day dawned, he opened the doors of his court, and the nobles stood about him, each man according to his rank. And presently there came from Cabul Mihrab the King to tender morning greeting to the stranger without his gates. And Zal desired that Mihrab should crave a boon at his hands. Then spake Mihrab unto him saying-

"O ruler mighty and great, I have but one desire, and to bring it to pass is easy. For I crave thee that thou dwell as guest beneath my roof, and let my heart rejoice in thy presence."

Then Zal said unto him, "O King, ask not this boon at my hands, I pray thee, for it can in nowise be accomplished. The Shah and Saum would be angered should they learn that I had eaten under the roof of Zohak. I beg of thee ask aught but this."

When Mihrab heard these words he was sorrowful, and bent low before Zal, and departed from out the tents. And the eye of Zal looked after him, and yet again he spake his praises. Then he bethought him of the King's daughter, and how that she was fair, and he was sunk in brooding and desire, and the days passed unheeded over his head.

Now it came to pass that on a certain morning Mihrab stepped forth from his palace to the house of the women to visit Sindokht his wife, and her daughter Rudabeh. Truly the house was like to a garden for colour and perfume, and over all shone those moons of beauty. Now when Mihrab had greeted Rudabeh he marvelled at her loveliness, and called down the blessings of Heaven upon her head. Then Sindokht opened her lips and questioned Mihrab concerning the stranger whose tents were without their gates. And she said-

"I pray thee tell unto me what manner of man is this white-haired son of Saum, and is he worthy the nest or the throne? "

Then Mihrab said unto her, "O my fair cypress, the son of Saum is a hero among men. His heart is like unto a lion's, his strength is as an elephant's, to his friends he is a gracious Nile, unto his enemies a wasting crocodile. And in him are even blemishes turned to beauties, his white locks but enhance his glory."

When Rudabeh had listened to these words her heart burned with love for Zal, so that she could neither eat nor rest, and was like unto one that hath changed her shape. And after a while, because that she could bear the burden thereof no longer, she told her secret to the slaves that loved and served her. And she charged them tell no man, and entreated of them that they would aid her to allay the troubles of her heart. And when the slaves had listened to her story, they were filled with fear, and with one accord entreated her that she would dismiss from her heart one branded among men, and whom his own father had cast out. But Rudabeh would not listen to their voice. And when they beheld that she was firm in her spirit, and that their words were vain, they cast about how they might serve her. And one among them who was wise above the rest opened her lips and spake-

"O moon-faced beauty, slender cypress, it shall be done at thy desire.

Thy slaves will neither rest nor slumber until the royal youth shall have become the footstool to thy feet."

Then Rudabeh was glad and said-

"An the issue be happy, there shall be planted for thee a noble tree, and it shall bear riches and jewels, and wisdom shall cull its fruits."

Then the slaves pondered in their hearts how they should compass their end, for they knew that only by craft could it be brought about. Straightway they clothed themselves in costly raiment, and went forth blithely into the garden of flowers that was spread beside the river's bank without the city. And they gathered roses, and decked their hair with blossoms, and threw them into the stream for sooth-telling; and as they gathered they came unto the spot over against which were pitched the tents of Zal. Now Zal beheld them from his tent, and he questioned them concerning these rose-gatherers. And one uprose and said unto him-

"They are slaves sent forth by the moon of Cabul into the garden of flowers."

Now when Zal heard this his heart leaped for joy, and he set forth unto the river's bank with only one page to bear him company. And seeing a water-bird fly upwards, he took his bow and shot it through the heart, and it fell among the rose-gatherers. Then Zal bade the boy cross the water and bring him the bird. And when he had landed, the moon-faced women pressed about him and questioned him, saying-

"O youth, tell us the name of him who aimeth thus surely, for verily he is a king among men."

Then the boy answering said, "What! know ye not the son of Saum the hero? The world hath not his equal for strength and beauty."

But the girls reproved him, and said, "Not so, boast not thus vainly, for the house of Mihrab holdeth a sun that o'ershines all besides."

And the page smiled, and the smile yet lingered on his lips when he came back to Zal. And Zal said-

"Why smilest thou, boy? What have they spoken unto thee that thou openest thy lips and showest thy ivory teeth?"

Then the boy told unto him the speech of the women. And Zal said-

"Go over yet again and bid them tarry, that they may bear back jewels with their roses."

And he chose forth from among his treasures trinkets of pearl and gold, and sent them to the slaves. Then the one who had sworn to serve Rudabeh above the rest craved that she might look upon the face of the hero, for she said-

"A secret that is known to three is one no longer."

And Zal granted her desire, and she told him of Rudabeh and of her beauty, and his passion burned the more. And he spake-

"Show unto me, I pray thee, the path by which I may behold this fair one, for my heart is filled with longing."

Then the slave said, "Suffer that we go back to the house of the women, and we will fill the ears of Rudabeh with praises of the son of Saum, and will entangle her in the meshes of our net, and the lion shall rejoice in his chase of the lamb."

Then Zal bade her go forth, and the women returned to the house rejoicing and saying-

"The lion entereth the snare spread forth to entrap him, and the wishes of Rudabeh and Zal will be accomplished."

But when they were come to the gates the porter chid them that they were gone without while the stranger sojourned in Cabul, and they were troubled and sore afraid for their secret. But they stilled his wrath and came unto where Rudabeh awaited them. And they told her of Zal, the son of Saum, and of his beauty and his prowess. And Rudabeh smiled and said-

"Wherefore have ye thus changed your note? For a while back ye spake with scorn of this bird-reared youth, on whose head hang the locks of a sage, but now are ye loud in his praises."

Then Rudabeh began privily to deck her house that it might be worthy a guest. With brocades of Roum and carpets of Ind did she hang it, and she perfumed it with musk and ambergris, and flowers did she cause to bloom about the rooms. And when the sun was sunk, and the doors of the house were locked and the keys withdrawn, a slave went forth unto Zal, the son of Saum. And she spake unto him in a low voice-

"Come now, for all is ready."

And Zal followed after her. And when they were come to the house of the women Zal beheld the daughter of the King standing upon the roof, and her beauty was like unto a cypress on which the full moon shineth. And when she beheld him, she spake and said-

"I bid thee welcome, O young man, son of a hero, and may the blessing of Heaven rest upon thee."

And Zal answered her benison, and prayed that he might enter into nearer converse, for he was on the ground and she was on the roof. Then the Peri-faced loosened her tresses, and they were long, so that they fell from the battlements unto the ground. And she said unto Zal-

"Here hast thou a cord without flaw. Mount, O Pehliva, and seize my black locks, for it is fitting that I should be a snare unto thee."

But Zal cried, "Not so, O fair one, it would beseem me ill to do thee hurt."

And he covered her hair with kisses. Then he called for a cord and made a running knot, and threw it upwards and fastened it to the battlements. And with a bound he swung himself upon the roof. Then Rudabeh took his hand and they stepped down together into the golden chambers, and the slaves stood round about them. And they gazed upon each other and knew that they excelled in beauty, and the hours slipped by in sweet talk, while love was fanned in their hearts. Then Zal cried-

"O fair cypress, musk-perfumed, when Minuchihr shall learn of this he will be angered and Saum also will chide. And they will say I have forgotten my God, and will lift their hands against me. But I swear unto thee that this life is to me vile if it be not spent in thy presence. And I call upon Heaven to hear me that none other but thee will I call my bride."

And Rudabeh said, "I too will swear unto thee this oath."

So the hours sped, and there arose from out the tents of the King the sound of drums that announce the coming of the day. Then cried Zal and Rudabeh of one accord-

"O glory of the world, tarry yet a while, neither arrive so quickly."

But the sun gave no ear to their reproaches, and the hour to part was come. Then Zal swung himself from the battlements unto the ground, and quitted the house of his beloved.

Now when the earth was flooded with light, and the nobles and chiefs had tendered unto Zal their morning greetings as was their wont, he called about him his Mubids, and laid before them how that he was filled with love for a daughter of the Serpent. And the Mubids when they heard it were troubled, and their lips were closed, and the words were chained upon their tongues. For there was none of them that listed to mingle poison in the honey of this love. Whereupon Zal reproved them, and said that he would bestow on them rich gifts if they would open their mouths. Then they spake and said unto him that the honour of a king could not suffer by a woman, and though Mihrab be indeed of Zohak's race, he was noble and valiant. And they urged him to write unto his father and crave Saum to wait upon the Shah.

Then Zal called unto him a scribe and bade him write down the words that he spake. And he told unto Saum his love and his fears. And he recalled unto him how that he had cast him out, and how that he had lived in a nest, and a bird had reared him, and the sun had poured down upon his head, and raw flesh had been his nourishment the while his father had sat within a goodly house clothed in silk. And he recalled the promise given to him by Saum. Neither did he seek to justify that which was come about. Then he gave the letter to a messenger, and bade him ride until he should be come into the presence of Saum.

When Saum had heard the words of his son his spirit was troubled, and he cried-

"Woe unto me, for now is clear what hath so long been hidden. One whom a wild bird hath reared looketh for the fulfilment of wild desires, and seeks union with an accursed race."

And he pondered long what he should answer. For he said, "If I say, Abandon this desire, sow no discord, return to reason, I break my oath and God will punish me. Yet if I say, Thy desire is just, satisfy the passions of thy heart, what offspring can come to pass from the union of a Deev and the nursling of a bird?"

And the heart of Saum was heavy with care. So he called unto him his Mubids that they should search the stars, for he said-

"If I mingle fire and water I do ill, and ill will come of it."

Then all that day the Wise Men searched the secrets of Fate, and they cast the horoscope of Zal and Rudabeh, and at even they returned to the King rejoicing. And they found him torn with anguish. Then they said-

"Hail unto thee, O Saum, for we have followed the movement of the stars and counted their course, and we have read the message of the skies. And it is written, 'A clear spring shall issue into the day, a son shall be born to Zal, a hero full of power and glory, and there shall not be his like in Iran.'"

Now when Saum had drunk in these words, his soul was uplifted, and he poured gifts upon the Mubids. Then he called to him the messenger of Zal, and he gave him pieces of silver, and bade him return unto his master and say-

"I hold thy passion folly, O my son, but because of the oath that I have sworn to thee it shall be done at thy desire. I will hie me unto Iran and lay thy suit before the Shah."

Then Saum called together his army and set forth for Iran, and the sound of trumpets and cymbals went before him.

Now when the messenger was come back to Zal, he rejoiced and praised God, and gave gold and silver to the poor, and gifts unto his servants. But when night was come he could not close his eyes in slumber, nor could he rest during the day. Neither did he drink wine nor demand the singers, for his soul was filled with longing after his love. And presently there came out to him a slave, and he gave unto her Saum's letter that she might bear it to Rudabeh. And Rudabeh rejoiced also, and chose from among her treasures a costly crown and a ring of worth, and bade the woman bear them unto Zal. Now as she quitted the chamber she met Sindokht. And the Queen questioned her and said-

"Whence comest thou? Reply to all my questions, neither seek thou to deceive me, for already a long time do I suspect thy passing to and fro."

And the woman trembled as she heard these words, and fell down and kissed the feet of the Queen, and said-

"Have pity on thine handmaiden, who is poor and gaineth her bread as she can. I go into the houses of the rich and sell to them robes and jewels. And Rudabeh hath this day bought of me a tiara and a bracelet of gold."

Then said Sindokht, "Show unto me the money thou hast received for the same, that my anger be appeased."

And the woman answered and said, "Demand not that I show unto thee that which I have not, for Rudabeh will pay me to-morrow."

Now Sindokht knew that these words were feigned, and she searched the sleeve of the woman, and lo! she found therein the tiara that Rudabeh had broidered with her hands. Then she was angered, and commanded that the slave should be bound in chains. And she desired that her daughter be brought into her presence. And when she was come, Sindokht opened her mouth and spake, saying-

"O moon of noble race, to whom hath been taught naught but that which is good, how hast thou gone astray upon the paths of evil? O my daughter, confide unto thy mother thy secrets. From whom cometh this woman? For what man are destined thy gifts?"

When she had heard, Rudabeh was abashed, but after a while she told all unto Sindokht. Now when the Queen had heard she was confounded, for she feared the wrath of the Shah, and that he would raze Cabul to the dust for this mischance. And she went into her rooms and wept in her sorrow. Then presently Mihrab the King came in to Sindokht, and he was of joyful mind, for Zal had received him graciously. But when he beheld her tears he questioned of her grief. Then she told him how that his daughter was filled with love for Zal, the son of Saum. And when Mihrab had heard her to an end, his heart also was troubled, for he knew that Cabul could not stand before the Shah.

Minuchihr, too, when he had heard these things, was troubled, for he beheld in them the device of Ahriman, and feared lest this union should bring evil upon Iran. And he bade Nauder call Saum before him. Now when Saum heard the desire of the Shah, he spake and said-

"I obey, and the sight of the King will be a banquet unto my soul."

Then Saum went into the presence of Minuchihr, and he kissed the ground, and called down blessings upon the head of the Shah. But Minuchihr raised him and seated him beside him on the throne, and straightway began to question him concerning the war, and the Deevs of Mazinderan. Then Saum told him all the story of his battles. And Minuchihr listened with joy though the tale was long, and when Saum had ended he praised his prowess. And he lifted his crown unto heaven and rejoiced that his enemies were thus confounded. Then be bade a banquet be spread, and all night long the heroes feasted and shortened the hours with wine. But when the first rays of morn had shed their light, the curtains of the Shah's house were opened, that he might hold audience and grant the petitions of his people. And Saum the Pehliva came the first to stand before the King, for he desired to speak to him of Zal. But the Shah of the world would not suffer him to open his lips, but said unto him-

"Go hence, O Saum, and take with thee thine army, for I command thee to go yet again to battle. Set forth unto Cabul and burn the house of Mihrab the King, and utterly destroy his race and all who serve him, nor suffer that any of the seed of Zohak escape destruction, for I will that the earth be delivered of this serpent brood."

When Saum heard these words he knew that the Shah was angered, and that speech would avail him naught. So he kissed the throne and touched the earth with his forehead, and said, "Lord, I am thy servant, and I obey thy desires." And he departed, and the earth trembled under the stamping of footmen and of hoofs, and the air of the city was darkened with his spears.

Now the news of Saum's intent reached even unto Cabul, and the land was sunk in woe, and weeping filled the house of the King. But Zal was wroth, and he went forth to meet his father. And when he was come to the spot where he had encamped his army, he craved an audience. And Saum granted it, and Zal reminded him yet again of his oath, and desired that he would spare the land of Cabul, nor visit his judgments upon the innocent. When Saum had listened, his heart was moved, and he said-

"O my son, thou speakest that which is right. To thee have I been unjust from the day of thy birth. But stay thy wrath, for surely I will find a remedy, and thy wishes shall yet be accomplished. For thou shalt bear a letter unto the Shah, and when he shall have looked on thy face, he will be moved with compassion and cease to trouble thee."

Then Zal kissed the ground before his father and craved the blessings of God upon his head. And Saum dictated a letter to the Shah, and he spoke therein of all he had done for Minuchihr, and how he had killed the dragon that had laid waste the land, how he had ever subdued the foes of Iran, and how the frontiers were enlarged by his hands. Yet now was he waxing old, and could no longer do doughty deeds. But a brave son was his, worthy and true, who would follow in his footsteps. Only his heart was devoured of love, and perchance he would die if his longing were unsatisfied. And therewith he commended to the wisdom of the Shah the affairs of Zal.

When the letter was ended Zal set forth with it unto the court, and the flower of his army went with him.

But the fear of Minuchihr was great in Cabul, and Mihrab pondered how he should quench the wrath of the King of kings. And he spake to Sindokht and said-

"For that the King is angered against me because of thee and thy daughter, and because I cannot stand before him, I will lead Rudabeh unto his court and kill her before his eyes. Perchance his anger may be thus allayed."

Sindokht listened to his words in silence, and when he had ended she cast about her for a plan, for she was quick of wit. And when she had found one she came again into the presence of Mihrab, and she craved of him that he should give her the key of his treasury. For she said-

"This is not the hour to be strait-handed; suffer that I take what seemeth good unto me and go before Saum, it may be that I move him to spare the land."

And Mihrab agreed to her demand because of the fear that devoured him. Then Sindokht went out to the house of Saum, and she took with her three hundred thousand pieces of gold, and sixty horses caparisoned in silver, bearing sixty slaves that held cups filled to the brim with musk and camphor, and rubies, and turquoise, and precious stones of every kind. And there followed two hundred dromedaries and four tall Indian elephants laden with carpets and brocades of Roum, and the train reached for two miles beyond the King's gates. Now when Sindokht was come to Seistan she bade the guardians of the door say unto Saum that an envoy was come from Cabul bearing a message. And Saum granted an audience, and Sindokht was brought into his presence. Then she kissed the ground at his feet and called upon Heaven to shower down blessings on his head.

And when she had done so, she caused her gifts to be laid before Saum, and when Saum beheld these treasures, he marvelled and thought within himself, "How cometh it that a woman is sent as envoy from a land that boasteth such riches? If I accept them the Shah will be angered, and if I refuse perchance Zal will reproach me that I rob him of his heritage." So he lifted his head and said-

"Let these treasures be given unto the treasurer of my son."

When Sindokht beheld that her gifts were accepted, she rejoiced and raised her voice in speech. And she questioned Saum, saying-

"Tell me, I pray thee, what wrong have the people of Cabul done unto thee that thou wouldst destroy them?"

Then answered Saum the hero, "Reply unto my questions and lie not. Art thou the slave or the wife of Mihrab, and is it thy daughter whom Zal hath seen? If indeed it be so, tell me, I pray, of her beauty, that I may know if she be worthy of my son."

Then Sindokht said, "O Pehliva, swear to me first a great oath that thou wilt spare my life and the lives of those dear unto me. And when I am assured of thy protection I will recount all that thou desirest."

Then Saum took the hand of Sindokht, and he sware unto her a great oath, and gave her his word and his promise. And when she had heard it she was no longer afraid, and she told him all her secrets. And she said-

"I am of the race of Zohak, and wife unto the valiant Mihrab, and mother of Rudabeh, who hath found favour in the eyes of thy son. And I am come to learn of thy desire, and who are thine enemies in Cabul. Destroy the wicked, and those who merit chastisement, but spare, I pray thee, the innocent, or thy deeds will change day into night."

Then spake Saum, "My oath is sacred, and if it cost my life, thou and thine and Cabul may rest assured that I will not harm them. And I desire that Zal should find a wife in Rudabeh, though she be of an alien race."

And he told her how that he had written to the Shah a letter of supplication such as only one in grief could pen, and how Zal was absent with the message, and he craved her to tell him of Rudabeh.

But Sindokht replied, "If the Pehliva of the world will make the hearts of his slaves rejoice, he will visit us and look with his own eyes upon our moon."

And Saum smiled and said, "Rest content and deliver thine heart of cares, for all shall end according unto thy desires."

When Sindokht heard this she bade him farewell and made all haste to return. And Saum loaded her with gifts and bade her depart in peace. And

Sindokht's face shone brightly, like unto the moon when she hath been eclipsed, and hope once more reigned in her breast.

Now listen to what happened to Zal while these things were passing in Seistan. When he was come to the court of Minuchihr he hastened into his presence, and kissed the ground at his feet, and lay prostrate before him in the dust. And when the Shah saw this he was moved, and bade his servants raise Zal, and pour musk before him. Then Zal drew nigh unto the throne and gave to the King the letter written by Saum the son of Neriman. And when Minuchihr had read it he was grieved, and said-

"This letter, written by Saum thy father in his sorrow, hath awakened an old pain within me. But for the sake of my faithful servant I will do unto thee that which is thy desire. Yet I ask that thou abide with me a little while that I may seek counsel about thee."

Then the cooks brought forth a table of gold, and Zal was seated beside the Shah and all the nobles according to their rank, and they ate flesh and drank wine together. Then when the mantle of night was fallen over the earth Zal sprang upon his steed and scoured the land in the unrest of his spirit, for his heart was full of thoughts and his mouth of words. But when morning was come he presented himself before the Shah in audience. And his speech and mien found favour in the eyes of the Shah, and he called unto him his Wise Men and bade them question the stars of this matter. Three days and three nights did the Mubids search the heavens without ceasing, and on the fourth they came before the Shah and spake. And they said unto him-

"Hail to thee, hero of the golden girdle, for we bring unto thee glad tidings. The son of Saum and the daughter of Mihrab shall be a glorious pair, and from their union shall spring a son like to a war-elephant, and he shall subdue all men by his sword and raise the glory of Iran even unto the skies. And he shall uproot the wicked from the earth so that there shall be no room for them. Segsars and Mazinderan shall feel the weight of his mace, and he shall bring much woe upon Turan, but Iran shall be loaded with prosperity at his hands. And he will give back sleep to the unhappy, and close the doors of discord, and bar the paths of wrong-doing. The kingdom will rejoice while he lives; Roum, Ind, and Iran will grave his name upon their seals."

When the Shah had heard this he charged the Mubids that they keep secret that which they had revealed unto him. And he called for Zal that he might question him and test his wisdom. And the Wise Men and the

Mubids were seated in a circle, and they put these questions to the son of Saum.

And the first opened his mouth and said-

"Twelve trees, well grown and green, Fair and lofty, have I seen; Each has sprung with vigorous sprout, Sending thirty branches out; Wax no more, nor wane, they can In the kingdom of Iran."

And Zal pondered a while and then answered and said-

'Twelve moons in the year, and each I praise As a new-made king on a new throne's blaze: Each comes to an end in thirty days."

Then the second Mubid questioned him and said-

"Thou whose head is high in air, Rede me now of coursers twain; Both are noble, swift to speed; Black as storms in the night one steed, The other crystal, white and fair, They race for ever and haste in vain, Towards a goal they never gain."

And Zal thought again yet a while and answered-

"Two shining horses, one black, one white. That run for ever in rapid flight; The one is the day, the other the night, That count the throbs of the heavens height, Like the hunted prey from the following chase They flee, yet neither wins the race."

Then the third Mubid questioned him and said-

"Thirty knights before the king Pass along. Regard the thing Closely; one is gone. Again Look- the thirty are in train."

And Zal answered and spake-

"Thirty knights of whom the train Is full, then fails, then fills again, Know, each moon is reckoned thus, So willed by God who governs us, And thy word is true of the faint moon's wane, Now failing in darkness, now shining plain."

Then the fourth Mubid questioned him and said-

"See a green garden full of springs; A strong man with a sickle keen Enters, and reaps both dry and green; No word thine utmost anguish wrings."

And Zal bethought him and replied-

"Thy word was of a garden green, A reaper with a sickle keen, Who cuts alike the fresh and the dry Nor heedeth prayer nor any cry: Time is the reaper, we the grass; Pity nor fear his spirit has, But old and young he reaps alike. No rank can stay his sickle's strike, No love, but he will leave it lorn, For to this end all men are born. Birth opes to all the gate of Life, Death shuts it down on love and strife, And Fate, that counts the breath of man, Measures to each a reckoned span."

Then the fifth Mubid questioned him and said-

"Look how two lofty cypresses Spring up, like reeds, from stormy seas, There builds a bird his dwelling-place; Upon the one all night he stays, But swift, with the dawn, across he flies; The abandoned tree dries up and dies, While that whereon he sets his feet Breathes odours out, surpassing sweet. The one is dead for ever and aye, The other lives and blooms alway."

Then Zal yet again bethought him before he said-

"Hear of the sea-born cypresses, Where builds a bird, and rests, and flees. From the Ram to the Scales the earth o'erpowers, Shadows obscure of the night that lowers, But when the Scales' sign it must quit, Darkness and gloom o'ermaster it; The sides of heaven thy fable shows Whence grief to man or blessing flows, The sun like a bird flies to and fro, Weal with him bringing, but leaving woe."

Then the sixth Mubid questioned him, and it was the last question that he asked, and he deemed it the hardest of all to answer. And all men hung upon his words and listened to the answer of Zal. And the Mubid said-

"Built on a rock I found A town. Men left the gate and chose A thicket on the level ground. Soon their soaring mansions rose Lifting roofs that reach the moon, Some men slaves, some kings, became, Of their earlier city soon The memory died in all. Its name None breathed. But hark! an earthquake; down, Lost in the chasm lies the land- Now long they for their rock-built town, Enduring things they understand. Seek in thy soul the truth of this; This before kings proclaim, I was, If rightly thou the riddle rede, Black earth to musk thou hast changed indeed."

And Zal pondered this riddle but a little while, and then opened his mouth and said-

"The eternal, final world is shown By image of a rock-built town; The thicket is our passing life, A place of pleasure and of pain, A world of dreams and eager strife, A time for labour, and loss, and gain; This counts thy heart-beats, at its will Prolongs their pulse or makes it still. But winds and earthquake rouse: a cry Goes up of bitterness and woe, Now we must leave our homes below And climb the rocky fastness high. Another reaps our fruit of pain, That yet to another leaves his gain; So was it aye, must so remain. Well for us if our name endure, Though we shall pass, beloved and pure, For all the evil man hath done, Stalks, when he dies, in the sight of the sun; When dust is strown on breast and head, Then desolation reigns with dread."

When Zal had spoken thus the Shah was glad, and an the assembly were amazed, and lauded the son of Saum. And the King bade a great banquet be prepared, and they drank wine until the world was darkened, and the heads of the drinkers were troubled. Then when morn was come Zal prayed that the Shah would dismiss him. But Minuchihr said-

"Not so, abide with me yet another day," and he bade the drums be beaten to call together his heroes, for he desired to test Zal also in feats of strength. And the Shah sat upon the roof of his house and looked down upon the games, and he beheld Zal, the son of Saum, do mighty deeds of prowess. With his arrow did he shoot farther and straighter than the rest, and with his spear he pierced all shields, and in wrestling he overcame the strongest who had never known defeat. When the nobles beheld these doughty deeds they shouted and clapped their hands, and Minuchihr loaded Zal with gifts. Then he prepared a reply unto the letter of Saum. And he wrote-

"O my Pehliva, hero of great renown, I have listened to thy desires, and I have beheld the youth who is worthy to be thy son. And he hath found favour in my sight, and I send him back to thee satisfied. May his enemies be impotent to harm him."

Then when the Shah had given him leave to go, Zal set forth, and he bare his head high in the joy of his heart. And when he came before his father and gave to him the letter of the Shah, Saum was young again for happiness. Then the drums sounded the signal to depart, and the tents were prepared, and a messenger, mounted on a fleet dromedary, was sent unto Mihrab to tell him that Saum and Zal were setting forth for Cabul. And when Mihrab heard the tidings his fears were stilled, and he commanded that his army be clad in festal array. And silken standards of bright colour decked the city, and the sounds of trumpets, harps, and cymbals filled the air. And Sindokht told the glad tidings to Rudabeh, and they made ready the house like unto a paradise. Carpets broidered with gold and precious stones did they lay down upon its floors, and set forth thrones of ivory and rich carving. And the ground they watered with rose-water and wine.

Then when the guests were come near unto Cabul, Mihrab went forth to meet them, and he placed upon the head of Zal a crown of diamonds, and they came into the city in triumph. And all the people did homage before them, and Sindokht met them at the doors of the King's house, and poured out musk and precious stones before them. Then Saum, when he had replied to their homage, smiled, and turned to Sindokht and said-

"How much longer dost thou think to hide Rudabeh from our eyes?"

And Sindokht said, "What wilt thou give me to see the sun?"

Then Saum replied, "All that thou wilt, even unto my slaves and my throne, will I give to thee."

Then Sindokht led him within the curtains, and when Saum beheld

Rudabeh he was struck dumb with wonder, for her beauty exceeded dreams, and he knew not how he could find words to praise her. Then he asked of Mihrab that he would give unto him her hand, and they concluded an alliance according to custom and the law. And the lovers were seated upon a throne, and Mihrab read out the list of the gifts, and it was so long the ear did not suffice to hear them. Then they repaired unto the banquet, and they feasted seven days without ceasing. And when a month had passed Saum went back to Seistan, and Zal and Rudabeh followed after him. And speedily did he set forth again to battle, and left the kingdom in the hands of his son, and Zal administered it with wisdom and judgment. And Rudabeh sat beside him on the throne, and he placed a crown of gold upon her head.

RUSTEM

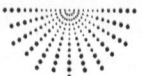

*N*ow ere the son of Zal was born, Rudabeh was sore afflicted, and neither by day nor night could she find rest. Then Zal in his trouble bethought him of the Simurgh, his nurse, and how she had given unto him a feather that he might use it in the hour of his need. And he cast the feather into the fire as she had commanded, and straightway a sound of rushing wings filled the air, and the sky was darkened and the bird of God stood before Zal. And she said unto him-

"O my son, wherefore art thou troubled, and why are the eyes of this lion wet with tears?"

Then he told her of his sorrow, and she bade him be of good cheer, "For verily thy nurse who shielded thee, and reared thee when thy father cast thee out, is come yet again to succour thee."

And she told him how he should act, and when she had done speaking she turned her once more towards her nest. But Zal did as she had commanded, and there was born to him a son comely of limb. And when Rudabeh beheld the babe, she smiled and said-

"Verily he shall be called Rustem (which, being interpreted, meaneth delivered), for I am delivered of my pains."

And all the land was glad that a son was come unto Zal the hero, and the sounds of feasting and joy were heard throughout its breadth.

Then fleet messengers brought the sweet tidings unto Saum. And they bare with them an image of Rustem sewn of silk, whereon were traced the features of this lion's whelp, and a club was put into its hands, and it was mounted upon a dromedary. Now when Saum beheld the image his heart leaped up within him. He poured mountains of gold before the messengers, and gave thanks unto Ormuzd that he had suffered his eyes to look upon this child.

And when eight summers had rolled above their heads, Saum learned that Rustem was mighty of stature and fair of mien, and his heart yearned towards him. He therefore made ready a mighty host and passed unto Zaboulistan, that he might look upon his son. And Rustem rode forth to meet his sire, mounted upon an elephant of war, and when he beheld Saum he fell upon his face and craved his blessing. And Saum blessed Rustem, the son of Zal.

Then Rustem spake unto Saum and said, "O Pehliva, I rejoice in that I am sprung from thee, for my desires are not after the feast, neither do I covet sleep or rest. My heart is fixed upon valour, a horse do I crave and a saddle, a coat of mail and a helmet, and my delight is in the arrow. Thine enemies will I vanquish, and may my courage be like unto thine."

And Saum, when he had heard these words, was astonished, and blessed Rustem yet again. And his eyes could not cease from gazing upon the face of the boy, and he lingered in the land until a moon had run her course.

Now it befell that when yet two springs had passed, Rustem was awakened from his slumber by a mighty roaring that shook the walls of the house, even unto the foundation, and a cry went forth that the white elephant of the King had broken its chain in fury, and that the housemates were in danger. And Rustem, when he learned it, sprang from his bed, and desired of the guards that they should suffer him to pass into the court that he might conquer the beast. But the guards barred the way from him, saying-

"How can we answer for it before the King if thou run into danger?"

But Rustem would not listen to their voice. He forced a passage for himself with his mighty arms, with his strong fists he broke down the barriers of the door. And when he was without he beheld how that all the warriors were sore afraid of the elephant, because that he was mad with rage. And Rustem was ashamed for them in his soul, and he ran towards the beast with a loud cry. Then the elephant, when he saw him, raised his trunk to strike him, but Rustem beat him upon the head with his club, and smote him that he died. And when he had done this deed, he returned unto his bed and slept until the morning. But the news of his prowess spread throughout the house of the King and far into the land, even unto the realms of Saum. And Zal, and all men with him, rejoiced because a hero was arisen in Iran.

Now, while these things were passing in the house of Zal, in the land of Zaboulistan, Minuchihr made him ready to pass from the world, for he had reached twice sixty years. He called before him Nauder his son, and gave him wise counsels, and exhorted him that he should ever walk in the paths of wisdom. And he bade him rest his throne upon the strength of Saum and Zal, and the child that was sprung from their loins. Then when he had spoken, Minuchihr closed his eyes and sighed, and there remained of him only a memory in the world.

But Nauder forgot the counsels of his father. He vexed the land and reigned in anger, and cruel deeds were committed in his name, so that the people rose up and cried against the King. And men of might came unto Saum and laid before him their plaints, and the petitions of the people, and they prayed that he would wrest the crown from the head of Nauder, and place it upon his own. But Saum was sore grieved when he had heard these words, and he spake, saying-

"Not so, for it beseemeth me not to put out my hand after the crown, for Nauder is of the race of the Kaianides, and unto them is given majesty and might."

Then he girt his sword about his loins, and took with him a host, and rode before the face of the Shah. And when he was come unto him, Saum exhorted him with prayers and tears that he would turn him from the paths of evil. And Nauder listened unto the voice of Saum the Pehliva, and joy was abroad once more.

But the tidings spread, even into Turan, that Minuchihr the just was departed, and that the hand of Nauder was heavy upon the land. And Poshang, who was of the race of Tur, heard the news thereof with gladness, for he deemed that the time was ripe to remember the vengeance that was due unto the blood of his sire. Therefore he called about him his warriors, and bade them go forth to war against Iran, saying the time was come to avenge his father and draw unto himself the heritage. And while his son Afrasiyab made ready the host to fulfil the desire of his father, there spread the news that Saum the Pehliva had been gathered unto the dust, and that Zal tarried in his house to build him a tomb. And the news gave courage unto Afrasiyab and his men, and they made haste to gain the frontier.

But the grandson of Feridoun had learned of their coming, and he prepared him to meet the foes of his land. Then he sent forth an army that overshadowed the earth in its progress. But the army of Afrasiyab was great also, and it covered the ground like unto ants and locusts. And both hosts pitched their tents in the plains of Dehstan, and made them ready for the fight. And the horses neighed loud, and the pawing of their hoofs shook the deep places of the earth, and the dust of their trampling uprose even unto heaven. Then when they had put their men into array, they fell upon each other, and for two days did they rage in fierce combat, neither did the victory lean to either side. And the clamour and confusion were mighty, and earth and sky seemed blended into one. And the carnage was great, and blood flowed like water, and heads fell from their trunks like unto autumn leaves that are withered. But on the third day it came about that the upper hand was given unto the men of Turan, and Nauder the King, and the flower of his army with him, fell into the hands of the foe.

Then Afrasiyab cut off the head of Nauder the Shah, and sat himself down upon the throne of light. And he proclaimed himself lord of Iran, and required of all men that they should do him homage, and pour gifts before his face. But the people would not listen unto his voice, and they sent messengers into Seistan, and craved counsel of the Pehliva in their distress. And Zal, when he heard their tidings, cast aside the sorrow for Saum his father, and girded his loins in enmity against the son of Tur. And he bade the Iranians choose out Zew, the son of Thamasp, of the blood of Feridoun, of wisdom in speech, that he should rule over them on the throne of the Kaianides. And the people did as Zal commanded.

Now the throne of Feridoun grew young again under the sway of Zew. With power did he beat back the host of Turan, a covenant of peace did he wring from their hands. And it was written that the Jihun should divide the lands, and that the power of Zal the Pehliva should end where men take up their abode in tents. And Zew ruled rightly in the sight of Ormuzd, and God gave unto the land the key of abundance. Yet few were the years that he commanded with equity, and Garshasp his son reigned in his stead. But neither to him was it given to reign long with glory, and bitter fruit sprouted yet again from the tree of misfortune. For the throne of the Kaianides was empty, and Afrasiyab, when he learned thereof, followed the counsels of Poshang his father, and hurried him unto the land of Iran, that he might place himself upon the seat of power. And all the men of Iran, when they learned thereof, were sore afraid, and they turned them once again unto the son of Saum. And they spake unto him hard words, and heaped reproaches upon him that he had not averted these dangers

FERDOWSI

from their heads. And Zal in his heart smiled at their ingratitude and lipwisdom, but he also sorrowed with them and with his land. And he spake, saying-

"I have ever done for you what was fitting and right, and all my life have I feared no enemy save only old age. But that enemy is now upon me, therefore I charge you that ye look unto Rustem to deliver you. Howbeit he shall be backed by the counsels of his father."

Then he called before him his son, who was yet of tender age, and he said unto him-

"O my son, thy lips still smell of milk, and thy heart should go out to pleasure. But the days are grave, and Iran looketh unto thee in its danger. I must send thee forth to cope with heroes."

And Rustem answered and said, "Thou knowest, O my father, that my desires are rather after war than pleasures. Give unto me, therefore, a steed of strength and the mace of Saum thy father, and suffer that I go out to meet the hosts of Ahriman."

Then Zal's heart laughed within him when he heard these words of manhood. And he commanded that all the flocks of horses, both from Zaboulistan and Cabul, be brought before his son, that he might choose from their midst his steed of battle. And they were passed in order before Rustem, and he laid upon the backs of each his hand of might to test them if they could bear his weight of valour. And the horses shuddered as they bent beneath his grasp, and sank upon their haunches in weakness. And thus did he do with them all in turn, until he came unto the flocks of Cabul. Then he perceived in their midst a mare mighty and strong, and there followed after her a colt like to its mother, with the chest and shoulders of a lion. And in strength it seemed like an elephant, and in colour it was as rose leaves that have been scattered upon a saffron ground. Now Rustem, when he had tested the colt with his eyes, made a running knot in his cord and threw it about the beast. And he caught the colt in the snare, though the mare defended it mightily. Then the keeper of the flock came before Rustem and said-

"O youth puissant and tall, take not, I counsel thee, the horse of another."

And Rustem answered him and asked, "To whom then pertaineth this steed? I see no mark upon its flanks."

And the keeper said, "We know not its master, but rumours are rife anent it throughout the land, and men name it the Rakush of Rustem. And I warn thee, the mother will never permit thee to ride on it. Three years has it been ready for the saddle, but none would she suffer to mount thereon."

Then Rustem, when he heard these words, swung himself upon the colt with a great bound. And the mare, when she saw it, ran at him and would have pulled him down, but when she had heard his voice she suffered it. And the rose-coloured steed bore Rustem along the plains like unto the wind. Then when he was returned, the son of Zal spake and said to the keeper-

"I pray thee, tell unto me what is the price of this dragon?"

But the keeper replied, "If thou be Rustem, mount him, and retrieve the sorrows of Iran. For his price is the land of Iran, and seated upon him thou wilt save the world."

And Rustem rejoiced in Rakush (whose name, being interpreted, meaneth the lightning), and Zal rejoiced with him, and they made them ready to stand against Afrasiyab.

Now it was in the time of roses, and the meadows smiled with verdure, when Zal led forth his hosts against the offspring of Tur. And the standard of Kawah streamed upon the breeze, and Mihrab marched on the left, and Gustahem marched on the right, and Zal went in the midst of the men, but Rustem went at the head of all. And there followed after him a number like to the sands of the sea, and the sounds of cymbals and bells made a noise throughout the land like unto the day of judgment, when the earth shall cry unto the dead, "Arise." And they marched in order even unto the shores of the river Rai, and the two armies were but some farsangs apart.

Albeit, when Afrasiyab heard that Rustem and Zal were come out against him, he was in nowise dismayed, for he said, "The son is but a boy, and the father is old; it will not, therefore, be hard for me to keep my power in Iran." And he made ready his warriors with gladness of heart.

But Zal, when he had drawn up his army in battle array, spake unto them, saying-

"O men valiant in fight, we are great in number, but there is wanting to us a chief, for we are without the counsels of a Shah, and verily no labour succeedeth when the head is lacking. But rejoice, and be not downcast in your hearts, for a Mubid hath revealed unto me that there yet liveth one of the race of Feridoun to whom pertaineth the throne, and that he is a youth wise and brave."

And when he had thus spoken, he turned him to Rustem and said-

"I charge thee, O my son, depart in haste for the Mount Alberz, neither tarry by the way. And wend thee unto Kai Kobad, and say unto him that his army awaiteth him, and that the throne of the Kaianides is empty."

And Rustem, when he had heard his father's command, touched with his eyelashes the ground before his feet, and straightway departed. In his hand he bare a mace of might, and under him was Rakush the swift of foot. And he rode till he came within sight of the Mount Alberz, whereon had stood the cradle of his father. Then he beheld at its foot a house beauteous like unto that of a king. And around it was spread a garden whence came the sounds of running waters, and trees of tall stature uprose therein, and under their shade, by a gurgling rill, there stood a throne, and a youth, fair like to the moon, was seated thereon. And round about him leaned knights girt with red sashes of power, and you would have said it was a paradise for perfume and beauty.

Now when those within the garden beheld the son of Zal ride by, they came out unto him and said—

"O Pehliva, it behoveth us not to let thee go farther before thou hast permitted us to greet thee as our guest. We pray thee, therefore, descend from off thy horse and drink the cup of friendship in our house."

But Rustem said, "Not so, I thank you, but suffer that I may pass unto the mountain with an errand that brooketh no delay. For the borders of Iran are encircled by the enemy, and the throne is empty of a king. Wherefore I may not stay to taste of wine."

Then they answered him, "If thou goest unto the mount, tell us, we pray thee, thy mission, for unto us is it given to guard its sides."

And Rustem replied, "I seek there a king of the seed of Feridoun, who cleansed the world of the abominations of Zohak, a youth who reareth high his head. I pray ye, therefore, if ye know aught of Kai Kobad, that ye give me tidings where I may find him."

Then the youth that sat upon the throne opened his mouth and said, "Kai Kobad is known unto me, and if thou wilt enter this garden and rejoice my soul with thy presence I will give thee tidings concerning him."

When Rustem heard these words he sprang from off his horse and came within the gates. And the youth took his hand and led him unto the steps of the throne. Then he mounted it yet again, and when he had filled a cup with wine, he pledged the guest within his gates. Then he gave a cup unto Rustem, and questioned him wherefore he sought for Kai Kobad, and at whose desire he was come forth to find him. And Rustem told him of the Mubids, and how that his father had sent him with all speed to pray the young King that he would be their Shah, and lead the host against the enemies of Iran. Then the youth, when he had listened to an end, smiled and said-

"O Pehliva, behold me, for verily I am Kai Kobad of the race of Feridoun!"

And Rustem, when he had heard these words, fell on the ground before his feet, and saluted him Shah. Then the King raised him, and commanded that the slaves should give him yet another cup of wine, and he bore it to his lips in honour of Rustem, the son of Zal, the son of Saum, the son of Neriman. And they gave a cup also unto Rustem, and he cried-

"May the Shah live for ever!"

Then instruments of music rent the air, and joy spread over all the assembly. But when silence was fallen yet again, Kai Kobad opened his mouth and said-

"Hearken, O my knights, unto the dream that I had dreamed, and ye will know wherefore I called upon you this day to stand in majesty about my throne. For in my sleep I beheld two falcons white of wing, and they came out unto me from Iran, and in their beaks they bare a sunny crown. And the crown they placed upon my head. And behold now is Rustem come out unto me like to a white bird, and his father, the nursling of a bird, hath sent him, and they have given unto me the crown of Iran."

And Rustem, when he had heard this dream, said, "Surely thy vision was given unto thee of God! But now, I pray thee, up and tarry no longer, for the land of Iran groaneth sore and awaiteth thee with much travail."

So Kai Kobad listened to the desires of Rustem, and swung him upon his steed of war; and they rode day and night, until they came down from the hills unto the green plains that are watered by murmuring streams. And Rustem brought the King safely through the outposts of the enemy; and when the night was fallen, he led him within the tents of Zal, and none knew that he was come save only the Mubids. For seven days did they hold counsel together, and on the eighth the message of the stars was received with joy. And Zal made ready a throne of ivory and a banquet, and the crown of Iran was placed upon the head of the young Shah. Then the nobles came and did homage before him, and they revelled in wine till the night was far spent. And they prayed him that he would make him ready to lead them against the Turks. And Kai Kobad mustered the army and did as they desired.

And soon the battle raged hot and strong many days, and deeds of valour were done on either side; but the men of Turan could not stand against the men of Iran, neither could the strength of Rustem be broken. For he put forth the power of a lion, and his shadow extended for miles.

And from that day men named him Tehemten (which being interpreted, meaneth the strong-limbed), for he did deeds of prowess in the sight of men. And Afrasiyab was discomfited, and fled before him, and his army followed after, and their hearts were bruised and full of care.

But the Iranians, when they beheld that their foes had vanished before them, turned them unto Kai Kobad and did homage before his throne. And Kai Kobad celebrated the victory with much pomp, as is the manner of kings; and he placed Rustem upon his right hand and Zal upon his left, and they feasted and made them merry with wine.

In the meantime Afrasiyab returned him unto Poshang his father, who was of the race of Tur. And he came before him right sorrowful and spake, saying-

"O King, whose name is glorious, thou didst evil to provoke this war. The land which Feridoun the great did give in ancient time unto Tur the valiant, it hath been delivered unto thee, and the partition was just. Why, therefore, seekest thou to enlarge thy border? Verily I say, if thou haste not to make peace with Iran, Kai Kobad will send out against us an army from the four quarters of the earth, and they will subdue us, and by our own act we shall make the land too narrow for us. For the world is not delivered of the race of Irij, and the noxious poison hath not been converted into honey. For when one dieth another taketh his place, and never do they leave the world without a master. And there is arisen of the race of Saum a warrior called Rustem, and none can withstand him. He hath broken the power of thine host, and the world hath not seen his like for stoutness; and withal he is but little more than a weanling. Ponder therefore, O King, how shall it be when he may be come to years of vigour. Surely I am a man who desireth to possess the world, the stay of thine army, and thy refuge in danger, but before this boy my power fadeth like unto the mists that rise above the hills."

When the King of Turan had listened to these words, the tears of bitterness fell from his eyes. Then he called before him a scribe and he bade him write a letter unto Kai Kobad, the Shah. And the scribe adorned it with many colours and fair designs. And the scribe wrote-

"In the name of Ormuzd, the ruler of the sun and moon, greeting and salutation unto Kai Kobad the gracious from the meanest of his servants. Listen unto me, O valiant Shah, and ponder the words that I shall write. May grace fall upon the soul of Feridoun, who wove the woof of our race! Why should we any longer hold the world in confusion? That which he fixed, surely it was right, for he parted the world with equity, and we do wrong before him when we depart from the grooves that he hath shaped. I pray thee, therefore, let us no longer speak of Tur and his evil acts unto Irij, for if Irij was the cause of our hates, surely by Minuchihr hath he been avenged. Let us return, then, within the bounds that Feridoun hath blest, and let us part the world anew, as it was parted for Tur, and Selim, and Irij. For wherefore should we seek the land of another, since in the end each will receive in heritage a spot no larger than his body? If then Kai Kobad will listen unto my prayer, let the Jihun be the boundary between us, and none of my people shall behold its waters, nay, not even in a dream, neither shall any Iranian cross its floods, save only in amity."

And the King put his seal upon the letter and sent it unto Kai Kobad, and the messenger bare with him rich gifts of jewels and steeds of Araby. And when Kai Kobad had read the letter he smiled in his spirit and said—

"Verily not my people sought out this war but Afrasiyab, who deemed that he could wrest unto himself the crown of Iran, and could subdue the masterless land unto his will. And he hath but followed in the footsteps of Tur his father, for even as he robbed the throne of Irij, so did Afrasiyab take from it Nauder the Shah. And I say to you that I need not make peace with you because of any fear, but I will do it because war is not pleasing unto me. I will give unto you, therefore, the farther side of the river, and it shall be a boundary between us, and I pray that Afrasiyab may find rest within his borders."

And Kai Kobad did according to his word. He drew up a fresh covenant between them, and planted a new tree in the garden of power. And the messenger took the writing unto Poshang, King of Turan, and Kai Kobad proclaimed that there was peace throughout the land.

Now for the space of an hundred years did Kai Kobad rule over Iran, and he administered his realm with clemency, and the earth was quiet before him, and he gat his people great honour, and I ask of you what king can be likened unto him? But when this time had passed, his strength waned, and he knew that a green leaf was about to fade. So he called before him Kai Kaous his son, and gave unto him counsels many and wise. And when he had done speaking he bade them make ready his grave, and he exchanged the palace for the tomb. And thus endeth the history of Kai Kobad the glorious. It behoveth us now to speak of his son.

THE MARCH INTO MAZINDERAN

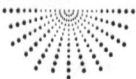

*K*ai aous seated him on the crystal throne, and the world was obedient to his will. But Ahriman was angry that his power was so long broken in Iran, and he sware unto himself that happiness should no longer smile upon the land. And he imagined guile in his black heart.

Now it came about one day that the Shah sat in his trellised bower in the garden of roses, drinking wine and making merry with his court. Then Ahriman, when he beheld that they were thus forgetful of care, saw that the time served him. So he sent forth a Deev clad as a singer, and bade him ask for audience before the Shah. And the Deev did as he was bidden. And he came before the servants of the King, and begged for entrance into the arbour of flowers.

"For verily," he said, "I am a singer of sweet songs, and I come from Mazinderan, and desire to pour my homage at the throne of my lord."

Now when Kai Kaous learned that a singer waited without, he commanded that he should be brought in. Then he gave him wine and permitted him to open his mouth before him. Now the Deev, when he had done homage before the Shah, warbled unto his lyre words of deep cunning. And he sang how that no land was like unto his own for beauty and riches, and he inflamed the desires of the Shah after Mazinderan. And Ahriman fanned the flame within the mind of the King, and when the Deev had ended, Kai Kaous was become uplifted in his heart, like unto Jemshid. So he turned him unto his warriors and said-

"O my friends, mighty and brave, we have abandoned ourselves unto feasting, we have revelled in the arms of peace. But it behoveth not men to live long in this wise, lest they grow idle and weak. And above all it behoveth not me that am a Shah, for the Shah is called to be a hero among men, and the world should be his footstool. Now verily the power and splendour of Jemshid was lower than mine, and my wealth surpasseth that of Zohak and Kai Kobad. It beseemeth me therefore to be greater also than they in prowess, and to be master of Mazinderan, which ever resisted their might. I bid you therefore make ready for combat, and I will lead you into the land whereof this singer hath sung so sweetly."

Now the nobles, when they had heard these words, grew pale with fear, for there was not one among them who listed to combat with Deevs. But none durst open their lips in answer, yet their hearts were full of fear and their mouths of sighs. But at last, when they could keep silence no longer, some spake and said-

"Lord, we are thy servants, and that which thou biddest surely we must do."

But among themselves they took counsel how they should act if the Shah held firm by his desire. And they recalled how not even Jemshid in his pride had thought to conquer the Deevs of Mazinderan, before whom the sword hath no power and wisdom no avail, neither had Feridoun, learned in magic, or Minuchihr the mighty, ventured on this emprise. Then they bethought them of Zal the son of Saum, and they sent forth a wind-footed dromedary and a messenger. And they said unto Zal-

"Haste, we pray thee, neither tarry to cleanse thine head though it be covered with dust; for Ahriman hath strown evil seed in the heart of Kai Kaous, and it ripeneth to fruit already, and already it hath borne fruit, and Iran is threatened with danger. But we look to thee that thou speak words of good counsel unto the Shah, and avert these sorrows from our heads."

Now Zal was sore distressed when he learned that a leaf on the tree of the Kaianides was thus faded. And he said-

"Kai Kaous is void of knowledge, and the sun must revolve yet oft above his head before he learneth the wisdom of the great. For unto true wisdom alone is it given to know when to strike and when to tarry. But he is like unto a child who deemeth the world will tremble if it but upraiseth its sword. And but for my duty unto God and unto Iran, I would abandon him to his folly."

Then Zal revolved in his mind this trouble even until the sun was set.

But when the glory of the world was arisen yet again, he girt his sash about his loins, and took in his hand the mace of might and set forth unto the throne of the Shah. And he craved for audience, and prostrated himself before the King. And when Kai Kaous permitted it, Zal opened his mouth and spake words of wisdom. And he said-

"O King powerful and great, word is come unto me, even unto Seistan, of thy device. But it seemeth unto me that mine ears have not heard aright. For Mazinderan is the abode of Deevs, and no man can overcome their skill. Give not, therefore, unto the wind thy men and thy treasures. Turn, I pray thee, from this scheme, neither plant in the garden of Iran the tree of folly, whose leaves are curses and whose fruits are evil, for thus did not the kings before thee."

Then Kai Kaous, when he had listened, said, "I despise not thy counsel, nor do I bid thee hold thy peace, for thou art a pillar unto Iran. But neither shall thy words divert me from my desire, and Mazinderan shall pay tribute to my hands. For thou considerest not how that my heart is bolder and my might more great than that of my fathers before me. I go, therefore, and the kingdom will I leave between thy hands and those of Rustem thy son."

When Zal heard these words, and beheld that Kai Kaous was firm in his purpose, he ceased from opposing. Then he bowed him unto the dust, and spake, saying-

"O Shah, it is thine to command, and whether it be just or unjust, thy servants serve thee even unto death. I have spoken the words that weighed upon my heart. Three things it is not given to do, even unto a king: to elude death, to bind up the eye of destiny, to live without nurture. Mayst thou never repent thee of thy resolve, mayst thou never regret my counsels in the hour of danger, may the might of the Shah shine for ever!"

And when he had ended, Zal went out of the presence of the King, and he was right sorrowful, and the nobles mourned with him when they learned how nought had been accomplished.

Then, ere the day succeeded unto the night, Kai Kaous set forth with his horsemen unto Mazinderan.

Now when they were come within its borders, Kai Kaous commanded Gew that he should choose forth a strong band from out their midst, and go before the city with mighty clubs. And he bade him destroy the dwellers of the town, neither should they spare the women nor the young, because that they too were the children of Deevs. And Gew did as the

Shah commanded. Then clubs rained down upon the people like to hail, and the city that resembled a garden was changed into a desert, and all the inmates thereof perished at the hands of the enemy, neither did they find any mercy in their eyes. But when the men of Iran had ceased from killing, they sent news thereof unto the Shah, and told him of the riches that were hidden within the palaces.

And Kai Kaous said, "Blessed be he who sang to me of the glories of this realm."

And he marched after Gew with the rest of his host, and seven days did they never cease from plundering, neither could they be sated with the gold and jewels that they found. But on the eighth the tidings of their deeds pierced unto the King of Mazinderan, and his heart was heavy with care. He therefore sent a messenger unto the mountains where dwelt the White Deev, who was powerful and strong, and he entreated him that he would come unto his succour, or verily the land would perish under the feet of Iran.

The White Deev, when he heard the message, uprose like to a mountain in his strength, and he said-

"Let not the King of Mazinderan be troubled, for surely the hosts of Iran shall vanish at my approach."

Then, when the night was fallen, he spread a dark cloud, heavy and thick, over the land, and no light could pierce it, neither could fires be seen across its midst, and you would have said the world was steeped in pitch. And the army of Iran was wrapt in a tent of blackness. Then the Deev caused it to rain stones and javelins, and the Iranians could not behold their source, neither could they defend themselves or stand against the arts of magic. And they wandered astray in their distress, and no man could find his fellow, and their hearts were angered against the Shah for this emprise. But when the morning was come, and glory was arisen upon the world, they could not see it, for the light of their eyes was gone out. And Kai Kaous too was blinded, and he wept sore, and the whole army wept with him in their anguish. And the Shah cried in his distress-

"O Zal, O my Pehliva wise and great, wherefore did I shut mine ear unto thy voice!"

And the army echoed his words in their hearts, but their lips were silent for boundless sorrow.

Then the White Deev spake unto Kai Kaous with a voice of thunder, and he said-

"O King, thou hast been struck like to a rotten trunk, on thine own head alone resteth this destruction, for thou hast attained unto Mazinderan, and entered the land after which thy heart desired."

And he bade his legion guard the Shah and all his army, and he withheld from them wine and good cheer, and gave unto them but enough for sustenance, for he desired not that they should die, but gloried in their wretchedness. Then when he had so done he sent tidings thereof unto the King of Mazinderan. And he bade the King take back the booty and rejoice in the defeat of Iran. And he counselled him that he suffer not Kai Kaous to perish, that he might learn to know good fortune from ill. And the White Deev bade the King sing praises unto Ahriman the mighty, who had sent him unto his aid. And having spoken thus he returned him unto his home in the mountains, but the King of Mazinderan rejoiced in his spoils.

Now Kai Kaous remained in the land after which he had yearned, and his heart was heavy with bitterness. And the eyes of his soul were opened, and he cried continually, "This fault is mine;" and he cast about in his spirit how he might release his host from the hands of the Deevs. But the Deevs guarded him straitly, and he could send no messenger into Iran. Howbeit it came about that a messenger escaped their borders, and bore unto Zal the writing of Kai Kaous the afflicted. And Kai Kaous bowed himself in his spirit unto the dust before Zal, and he wrote to him all that was come about, and how that he and his host were blind and captive, and he poured forth his repentance, and he said-

"I have sought what the foolish seek, and found what they find. And if thou wilt not gird thy loins to succour me, I perish indeed."

When Zal heard this message he gnawed his hands in vexation. Then he called before him Rustem, and said-

"The hour is come to saddle Rakush and to avenge the world with thy sword. As for me, I number two hundred years, and have no longer the strength to fight with Deevs. But thou art young and mighty. Cast about thee, therefore, thy leopard-skin and deliver Iran from bondage."

And Rustem said, "My sword is ready, and I will go hence as thou dost bid. Yet of old, O my father, the mighty did not go forth of their own will to fight the powers of hell, neither doth one who is not weary of this world go into the mouth of a hungry lion. But if God be with me I shall overcome the Deevs and gird our army anew with the sashes of might. And I pray that His blessing rest upon me."

Then Zal, when he heard these noble words, blessed his son, and prayed that Ormuzd too would give him his blessing. And he bestowed on him wise counsel, and told him how he could come unto the land of Mazinderan. And he said-

"Two roads lead unto this kingdom, and both are hard and fraught with danger. The one taken of Kai Kaous is the safest, but it is long, and it behoveth vengeance to be fleet. Choose therefore, I charge thee, the shorter road, though it be beset with baleful things, and may Ormuzd return thee safe unto mine arms."

When Rustem had drunk in the counsels of his father he seated him on Rakush the fleet of foot. But when he would have departed, his mother came out before him, and she made great wailing that Rustem should go before the evil Deevs. And she would have hindered him, but Rustem suffered her not. He comforted her with his voice, and bade her be of good cheer. He showed unto her how that he had not of his own choice chosen this adventure. And he bade her rest her hopes in God. And when he had done speaking she let him depart, but the heart of Rudabeh yearned after her son, and her eyes were red with weeping many days.

In the meanwhile the young hero of the world sped forth to do his duty unto the Shah. And Rakush caused the ground to vanish under his feet, and in twelve hours was a two days' journey accomplished. Then when eve was fallen, Rustem ensnared a wild ass, and made a fire and roasted it for his meal. And when he had done he released Rakush from the bonds of his saddle and prepared for himself a couch among the reeds, neither was he afraid of wild beasts or of Deevs.

But in the reeds was hidden the lair of a fierce lion, and the lion when he returned unto his haunt beheld the tall man and the horse that watched beside him. And he rejoiced at the fat meal that he held was in store. And he thought within his mind, "I will first subdue the steed, then the rider will be an easy prey." And he fell upon Rakush. But Rakush defended himself mightily. With his hoofs did he trample upon the forehead of the lion, with his sharp teeth did he tear his skin, and he trampled upon him till he died. But the noise of the struggle had wakened Rustem, and when he beheld the body of the lion, and Rakush standing beside it, he knew what had been done. Then he opened his mouth in reproof, and said-

"O thoughtless steed, who bade thee combat lions? Wherefore didst thou not wake me? for if thou hadst been overcome, who, I pray thee, could have borne my weight into Mazinderan, whither I must hie me to deliver the Shah?

FERDOWSI

When he had thus spoken he turned again to sleep, but Rakush was sorrowful and downcast in his spirit.

Now when morn was come they set forth once again upon their travels. And all day long they passed through a desert, and the pitiless sun burned down upon their heads, and the sand was living fire, and the steed and rider were like to perish of thirst, and nowhere could Rustem find the traces of water. So he made him ready to die, and commended his soul unto God, and prayed Him to remember Kai Kaous, His servant, nor abandon him in his distress. Then he laid him down to await the end. But lo! when he thought it was come, there passed before him a ram, well nourished and fat. And Rustem said unto himself-

"Surely the watering-place of this beast cannot be distant."

Then he roused him and led Rakush and followed in the footsteps of the ram, and behold, it led him unto a spring of water, cool and clear. And Rustem drank thereof with greed, and he gave unto Rakush, and bathed him in the waters, and when they were both refreshed he sought for the traces of the ram. And they were nowhere to be found. Then Rustem knew that Ormuzd had wrought a wonder for his sake, and he fell upon the ground and lifted up his soul in thankfulness. Then when he had caught and eaten a wild ass, he laid him down to slumber. And he spake and said unto Rakush-

"I charge thee, O my steed, that thou seek no strife during my slumbers. If an enemy cometh before thee, come unto me and neigh beside mine ear, and verily I will waken and come to thine aid."

And Rakush listened, and when he saw that Rustem slumbered, he gambolled and grazed beside him. But when some watches of the night were spent, there came forth an angry dragon whose home was in this spot, a dragon fierce and fiery, whom even the Deevs dared not encounter. And when he beheld Rakush and Rustem he was astonished that a man should slumber softly beside his lair. And he came towards them with his breath of poison. Then Rakush, when he saw it, stamped his hoofs upon the ground and beat the air with his tail, so that the noise thereof resounded wide, and Rustem was awakened with the din. And he was angry with Rakush that he had wakened him, for the dragon had vanished, and he could see no cause for fear. And he said-

"It is thy fault, O unkind steed, that slumber is fled from me."

Then he turned him to sleep once again. But when the dragon saw it he came forth once more, and once more did Rakush wake Rustem, and once more did the dragon vanish ere the eyes of Rustem were opened. And when Rakush had thus awakened the hero yet three times, Rustem was beside him with anger, and wisdom departed from its dwelling. He piled reproaches upon the horse, and hurled bitter words upon his head, and he sware that if he acted thus again he would slay him with his arm of power, and would wander on foot unto Mazinderan. And he said-

"I bade thee call upon me if dangers menaced, but thou sufferest me not to slumber when all is well."

Then Rustem drew his leopard-skin about him and laid him down again to sleep. But Rakush was pained in his spirit, and pawed the ground in his vexation. Then the dragon came forth yet again, and was about to fall upon Rakush, and the steed was sore distressed how he should act. But he took courage and came beside Rustem once more, and stamped upon the ground and neighed and woke him. And Rustem sprang up in fury, but this time it was given unto him to behold the dragon, and he knew that Rakush had done that which was right. And he drew his armour about him and unsheathed his sword, and came forth to meet the fiery beast. Then the dragon said-

"What is thy name, and who art thou that dost venture against me? for verily the woman that bore thee shall weep."

And the Pehliva answered, "I am Rustem, of the seed of Zal, and in myself I am an host, and none can withstand my might."

But the dragon laughed at his words, and held them to be vain boasting. Then he fell upon Rustem, the son of Zal, and he wound himself about his body, and would have crushed him with his writhings, and you would have said that the end of this hero was come. But Rakush, when he beheld the straits of his master, sprang upon the dragon from the rear, and he tore him as he had torn the lion, and Rustem pierced the beast with his sword, and between them the world was delivered of this scourge. Then Rustem was glad, and he praised Rakush, and washed him at the fountain, and gave thanks to God who had given unto him the victory. And when he had so done he sprang into his saddle, and rode until they were come unto the land of the magicians.

Now when evening was fallen over the land they came unto a green and shady vale, and a brook ran through it, and cool woods clothed its sides. And beside a spring there was spread a table, and wine and all manner of good cheer stood thereon. And Rustem, when he saw it, loosened his saddle and bade Rakush graze and drink, and he seated him beside the table and enjoyed its fare. And his spirit laughed with pleasure that he had found a table ready dressed within the desert, for he knew not that it was the table of the magicians, who were fled on his approach. And he ate and drank, and when he had stilled his hunger he took up a lyre that lay beside him, and he lilted to it in his ease of heart. And he sang—

"Rustem is the scourge of the base, Not for him were pleasures meant; Rare are his feasts and holidays, His garden is the desert place, The battlefield his tournament.

"There the sword of Rustem cleaves Not the armour of jousting knights, But the skulls of dragons and Deevs; Nor shall Rustem, as he believes, Ever be quit of the foes he fights.

"Cups of wine and wreaths of rose, Gardens where cool arbours stand, Fortune gave such gifts as those Not to Rustem, but hurtling foes, Strife, and a warrior's heart and hand."

Now the song of Rustem was come to the ears of one of the witches, and she changed herself into a damsel with a face of spring. And she came before Rustem and asked him his name, and toyed with him, and he was pleased with her company. And he poured out wine and handed it unto her, and bade her drink unto Ormuzd. But the magician, when she heard the name of God, fell into a tremble and her visage changed, and Rustem beheld her in all her vileness. Then his quick spirit knew her for what she was, and he made a noose and caught her in his snare, and severed her in twain. And all the magicians, when they saw it, were afraid, and none durst come forth to meet the hero. But Rustem straightway departed from this spot.

And Rustem rode till that he was come unto a land where the sun never shineth, neither stars lighten the blackness, and he could not see his path. So he suffered Rakush to lead him at his will. And they stumbled along amid the blackness, but at the end they came out again into the light. And Rustem beheld a land that was swathed in verdure, and fields wherein the crops were sprouting. Then he loosened Rakush and bade him graze, and laid himself down to slumber awhile.

Now Rakush went forth to graze in a field that had been sown, and the guardian thereof, when he saw it, was angry, and ran unto the spot where Rustem was couched, and beat the soles of his feet with a stick and woke him. And he flung reproaches and evil words upon him for that his horse was broken into the pastures. Then Rustem was angry, and fell upon the man, and took him by the ears and tore them from his body. And the man fled, howling in his agony, and came before Aulad, the ruler of the land, and laid his plaints before him. And Aulad also was angry, and went forth to seek Rustem, and demand his name and mission, and wherefore he had thus disturbed their peace. And Aulad sware that he would destroy him for this deed.

Then Rustem answered, "I am the thunder-cloud that sendeth forth lightnings, and none can stand before my strength. But if thou shouldest hear my name, the blood would stand still within thy veins. Thou art come against me with an host, see therefore how I shall scatter them like the wind."

And when he had thus spoken, Rustem fell upon the warriors of Aulad, and he beat them down before him, and their heads fell under the blows of his sword of death. And the army was routed at the hands of one man. Now Aulad, when he saw it, wept and fled; but Rustem pursued him, and threw his noose about him, and caught him in the snare. And the world became dark unto Aulad. Then Rustem bound him, and threw him on the ground, and said-

"If thou speak unto me that which is true, verily I will release thee; and when I shall have overcome the Deevs, I will give the land of Mazinderan into thy hands. Tell me, therefore, where dwelleth the White Deev, and where may I find the Shah and his men, and how can I deliver them from bondage?"

Then Aulad answered and told Rustem how it was an hundred farsangs unto the spot where Kai Kaous groaned in his bondage, and how it was yet another hundred unto the mountain pass where dwelt the Deev. And he told him how the passes were guarded by lions and magicians and mighty men, and how none had ever pierced thereunto. And he counselled him to desist from this quest.

But Rustem smiled, and said, "Be thou my guide, and thou wilt behold an elephant overcome the might of evil."

And when he had thus spoken he sprang upon Rakush, and Aulad in his bonds ran after him, and they sped like the wind, neither did they halt by night or day till they were come unto the spot where Kai Kaous had been smitten by the Deevs. And when they were come there they could behold the watch-fires of Mazinderan. Then Rustem laid him down to sleep, and he tied Aulad unto a tree that he should not escape him. But when the sun was risen he laid the mace of Saum before his saddle, and rode with gladness towards the city of the Deevs.

Now when Rustem was come nigh unto the tents of Arzang, that led the army of Mazinderan, he uttered a cry that rent the mountains. And the cry brought forth Arzang from out his tent, and when he perceived Rustem he ran at him, and would have thrown him down. But Rustem sprang upon Arzang, and he seemed an insect in his grasp. And he overcame him, and parted his head from his body, and hung it upon his saddlebow in triumph. And fear came upon the army of Mazinderan when they saw it, and they fled in faintness of spirit, and so great was the confusion that none beheld whither he bent his steps. And fathers fell upon sons, and brothers upon brothers, and dismay was spread throughout the land.

Then Rustem loosened the bonds of Aulad, and bade him lead him into the city where Kai Kaous pined in his bondage. And Aulad led him. Now when they neared the city, Rakush neighed so loud that the sound pierced even unto the spot where Kai Kaous was hidden. And the Shah, when he heard it, rejoiced, for he knew that succour was come. And he told it unto his comrades. But they refused to listen unto these words, and deemed that grief had distraught his wits. In vain therefore did Kai Kaous insist unto them that his ears had heard the voice of Rakush. But not long did he combat their unbelief, for presently there came before him Tehemten, the stout of limb, and when the nobles heard his voice and his step they repented them of their doubts. And Kai Kaous embraced Rustem and blessed him, and questioned him of his journey and of Zal. Then he said—

"O my Pehliva, we may no longer waste the moments with sweet words. I must send thee forth yet again to battle. For when the White Deev shall learn that Arzang is defeated, he will come forth from out his mountain fastness, and bring with him the whole multitude of evil ones, and even thy might will not stand before them. Go therefore unto the Seven Mountains, and conquer the White Deev ere the tidings reach him of thy coming. Unto thee alone can Iran look for her succour, for I cannot aid thee, neither can my warriors assist thee with their arms, for our eyes are filled with darkness, and their light is gone out. Yet I grieve to send thee into this emprise alone, for I have heard it spoken that the dwelling of the Deevs is a spot of fear and terror, but alas! my grief is of no avail. And I conjure thee, slay the Deev, and bring unto me the blood of his heart, for a Mubid hath revealed unto me that only by this blood can our sight be restored. And go forth now, my son, and may Ormuzd be gracious unto thee, and may the tree of gladness sprout again for Iran!"

Then Rustem did as Kai Kaous commanded, and he rode forth, and Aulad went beside him to lead him in the way. And when they had passed the Seven Mountains and were come unto the gates of hell, Rustem spake unto Aulad, and said—

"Thou hast ever led me aright, and all that thou hast spoken I have surely found it true. Tell me, therefore, now how I shall vanquish the Deevs."

And Aulad said, "Tarry, I counsel thee, till that the sun be high in the heavens. For when it beateth fierce upon the earth the Deevs are wont to lay them down to slumber, and when they are drunk with sleep they shall fall an easy prey into thine hands."

Then Rustem did as Aulad bade him, and he halted by the roadside, and he bound Aulad from head to foot in his snare, and he seated himself upon the ends. But when the sun was high he drew forth his sword from out its sheath, and shouted loud his name, and flung it among the Deevs like to a thunderbolt. Then before they were well awakened from their sleep, he threw himself upon them, and none could resist him, and he scattered their heads with his sword. And when he had dispersed the guards he came unto the lair of the White Deev.

Then Rustem stepped within the rocky tomb wherein the Deev was hidden, and the air was murky and heavy with evil odours, and the Pehliva could not see his path. But he went on void of fear, though the spot was fearful and dangers lurked in its sides. And when he was come unto the end of the cave he found a great mass like to a mountain, and it was the Deev in his midday slumber. Then Rustem woke him, and the Deev was astonished at his daring, and sprang at the hero, and threw a great stone like a small mountain upon him. And Rustem's heart trembled, and he said unto himself, "If I escape to-day, I shall live for ever." And he fell on the Deev, and they struggled hot and sore, and the Deev tore Rustem, but Rustem defended himself, and they wrestled with force till that the blood and sweat ran down in rivers from their bodies. Then Rustem prayed to God, and God heard him and gave him strength, and in the end Rustem overcame the White Deev and slew him. And he severed his head from his trunk, and cut his heart from out his midst.

Then Rustem returned him unto Aulad and told him what he had done. And Aulad said—

"O brave lion, who hast vanquished the world with thy sword, release now, I pray thee, this thy servant, for thy snare is entered into my flesh. And suffer that I recall to thee how that thou hast promised to me a recompense, and surely thou wilt fulfil thy word."

And Rustem answered and said, "Ay, verily; but I have yet much to do ere that my mission be ended. For I have still to conquer the King of Mazinderan; but when these things shall be accomplished, in truth I will fulfil my words unto thee."

Then he bade Aulad follow him, and they retraced their steps until they were come unto the spot where Kai Kaous was held in bondage. And when Kai Kaous learned that Rustem was returned with victory upon his brow he shouted for joy, and all the host shouted with him, and they could not contain themselves for happiness. And they called down the blessings of Heaven upon the head of Rustem. But when the hero came before them, he took of the blood of the White Deev and poured it into their eyes, and the eyes of Kai Kaous and his men were opened, and they once again beheld the glory of the day. Then they swept the ground around them with fire, with swords they overcame their gaolers. But when they had finished, Kai Kaous bade them desist from further bloodshed.

Then Kai Kaous wrote a letter unto the King of Mazinderan, and he counselled him that he should conclude a peace. And he related to him how that his mainstay was broken, for Rustem had overcome Arzang and slain the White Deev. And he said that Rustem would slay him also if he should not submit unto Iran and pay tribute to its Shah. Then Kai Kaous sent a messenger with this writing unto the King of Mazinderan.

Now the King, when he had read the letter, and learned how that Arzang and the White Deev and all his train were slain, was sore troubled, and he paled in his spirit, and it seemed to him that the sun of his glory was about to set. Howbeit he suffered not the messenger to behold his distress, but wrote haughty words unto Kai Kaous, and dared him to come forth to meet him. And he boasted of his might and reproached Kai Kaous with his folly. And he threatened that he would raze Iran unto the dust.

When Kai Kaous had read this answer he was wroth, and his nobles with him. And Rustem spake and said-

"Permit me, O my Shah, that I go forth before the King of Mazinderan, and intrust unto me yet another writing."

Then Kai Kaous sent for a scribe, and the scribe cut a reed like to the point of an arrow, and he wrote with it the words that Kai Kaous dictated. And Kai Kaous made not many words. He bade the King lay aside his arrogance, and he warned him of the fate that would await his disobedience, and he said unto him that if he listened not he might hang his severed head on the walls of his own city. Then he signed the letter with his royal seal, and Rustem bore it forth from the camp.

Now when the King of Mazinderan learned that Kai Kaous sent him yet another messenger, he bade the flower of his army go forth to meet him. And Rustem, when he saw them come near, laid hold upon a tree of great stature and spreading branches that grew by the wayside. And he uprooted the tree from the earth, and brandished it in his hands like to a javelin. And those that saw it were amazed at his strength. Then Rustem, when he beheld their awe, flung the tree among them, and many a brave man was dismounted by this mace. Then there stepped forth from the midst of the host one of the giants of Mazinderan, and he begged that he might grasp Rustem by the hand. And when he had hold of the hand of the Pehliva he pressed it with all his might, for he thought that he could wring off this hand of valour. But Rustem smiled at the feebleness of his grasp, and he grasped him in return, and the giant grew pale, and the veins started forth upon his hands.

Then one set off to tell the King what he had seen. And the King sent forth his doughtiest knight, and bade him retrieve the honour of their strength. And Kalahour the knight said-

"Verily so will I do, and I will force the tears of pain from the eyes of this messenger."

And he came towards Rustem and wrung his hand, and his gripe was like to a vise, and Rustem felt the pang thereof, and he winced in his suffering. But he would not let the men of Mazinderan glory in his triumph. He took the hand of Kalahour in his own, and grasped it and crushed it till that the blood issued from its veins and the nails fell from off its fingers. Then Kalahour turned him and went before the Shah and showed unto him his hand. And he counselled him to make peace with the land that could send forth such messengers whose might none could withstand. But the King was loath to sue for peace, and he commanded that the messenger be brought before him.

Then the elephant-bodied stood before the King of Mazinderan. And the King questioned him of his journey, and of Kai Kaous, and of the road that he was come. And while he questioned he took muster of him with his eyes, and when he had done speaking he cried-

"Surely thou art Rustem, for thou hast the arms and breast of a Pehliva."

But Rustem replied, "Not so, I am but a slave who is not held worthy to serve even in his train; for he is a Pehliva great and strong, whose like the earth hath not seen." Then he handed unto the King the writing of his master. But when the King had read it he was wild with anger, and he said to Rustem-

"Surely he that hath sent thee is mad that he addresseth such words unto me. For if he be master in Iran, I am lord of Mazinderan, and never shall he call me his vassal. And verily it was his own overweening that let him fall between my hands, yet hath he learned no lesson from his disasters, but deemeth he can crush me with haughty words. Go, say unto him that the King of Mazinderan will meet him in battle, and verily his pride shall learn to know humility."

And when the King had thus spoken he dismissed Rustem from his presence, but he would have had him bear forth rich gifts. But Rustem would not take them, for he too was angered, and he spurred him unto Kai Kaous with a heart hungry for vengeance.

And Kai Kaous made ready his army, and the King of Mazinderan did likewise. And they marched forth unto the meeting-place, and the earth groaned under the feet of the war-elephants. And for seven days did the battle rage fast and furious, and all the earth was darkened with the black dust; and the fire of swords and maces flashed through the blackness like to lightning from a thundercloud. And the screams of the Deevs, and the shouts of the warriors, and the clanging of the trumpets, and the beating of drums, and the neighing of horses, and the groans of the dying made the earth hideous with noise. And the blood of the brave turned the plain into a lake, and it was a combat such as none hath seen the like. But victory leaned to neither side. Then on the eighth day Kai Kaous took from his head the crown of the Kaianides and bowed him in the dust before Ormuzd. And he prayed and said-

"O Lord of earth, incline thine ear unto my voice, and grant that I may overcome these Deevs who rest not their faith in Thee. And I pray Thee do this not for my sake, who am unworthy of Thy benefits, but for the sake of Iran, Thy kingdom."

Then he put the crown once more upon his head, and went out again before the army.

And all that day the hosts fought like lions, and pity and mercy were vanished from the world, and heaven itself seemed to rain maces. But Ormuzd had heard the prayer of His servant, and when evening was come the army of Mazinderan was faded like a flower. Then Rustem, perceiving the King of Mazinderan, challenged him to single combat. And the King consented, and Rustem overcame him, and raised his lance to strike him, saying-

"Perish, O evil Deev! for thy name is struck out of the lists of those who carry high their heads."

But when he was about to strike him, the King put forth his arts of magic, and he was changed into a rock within sight of all the army. And Rustem was confounded thereat, and he knew not what he should do. But Kai Kaous commanded that the rock should be brought before his throne. So those among the army who were strong of limb meshed it with cords and tried to raise it from the earth. But the rock resisted all their efforts and none could move it a jot. Then Rustem, the elephant-limbed, came forward to test his power, and he grasped the rock in his mighty fist, and he bore it in his hands across the hills, even unto the spot that Kai Kaous had named, and all the army shouted with amazement when they saw it.

Now when Rustem had laid down the stone at the feet of the Shah, he spake and said unto it-

"Issue forth, I command thee, O King of Mazinderan, or I will break thee into atoms with my mace."

When the King heard this threat he was afraid, and came out of the stone, and stood before Rustem in all his vileness. And Rustem took his hand and smiled and led him before Kai Kaous, and said-

"I bring thee this piece of rock, whom fear of my blows hath brought into subjection."

Then Kai Kaous reproached the King with all the evil he had done him, and when he had spoken he bade that the head of this wicked man should be severed from its trunk. And it was done as Kai Kaous commanded. Then Kai Kaous gave thanks unto God, and distributed rich gifts unto his army, to each man according to his deserts. And he prepared a feast, and bade them rejoice and make merry with wine. And at last he called before him Rustem, his Pehliva, and gave to him thanks, and said that but for his aid he would not have sat again upon his throne. But Rustem said-

"Not so, O King, thy thanks are due unto Aulad, for he it was who led me aright, and instructed me how I could vanquish the Deevs. Grant, therefore, now that I may fulfil my promise unto him, and bestow on him the crown of Mazinderan."

When Kai Kaous heard these words he did as Rustem desired, and Aulad received the crown and the land, and there was peace yet again in Iran. And the land rejoiced thereat, and Kai Kaous opened the doors of his treasures, and all was well within his borders. Then Rustem came before the Shah and prayed that he might be permitted to return unto his father. And Kai Kaous listened to the just desires of his Pehliva, and he sent him forth laden with rich gifts, and he could not cease from pouring treasure before him. And he blessed him, and said-

"Mayst thou live as long as the sun and moon, and may thy heart continue steadfast, mayst thou ever be the joy of Iran!"

Then when Rustem was departed, Kai Kaous gave himself up unto delights and to wine, but he governed his land right gloriously. He struck the neck of care with the sword of justice, he caused the earth to be clad with verdure, and God granted unto him His countenance, and the hand of Ahriman could do no hurt.

Thus endeth the history of the march into Mazinderan.

KAI KAOUS COMMITTETH MORE FOLLIES

*W*hilom the fancy seized upon the Shah of Iran that he would visit his empire, and look face to face upon his vassals, and exact their tribute. So he passed from Turan into China, and from Mikran into Berberistan. And wheresoever he passed men did homage before him, for the bull cannot wage battle with the lion. But it could not remain thus for ever, and already there sprang forth thorns in the garden of roses. For while the fortunes of the world thus prospered, a chieftain raised the standard of revolt in Egypt, and the people of the land turned them from the gates of submission unto Iran. And there was joined unto them the King of Hamaveran, who desired to throw off the yoke of Persia. But Kai Kaous, when the tidings thereof came unto him, got ready his army and marched against the rebels. And when he came before them, their army, that had seemed invincible, was routed, and the King of Hamaveran was foremost to lay down his arms and ask pardon of his Shah. And Kai Kaous granted his petition, and the King departed joyously from out his presence. Then one of those who stood about the Shah said unto him—

"Is it known to thee, O Shah, that this King hideth behind his curtains a daughter of beauty? It would beseem my lord that he should take this moon unto himself for wife."

And Kai Kaous answered, "Thy counsel is good, and I will therefore send messengers unto her father, and demand of him that he give me his daughter as tribute, and to cement the peace that hath been made between us."

When the King of Hamaveran heard this message his heart was filled with gall, and his head was heavy with sorrow, and he murmured in his spirit that Kai Kaous, who owned the world, should desire to take from him his chiefest treasure. And he hid not his grief from the Shah in his answer, but he wrote also that he knew it behoved him to do the thing that Kai Kaous desired. Then in his distress he called before him Sudaveh his daughter, whom he loved, and he told her all his troubles, and bade her counsel him how he should act. For he said-

"If I lose thee, the light of my life is gone out. Yet how may I stand against the Shah?"

And Sudaveh replied, "If there be no remedy, I counsel thee to rejoice at that which cannot be changed."

Now when her father heard these words he knew that she was not afflicted concerning that which was come about. So he sent for the envoy of Kai Kaous and assented unto his demands, and they concluded an alliance according to the forms of the land. Then when the King had poured gifts before the messenger, and feasted him with wine, he sent forth an escort to bear his daughter unto the tents of the Shah. And the young moon went forth in a litter, and she was robed in garbs of splendour, and when Kai Kaous beheld her loveliness he was struck dumb for very joy. Then he raised Sudaveh unto the throne beside him, and named her worthy to be his spouse. And they were glad in each other, and rejoiced; but all was not to be well thus quickly.

For the King of Hamaveran was sore in his heart that the light of his life was gone from him, and he cast about in his spirit how he should regain her unto himself. And when she had been gone but seven days, he sent forth a messenger unto Kai Kaous and entreated him that he would come and feast within his gates, so that all the land might rejoice in their alliance.

When Sudaveh heard this message her mind misgave her, and she feared evil. Wherefore she counselled the Shah that he should abstain from this feast. But Kai Kaous would not listen unto the fears of Sudaveh, he would not give ear unto her warning. Wherefore he went forth unto the city of the King of Hamaveran, and made merry with him many days. And the King caused gifts to be rained down upon Kai Kaous, and he flattered him, and cozened his vanity, and he made much of his men, and he darkened their wits with fair words and sweet wine. Then when he had lulled their fears, and caused them to forget wherefore and why and all knowledge of misfortune, he fell upon them and bound them with strong chains, and overthrew their glories and their thrones. And Kai Kaous did he send unto a fortress whose head touched the sky and whose foot was planted in the ocean. Then he sent forth a strong band into the camp of Iran, and veiled women went with them, and he charged them that they bring back Sudaveh unto his arms.

Now when Sudaveh saw the men and the women that went with them she guessed what was come about, and she cried aloud and tore her robes in anguish. And when they had brought her before her father she reproved him for his treachery, and she sware that none should part her from Kai Kaous, even though he were hidden in a tomb. Then the King was angered when he saw that her heart was taken from him and given to the Shah, and he bade that she be flung into the same prison as her lord. And Sudaveh was glad at his resolve, and she went into the dungeon with a light heart, and she seated herself beside the Shah, and served him and comforted him, and they bore the weight of captivity together.

After these things were come about, the Iranians, because that their Shah was held captive, returned unto Iran much discomfited. And when the news spread that the throne was empty many would have seized thereon. And Afrasiyab, when he learned it, straightway forgot hunger and sleep, and marched a strong army across the border. And he laid waste the land of Iran, and men, women, and children fell into bondage at his hands, and the world was darkened unto the kingdom of light. Then some arose and went before the son of Zal to crave his help in this sore need, saying unto him-

"Be thou our shield against misfortune, and deliver us from affliction, for the glory of the Kaianides is vanished, and the land which was a paradise is one no more."

Now Rustem, when he heard the news, was grieved for the land, but he was angered also against the Shah that he had thus once again run into danger. Yet he told the messengers that he would seek to deliver Kai Kaous, and that when he had done so he would remember the land of Iran. And forthwith he sent a secret messenger unto Kai Kaous, a man subtle and wise, and caused him to say unto the Shah-

"An army cometh forth from Iran to redeem thee. Rejoice, therefore, and cast aside thy fears."

And he also sent a writing unto the King of Hamaveran, and the writing was filled with threats, and spake only of maces and swords and combat. And Rustem loaded the King with reproaches because of his treachery, and he bade him prepare to meet Rustem the mighty.

When the King of Hamaveran had read this letter his head was troubled, and he defied Rustem, and threatened him that if he came forth against him he should meet at his hands the fate of the Shah. But Rustem only smiled when he heard this answer, and he said-

"Surely this man is foolish, or Ahriman hath filled his mind with smoke."

Then he mounted Rakush, and made ready to go into Hamaveran, and a vast train of warriors went after him. And the King of Hamaveran, when he saw it sent forth his army against him. But the army were afraid when they beheld Rustem and his might of mien, his mace, and his strong arms and lion chest, and their hearts departed from out their bodies, and they fled from before his sight, and returned them unto the King of Hamaveran.

Now the King was seated in the midst of his counsellors, and when he saw the army thus scattered before they had struck a blow, his heart misgave him, and he craved counsel of his chiefs. Then they counselled him that he should cast about him for allies. So the King of Hamaveran sent messengers of entreaty unto the Kings of Egypt and Berberistan, and they listened to his prayers, and sent out a great army unto his aid. And they drew them up against Rustem, and the armies stretched for two leagues in length, and you would have said the handful of Rustem could not withstand their force. Yet Rustem bade his men be not discomfited, and rest their hopes on God. Then he fell upon the armies of the Kings like to a flame that darteth forth, and the ground was drenched with gore, and on all sides rolled heads that were severed from their bodies; and wheresoever Rakush and Rustem showed themselves, there was great havoc made in the ranks. And ere the evening was come, the Kings of Egypt and Berberistan were his captives; and when the sun was set, the King of Hamaveran knew that a day of ill fortune was ended. So he sent forth to crave mercy at the hands of the Pehliva. And Rustem listened to his voice, and said that he would stay his hand if the King would restore unto him Kai Kaous, and the men and treasures that were his. Then the King of Hamaveran granted the just requests of Rustem. So Kai Kaous was led forth from his prison, and Sudaveh came with him. And when they beheld him, the King of Hamaveran and his allies declared their allegiance unto him, and they marched with him into Iran to go out against Afrasiyab. And Sudaveh went with the army in a litter clothed with fair stuffs, and encrusted with wood of aloes. And she was veiled that none might behold her beauty, and she went with the men like to the sun when he marcheth behind a cloud.

Now when Kai Kaous was come home again unto his land, he sent a writing unto Afrasiyab. And he said-

"Quit, I command thee, the land of Iran, nor seek to enlarge thyself at my cost. For knowest thou not that Iran is mine, and that the world pertaineth unto me?"

But Afrasiyab answered, "The words which thou dost write are not becoming unto a man such as thou, who didst covet Mazinderan and the countries round about. If thou wert satisfied with Iran, wherefore didst thou venture afield? And I say unto thee, Iran is mine, because of Tur my forefather, and because I subdued it under my hand."

When Kai Kaous had heard these words he knew that Afrasiyab would not yield save unto force. So he drew up his army into array, and they marched out to meet the King of Turan. And Afrasiyab met them with a great host, and the sound of drums and cymbals filled the air. And great was the strife and bloody, but Rustem broke the force of Turan, and the fortunes of its army were laid to rest upon the field of battle. And Afrasiyab, when he beheld it, was discomfited, and his spirit boiled over like to new wine that fermenteth. And he mourned over his army and the warriors that he had trained, and he conjured those that remained to make yet another onslaught, and he spake fair promises unto them if they would deliver unto his hands Rustem, the Pehliva. And he said-

"Whoever shall bring him alive before me, I will give unto him a kingdom and an umbrella, and the hand of my daughter in marriage."

And the Turks, when they heard these words, girded them yet again for resistance. But it availed them nought, for the Iranians were mightier than they, and they watered the earth with their blood until the ground was like a rose. And the fortunes of the Turks were as a light put out, and Afrasiyab fled before the face of Rustem, and the remnant of his army went after him.

Then Kai Kaous seated himself once more upon his throne, and men were glad that there was peace. And the Shah opened the doors of justice and splendour, and all men did that which was right, and the wolf turned him away from the lamb, and there was gladness through all the length of Iran. And the Shah gave thanks unto Rustem that he had aided him yet again, and he named him Jahani Pehliva, which being interpreted meaneth the champion of the world, and he called him the source of his happiness. Then he busied himself with building mighty towers and palaces, and the land of Iran was made fair at his hands, and all was well once more within its midst.

But Ahriman the wakeful was not pleased thereat, and he pondered how he could once again arouse the ambition of the Shah. So he held counsel with his Deevs how they might turn the heart of Kai Kaous from the right path. And one among them said-

"Suffer that I go before the Shah, and I will do thy behest."

And Ahriman suffered it. Then the Deev took upon him the form of a youth, and in his hand he held a cluster of roses, and he presented them unto the Shah, and he kissed the ground before his feet. And when Kai Kaous had given him leave to speak he opened his mouth and said-

"O Shah, live for ever! though such is thy might and majesty that the vault of heaven alone should be thy throne. All the world is submissive before thee, and I can bethink me but of one thing that is lacking unto thy glory."

Then Kai Kaous questioned him of this one thing, and the Deev said-

"It is that thou knowest not the nature of the sun and moon, nor wherefore the planets roll, neither the secret causes that set them in motion. Thou art master of all the earth, therefore shouldst thou not make the heavens also obedient to thy will?"

When Kai Kaous heard these words of guile his mind was dimmed, and he forgot that man cannot mount unto the skies, and he pondered without ceasing how he could fly unto the stars and inquire into their secrets. And he consulted many wise men in his trouble, but none could aid him. But at last it came about that a certain man taught him how he could perchance accomplish his designs. And Kai Kaous did according to his instructions. He built him a framework of aloe-wood, and at the four corners thereof he placed javelins upright, and on their points he put the flesh of goats. Then he chose out four eagles strong of wing, and bound them unto the corners of this chariot. And when it was done, Kai Kaous seated himself in the midst thereof with much pomp. And the eagles, when they smelt the flesh, desired after it, and they flapped their wings and raised themselves, and raised the framework with them. And they struggled sore, but they could not attain unto the meat; but ever as they struggled they bore aloft with them Kai Kaous and the throne whereon he sat. And so long as their hunger lasted, they strove after the prey. But at length their strength would hold no longer, and they desisted from the attempt. And behold! as they desisted the fabric fell back to earth, and the shock thereof was great. And but for Ormuzd Kai Kaous would have perished in the presumption of his spirit.

Now the eagles had borne the Shah even unto the desert of Cathay, and there was no man to succour him, and he suffered from the pangs of hunger, and there was nothing to assuage his longing, neither could his thirst be stilled. And he was alone, and sorrowful and shamed in his soul that he had yet again brought derision upon Iran. And he prayed to God in his trouble, and entreated pardon for his sins.

While Kai Kaous thus strove with repentance, Rustem learned tidings of him, and he set out with an army to seek him. And when he had found him he gave rein unto his anger, and he rebuked him for his follies, and he said-

"Hath the world seen the like of this man? Hath a more foolish head sat upon the throne of Iran? Ye would say there were no brains within this skull, or that not one of its thoughts was good. Kai Kaous is like a thing that is possessed, and every wind beareth him away. Thrice hast thou now fallen into mishap, and who can tell whether thy spirit hath yet learned wisdom? And it will be a reproach unto Iran all her days that a king puffed up with idle pride was seated upon her throne, a man who deemed in his folly that he could mount unto the skies, and visit the sun and moon, and count the stars one by one. I entreat of thee to bethink thee of thy forefathers, and follow in their steps, and rule the land in equity, neither rush after these mad adventures."

When Kai Kaous had listened to the bitter words spoken by Rustem, he was bowed down in his spirit and ashamed before him in his soul. And when at last he opened his mouth it was to utter words of humility. And he said unto Rustem-

"Surely that which thou speakest, it is true."

Then he suffered himself to be led back unto his palace, and many days and nights did he lie in the dust before God, and it was long before he held him worthy to mount again upon his throne. But when he deemed that God had forgiven him, he seated him upon it once again. In humility did he mount it, and he filled it in wisdom. And henceforth he ruled the land with justice, and he did that which was right in the sight of God, and bathed his face with the waters of sincerity. And kings and rulers did homage before him, and forgot the follies that he had done, and Kai Kaous grew worthy of the throne of light. And Iran was exalted at his hands, and power and prosperity increased within its borders.

RUSTEM AND SOHRAB

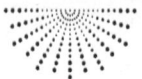

*G*ive ear unto the combat of Sohrab against Rustem, though it be a tale replete with tears.

It came about that on a certain day Rustem arose from his couch, and his mind was filled with forebodings. He bethought him therefore to go out to the chase. So he saddled Rakush and made ready his quiver with arrows. Then he turned him unto the wilds that lie near Turan, even in the direction of the city of Samengan. And when he was come nigh unto it, he started a herd of asses and made sport among them till that he was weary of the hunt. Then he caught one and slew it and roasted it for his meal, and when he had eaten it and broken the bones for the marrow, he laid himself down to slumber, and Rakush cropped the pasture beside him.

Now while the hero was sleeping there passed by seven knights of Turan, and they beheld Rakush and coveted him. So they threw their cords at him to ensnare him. But Rakush, when he beheld their design, pawed the ground in anger, and fell upon them as he had fallen upon the lion. And of one man he bit off the head, and another he struck down under his hoofs, and he would have overcome them all, but they were too many. So they ensnared him and led him into the city, thinking in their hearts, "Verily a goodly capture have we made." But Rustem when he awoke from his slumbers was downcast and sore grieved when he saw not his steed, and he said unto himself-

"How can I stand against the Turks, and how can I traverse the desert alone?"

And his heart was full of trouble. Then he sought for the traces of the horse's hoofs, and he followed them, and they led him even unto the gates of the city. Now when those within beheld Rustem, and that he came before them on foot, the King and the nobles came forth to greet him, and inquired of him how this was come about. Then Rustem told them how Rakush was vanished while he slumbered, and how he had followed his track even unto these gates. And he sware a great oath, and vowed that if his courser were not restored unto him many heads should quit their trunks. Then the King of Samengan, when he saw that Rustem was beside himself with anger, spoke words of soothing, and said that none of his people should do wrong unto the hero; and he begged him that he would enter into his house and abide with him until that search had been made, saying-

"Surely Rakush cannot be hid."

And Rustem was satisfied at these words, and cast suspicion from his spirit, and entered the house of the King, and feasted with him, and beguiled the hours with wine. And the King rejoiced in his guest, and encompassed him with sweet singers and all honour. And when the night was fallen the King himself led Rustem unto a couch perfumed with musk and roses, and he bade him slumber sweetly until the morning. And he declared to him yet again that all was well for him and for his steed.

Now when a portion of the night was spent, and the star of morning stood high in the arch of heaven, the door of Rustem's chamber was opened, and a murmur of soft voices came in from the threshold. And there stepped within a slave bearing a lamp perfumed with amber, and a woman whose beauty was veiled came after her. And as she moved musk was scattered from her robes. And the women came nigh unto the bed of the hero heavy with wine and slumber. And he was amazed when he saw them. And when he had roused him somewhat he spake and said-

"Who art thou, and what is thy name and thy desire, and what seekest thou from me in the dark night?"

Then the Peri-faced answered him, saying, "I am Tahmineh, the daughter of the King of Samengan, of the race of the leopard and the lion, and none of the princes of this earth are worthy of my hand, neither hath any man seen me unveiled. But my heart is torn with anguish, and my spirit

FERDOWSI

is tossed with desire, for I have heard of thy deeds of prowess, and how thou fearest neither Deev nor lion, neither leopard nor crocodile, and how thy hand is swift to strike, and how thou didst venture alone into Mazinderan, and how wild asses are devoured of thee, and how the earth groaneth under the tread of thy feet, and how men perish at thy blows, and how even the eagle dareth not swoop down upon her prey when she beholdeth thy sword. These things and more have they told unto me, and mine eyes have yearned to look upon thy face. And now hath God brought thee within the gates of my father, and I am come to say unto thee that I am thine if thou wilt hear me, and if thou wilt not, none other will I espouse. And consider, O Pehliva, how that love hath obscured mine understanding and withdrawn me from the bosom of discretion, yet peradventure God will grant unto me a son like to thee for strength and valour, to whom shall be given the empire of the world. And if thou wilt listen unto me, I will lead forth before thee Rakush thy steed, and I will place under thy feet the land of Samengan."

Now while this moon of beauty was yet speaking, Rustem regarded her. And he saw that she was fair, and that wisdom abode in her mind; and when he heard of Rakush, his spirit was decided within him, and he held that this adventure could not end save gloriously. So he sent a Mubid unto the King and demanded the hand of Tahmineh from her father. And the King, when he heard the news, was rejoiced, and gave his daughter unto the Pehliva, and they concluded an alliance according to custom and the rites. And all men, young and old, within the house and city of the King were glad at this alliance, and called down blessings upon Rustem.

Now Rustem, when he was alone with the Peri-faced, took from his arm an onyx that was known unto all the world. And he gave it to her, and said-

"Cherish this jewel, and if Heaven cause thee to give birth unto a daughter, fasten it within her locks, and it will shield her from evil; but if it be granted unto thee to bring forth a son, fasten it upon his arm, that he may wear it like his father. And he shall be strong as Keriman, of stature like unto Saum the son of Neriman, and of grace of speech like unto Zal, my father."

The Peri-faced, when she had heard these words, was glad in his presence. But when the day was passed there came in unto them the King her father, and he told Rustem how that tidings of Rakush were come unto his ears, and how that the courser would shortly be within the gates. And Rustem, when he heard it, was filled with longing after his steed, and when he knew that he was come he hastened forth to caress him. And with his own hands he fastened the saddle, and gave thanks unto Ormuzd, who had restored his joy between his hands. Then he knew that the time to depart was come. And he opened his arms and took unto his heart Tahmineh the fair of face, and he bathed her cheek with his tears and covered her hair with kisses. Then he flung him upon Rakush, and the swift-footed bare him quickly from out of her sight. And Tahmineh was sorrowful exceedingly, and Rustem too was filled with thoughts as he turned him back into Zaboulistan. And he pondered this adventure in his heart, but to no man did he speak of what he had seen or done.

Now when nine moons had run their course there was born unto Tahmineh a son in the likeness of his father, a babe whose mouth was filled with smiles, wherefore men called him Sohrab. And when he numbered but one month he was like unto a child of twelve, and when he numbered five years he was skilled in arms and all the arts of war, and when ten years were rolled above his head there was none in the land that could resist him in the games of strength. Then he came before his mother and spake words of daring. And he said-

"Since I am taller and stouter than my peers, teach unto me my race and lineage, and what I shall say when men ask me the name of my sire. But if thou refuse an answer unto my demands, I will strike thee out from the rolls of the living."

When Tahmineh beheld the ardour of her son, she smiled in her spirit because that his fire was like to that of his father. And she opened her mouth and said-

"Hear my words, O my son, and be glad in thine heart, neither give way in thy spirit to anger. For thou art the offspring of Rustem, thou art descended from the seed of Saum and Zal, and Neriman was thy forefather. And since God made the world it hath held none like unto Rustem, thy sire."

Then she showed to him a letter written by the Pehliva, and gave to him the gold and jewels Rustem had sent at his birth. And she spake and said-

"Cherish these gifts with gratitude, for it is thy father who hath sent them. Yet remember, O my son, that thou close thy lips concerning these things; for Turan groaneth under the hand of Afrasiyab, and he is foe unto Rustem the glorious. If, therefore, he should learn of thee, he would seek to destroy the son for hatred of the sire. Moreover, O my boy, if Rustem learned that thou wert become a mountain of valour, perchance he would demand thee at my hands, and the sorrow of thy loss would crush the heart of thy mother."

But Sohrab replied, "Nought can be hidden upon earth for aye. To all men are known the deeds of Rustem, and since my birth be thus noble, wherefore hast thou kept it dark from me so long? I will go forth with an army of brave Turks and lead them unto Iran, I will cast Kai Kaous from off his throne, I will give to Rustem the crown of the Kaianides, and together we will subdue the land of Turan, and Afrasiyab shall be slain by my hands. Then will I mount the throne in his stead. But thou shalt be called Queen of Iran. for since Rustem is my father and I am his son no other kings shall rule in this world, for to us alone behoveth it to wear the crowns of might. And I pant in longing after the battlefield, and I desire that the world should behold my prowess. But a horse is needful unto me, a steed tall and strong of power to bear me, for it beseemeth me not to go on foot before mine enemies."

Now Tahmineh, when she had heard the words of this boy, rejoiced in her soul at his courage. So she bade the guardians of the flocks lead out the horses before Sohrab her son. And they did as she had bidden, and Sohrab surveyed the steeds, and tested their strength like as his father had done before him of old, and he bowed them under his hand, and he could not be satisfied. And thus for many days did he seek a worthy steed. Then one came before him and told of a foal sprung from Rakush, the swift of foot. When Sohrab heard the tidings he smiled, and bade that the foal be led before him. And he tested it and found it to be strong. So he saddled it and sprang upon its back and cried, saying-

"Now that I own a horse like thee, the world shall be made dark to many."

Then he made ready for war against Iran, and the nobles and warriors flocked around him. And when all was in order Sohrab came before his grandsire and craved his counsel and his aid to go forth into the land of Iran and seek out his father. And the King of Samengan, when he heard these wishes, deemed them to be just, and he opened the doors of his treasures without stint and gave unto Sohrab of his wealth, for he was filled with pleasure at this boy. And he invested Sohrab with all the honours of a King, and he bestowed on him all the marks of his good pleasure.

Meantime a certain man brought news unto Afrasiyab that Sohrab was making ready an army to fall upon Iran, and to cast Kai Kaous from off his throne. And he told Afrasiyab how the courage and valour of Sohrab exceeded words. And Afrasiyab, when he heard this, hid not his contentment, and he called before him Human and Barman, the doughty. Then he bade them gather together an army and join the ranks of Sohrab, and he confided to them his secret purpose, but he enjoined them to tell no man thereof. For he said-

"Into our hands hath it been given to settle the course of the world. For it is known unto me that Sohrab is sprung from Rustem the Pehliva, but from Rustem must it be hidden who it is that goeth out against him, then peradventure he will perish by the hands of this young lion, and Iran, devoid of Rustem, will fall a prey into my hands. Then will we subdue Sohrab also, and all the world will be ours. But if it be written that Sohrab fall under the hand of Tehemten, then the grief he shall endure when he shall learn that he hath slain his son will bring him to the grave for sorrow."

So spake Afrasiyab in his guile, and when he had done unveiling his black heart he bade the warriors depart unto Samengan. And they bare with them gifts of great price to pour before the face of Sohrab. And they bare also a letter filled with soft words. And in the letter Afrasiyab lauded Sohrab for his resolve, and told him how that if Iran be subdued the world would henceforth know peace, for upon his own head would he place the crown of the Kaianides; and Turan, Iran, and Samengan should be as one land.

When Sohrab had read this letter, and saw the gifts and the aid sent out to him, he rejoiced aloud, for he deemed that now none could withstand his might. So he caused the cymbals of departure to be clashed, and the army made them ready to go forth. Then Sohrab led them into the land of Iran. And their track was marked by desolation and destruction, for they spared nothing that they passed. And they spread fire and dismay abroad, and they marched on unstayed until they came unto the White Castle, the fortress wherein Iran put its trust.

Now the guardian of the castle was named Hujir, and there lived with him Gustahem the brave, but he was grown old, and could aid no longer save with his counsels. And there abode also his daughter Gurdafrid, a warlike maid, firm in the saddle, and practised in the fight. Now when Hujir beheld from afar a dusky cloud of armed men he came forth to meet them. And Sohrab, when he saw him, drew his sword, and demanded his name, and bade him prepare to meet his end. And he taunted him with rashness that he was come forth thus unaided to stand against a lion. But Hujir

FERDOWSI

answered Sohrab with taunts again, and vowed that he would sever his head from his trunk and send it for a trophy unto the Shah. Yet Sohrab only smiled when he heard these words, and he challenged Hujir to come near. And they met in combat, and wrestled sore one with another, and stalwart were their strokes and strong; but Sohrab overcame Hujir as though he were an infant, and he bound him and sent him captive unto Human.

But when those within the castle learned that their chief was bound they raised great lamentation, and their fears were sore. And Gurdafrid too, when she learned it, was grieved, but she was ashamed also for the fate of Hujir. So she took forth burnished mail and clad herself therein, and she hid her tresses under a helmet of Roum, and she mounted a steed of battle and came forth before the walls like to a warrior. And she uttered a cry of thunder, and flung it amid the ranks of Turan, and she defied the champions to come forth to single combat. And none came, for they beheld her how she was strong, and they knew not that it was a woman, and they were afraid. But Sohrab, when he saw it, stepped forth and said-

"I will accept thy challenge, and a second prize will fall into my hands."

Then he girded himself and made ready for the fight. And the maid, when she saw he was ready, rained arrows upon him with art, and they fell quick like hail, and whizzed about his head; and Sohrab, when he saw it, could not defend himself, and was angry and ashamed. Then he covered his head with a shield and ran at the maid. But she, when she saw him approach, dropped her bow and couched a lance, and thrust at Sohrab with vigour, and shook him mightily, and it wanted little and she would have thrown him from his seat. And Sohrab was amazed, and his wrath knew no bounds. Then he ran at Gurdafrid with fury, and seized the reins of her steed, and caught her by the waist, and tore her armour, and threw her upon the ground. Yet ere he could raise his hand to strike her, she drew her sword and shivered his lance in twain, and leaped again upon her steed. And when she saw that the day was hers, she was weary of further combat, and she sped back unto the fortress. But Sohrab gave rein unto his horse, and followed after her in his great anger. And he caught her, and seized her, and tore the helmet from off her head, for he desired to look upon the face of the man who could withstand the son of Rustem. And lo! when he had done so, there rolled forth from the helmet coils of dusky hue, and Sohrab beheld it was a woman that had overcome him in the fight. And he was confounded. But when he had found speech he said-

"If the daughters of Iran are like to thee, and go forth unto battle, none can stand against this land."

Then he took his cord and threw it about her, and bound her in its snare, saying-

"Seek not to escape me, O moon of beauty, for never hath prey like unto thee fallen between my hands."

Then Gurdafrid, full of wile, turned unto him her face that was unveiled, for she beheld no other means of safety, and she said unto him-

"O hero without flaw, is it well that thou shouldest seek to make me captive, and show me unto the army? For they have beheld our combat, and that I overcame thee, and surely now they will gibe when they learn that thy strength was withstood by a woman. Better would it beseem thee to hide this adventure, lest thy cheeks have cause to blush because of me. Therefore let us conclude a peace together. The castle shall be thine, and all it holds; follow after me then, and take possession of thine own."

Now Sohrab, when he had listened, was beguiled by her words and her beauty, and he said-

"Thou dost wisely to make peace with me, for verily these walls could not resist my might."

And he followed after her unto the heights of the castle, and he stood with her before its gates. And Gustahem, when he saw them, opened the portal, and Gurdafrid stepped within the threshold, but when Sohrab would have followed after her she shut the door upon him. Then Sohrab saw that she had befooled him, and his fury knew no bounds. But ere he was recovered from his surprise she came out upon the battlements and scoffed at him, and counselled him to go back whence he was come; for surely, since he could not stand against a woman, he would fall an easy prey before Rustem, when the Pehliva should have learned that robbers from Turan were broken into the land. And Sohrab was made yet madder for her words, and he departed from the walls in his wrath, and rode far in his anger, and spread terror in his path. And he vowed that he would yet bring the maid into subjection.

In the meantime Gustahem the aged called before him a scribe, and bade him write unto Kai Kaous all that was come about, and how an army was come forth from Turan, at whose head rode a chief that was a child in years, a lion in strength and stature. And he told how Hujir had been bound, and how the fortress was like to fall into the hands of the enemy;

FERDOWSI

for there were none to defend it save only his daughter and himself and he craved the Shah to come to their aid.

Albeit when the day had followed yet again upon the night, Sohrab made ready his host to fall upon the castle. But when he came near thereto he found it was empty, and the doors thereof stood open, and no warriors appeared upon its walls. And he was surprised, for he knew not that in the darkness the inmates were fled by a passage that was hidden under the earth. And he searched the building for Gurdafrid, for his heart yearned after her in love, and he cried aloud-

"Woe, woe is me that this moon is vanished behind the clouds!"

Now when Kai Kaous had gotten the writing of Gustahem, he was sore afflicted and much afraid, and he called about him his nobles and asked their counsels. And he said-

"Who shall stand against this Turk? For Gustahem doth liken him in power unto Rustem, and saith he resembleth the seed of Neriman."

Then the warriors cried with one accord, "Unto Rustem alone can we look in this danger!"

And Kai Kaous hearkened to their voice, and he called for a scribe and dictated unto him a letter. And he wrote unto his Pehliva, and invoked the blessings of Heaven upon his head, and he told him all that was come to pass, and how new dangers threatened Iran, and how to Rustem alone could he look for help in his trouble. And he recalled unto Tehemten all that he had done for him in the days that were gone by, and he entreated him once again to be his refuge. And he said-

"When thou shalt receive this letter, stay not to speak the word that hangeth upon thy lips; and if thou bearest roses in thy hands, stop not to smell them, but haste thee to help us in our need."

Then Kai Kaous sent forth Gew with this writing unto Zaboulistan, and bade him neither rest nor tarry until he should stand before the face of Rustem. And he said-

"When thou hast done my behest, turn thee again unto me; neither abide within the courts of the Pehliva, nor linger by the roadside."

And Gew did as the Shah commanded, and took neither food nor rest till he set foot within the gates of Rustem. And Rustem greeted him kindly, and asked him of his mission; and when he had read the writing of the Shah, he questioned Gew concerning Sohrab. For he said-

"I should not marvel if such an hero arose in Iran, but that a warrior of renown should come forth from amid the Turks, I cannot believe it. But thou sayest none knoweth whence cometh this knight. I have myself a son in

Samengan, but he is yet an infant, and his mother writeth to me that he rejoiceth in the sports of his age, and though he be like to become a hero among men, his time is not yet come to lead forth an army. And that which thou sayest hath been done, surely it is not the work of a babe. But enter, I pray thee, into my house, and we will confer together concerning this adventure."

Then Rustem bade his cooks make ready a banquet, and he feasted Gew, and troubled his head with wine, and caused him to forget cares and time. But when morn was come Gew remembered the commands of the Shah that he tarry not, but return with all speed, and he spake thereof to Rustem, and prayed him to make known his resolve. But Rustem spake, saying-

"Disquiet not thyself, for death will surely fall upon these men of Turan. Stay with me yet another day and rest, and water thy lips that are parched. For though this Sohrab be a hero like to Saum and Zal and Neriman, verily he shall fall by my hands."

And he made ready yet another banquet, and three days they caroused without ceasing. But on the fourth Gew uprose with resolve, and came before Rustem girt for departure. And he said-

"It behoveth me to return, O Pehliva, for I bethink me how Kai Kaous is a man hard and choleric, and the fear of Sohrab weigheth upon his heart, and his soul burneth with impatience, and he hath lost sleep, and hath hunger and thirst on this account. And he will be wroth against us if we delay yet longer to do his behest."

Then Rustem said, "Fear not, for none on earth dare be angered with me."

But he did as Gew desired, and made ready his army, and saddled Rakush, and set forth from Zaboulistan, and a great train followed after him.

Now when they came nigh unto the courts of the Shah, the nobles came forth to meet them, and do homage before Rustem. And when they were come in Rustem gat him from Rakush and hastened into the presence of his lord. But Kai Kaous, when he beheld him, was angry, and spake not, and his brows were knit with fury; and when Rustem had done obeisance before him, he unlocked the doors of his mouth, and words of folly escaped his lips. And he said-

"Who is Rustem, that he defieth my power and disregardeth my commands? If I had a sword within my grasp I would split his head like to an orange. Seize him, I command, and hang him upon the nearest gallows, and let his name be never spoken in my presence."

When he heard these words Gew trembled in his heart, but he said, "Dost thou put forth thy hand against Rustem?"

And the Shah when he heard it was beside himself, and he cried with a loud voice that Gew be hanged together with the other; and he bade Tus lead them forth. And Tus would have led them out, for he hoped the anger of the Shah would be appeased; but Rustem broke from his grasp and stood before Kai Kaous, and all the nobles were filled with fear when they saw his anger. And he flung reproaches at Kai Kaous, and he recalled to him his follies, and the march into Mazinderan and Hamaveran, and his flight into Heaven; and he reminded him how that but for Rustem he would not now be seated upon the throne of light. And he bade him threaten Sohrab the Turk with his gallows, and he said-

"I am a free man and no slave, and am servant alone unto God; and without Rustem Kai Kaous is as nothing. And the world is subject unto me, and Rakush is my throne, and my sword is my seal, and my helmet my crown. And but for me, who called forth Kai Kobad, thine eyes had never looked upon this throne. And had I desired it I could have sat upon its seat. But now am I weary of thy follies, and I will turn me away from Iran, and when this Turk shall have put you under his yoke I shall not learn thereof."

Then he turned him and strode from out the presence-chamber. And he sprang upon Rakush, who waited without, and he was vanished from before their eyes ere yet the nobles had rallied from their astonishment. And they were downcast and oppressed with boding cares, and they held counsel among themselves what to do; for Rustem was their mainstay, and they knew that, bereft of his arm and counsel, they could not stand against this Turk. And they blamed Kai Kaous, and counted over the good deeds that Rustem had done for him, and they pondered and spake long. And in the end they resolved to send a messenger unto Kai Kaous, and they chose from their midst Gudarz the aged, and bade him stand before the Shah. And Gudarz did as they desired, and he spake long and without fear, and he counted over each deed that had been done by Rustem; and he reproached the Shah with his ingratitude, and he said how Rustem was the shepherd, and how the flock could not be led without its leader. And Kai Kaous heard him unto the end, and he knew that his words were the words of reason and truth, and he was ashamed of that which he had done, and confounded when he beheld his acts thus naked before him. And he humbled himself before Gudarz, and said-

"That which thou sayest, surely it is right."

And he entreated Gudarz to go forth and seek Rustem, and bid him forget the evil words of his Shah, and bring him back to the succour of Iran. And Gudarz hastened forth to do as Kai Kaous desired, and he told the nobles of his mission and they joined themselves unto him, and all the chiefs of Iran went forth in quest of Rustem. And when they had found him, they prostrated themselves into the dust before him, and Gudarz told him of his mission, and he prayed him to remember that Kai Kaous was a man devoid of understanding, whose thoughts flowed over like to new wine that fermenteth. And he said-

"Though Rustem be angered against the King, yet hath the land of Iran done no wrong that it should perish at his hands. Yet, if Rustem save it not, surely it will fall under this Turk."

But Rustem said, "My patience hath an end, and I fear none but God. What is this Kai Kaous that he should anger me? and what am I that I have need of him? I have not deserved the evil words that he spake unto me, but now will I think of them no longer, but cast aside all thoughts of Iran."

When the nobles heard these words they grew pale, and fear took hold on their hearts. But Gudarz, full of wisdom, opened his mouth and said-

"O Pehliva! the land, when it shall learn of this, will deem that Rustem is fled before the face of this Turk; and when men shall believe that Tehemten is afraid, they will cease to combat, and Iran will be downtrodden at his hands. Turn thee not, therefore, at this hour from thy allegiance to the Shah, and tarnish not thy glory by this retreat, neither suffer that the downfall of Iran rest upon thy head. Put from thee, therefore, the words that Kai Kaous spake in his empty anger, and lead us forth to battle against this Turk. For it must not be spoken that Rustem feared to fight a beardless boy."

And Rustem listened and pondered these words in his heart, and knew that they were good. But he said-

"Fear hath never been known of me, neither hath Rustem shunned the din of arms, and I depart not because of Sohrab, but because that scorn and insult have been my recompense."

Yet when he had pondered a while longer, he saw that he must return unto the Shah. So he did that which he knew to be right, and he rode till he came unto the gates of Kai Kaous, and he strode with a proud step into his presence.

Now when the Shah beheld Rustem from afar, he stepped down from off his throne and came before his Pehliva, and craved his pardon for that which was come about. And he said how he had been angered because

Rustem had tarried in his coming, and how haste was his birthright, and how he had forgotten himself in his vexation. But now was his mouth filled with the dust of repentance. And Rustem said-

"The world is the Shah's, and it behoveth thee to do as beseemeth thee best with thy servants. And until old age shall my loins be girt in fealty unto thee. And may power and majesty be thine for ever!"

And Kai Kaous answered and said, "O my Pehliva, may thy days be blessed unto the end!"

Then he invited him to feast with him, and they drank wine till far into the night, and held counsel together how they should act; and slaves poured rich gifts before Rustem, and the nobles rejoiced, and all was well again within the gates of the King.

Then when the sun had risen and clothed the world with love, the clarions of war were sounded throughout the city, and men made them ready to go forth in enmity before the Turks. And the legions of Persia came forth at the behest of their Shah, and their countless thousands hid the earth under their feet, and the air was darkened by their spears. And when they were come unto the plains where stood the fortress of Hujir, they set up their tents as was their manner. So the watchmen saw them from the battlements, and he set up a great cry. And Sohrab heard the cry, and questioned the man wherefore he shouted; and when he learned that the enemy were come, he rejoiced, and demanded a cup of wine, and drank to their destruction. Then he called forth Human and showed him the army, and bade him be of good cheer, for he said that he saw within its ranks no hero of mighty mace who could stand against himself. So he bade his warriors to a banquet of wine, and he said that they would feast until the time was come to meet their foes in battle. And they did as Sohrab said.

Now when night had thrown her mantle over the earth, Rustem came before the Shah and craved that he would suffer him to go forth beyond the camp that he might see what manner of man was this stripling. And Kai Kaous granted his request, and said that it was worthy a Pehliva of renown. Then Rustem went forth disguised in the garb of a Turk, and he entered the castle in secret, and he came within the chamber where Sohrab held his feast. Now when he had looked upon the boy he saw that he was like to a tall cypress of good sap, and that his arms were sinewy and strong like to the flanks of a camel, and that his stature was that of a hero. And he saw that round about him stood brave warriors. And slaves with golden bugles poured wine before them, and they were all glad, neither did they dream of sorrow. Then it came about that while Rustem regarded them, Zindeh changed his seat and came nigh unto the spot where Rustem was watching. Now Zindeh was brother unto Tahmineh, and she had sent him forth with her son that he might point out to him his father, whom he alone knew of all the army, and she did it that harm might not befall if the heroes should meet in battle. Now Zindeh, when he had changed his seat, thought that he espied a watcher, and he strode towards the place where Rustem was hid, and he came before him and said-

"Who art thou? Come forth into the light that I may behold thy face."

But ere he could speak further, Rustem had lifted up his hand and struck him, and laid him dead upon the ground.

Now Sohrab, when he saw that Zindeh was gone out, was disquieted, and he asked of his slaves wherefore the hero returned not unto the banquet. So they went forth to seek him, and when they had found him in his blood, they came and told Sohrab what they had seen. But Sohrab would not believe it; so he ran to the spot and bade them bring torches, and all the warriors and singing girls followed after him. Then when Sohrab saw that it was true he was sore grieved; but he suffered not that the banquet be ended, for he would not that the spirits of his men be damped with pity. So they went back yet again to the feast.

Meanwhile Rustem returned him to the camp, and as he would have entered the lines he encountered Gew, who went around to see that all was safe. And Gew, when he saw a tall man clad in the garb of a Turk, drew his sword and held himself ready for combat. But Rustem smiled and opened his mouth, and Gew knew his voice, and came to him and questioned him what he did without in the darkness. And Rustem told him. Then he went before Kai Kaous also and related what he had seen, and how no man like unto Sohrab was yet come forth from amid the Turks. And he likened him unto Saum, the son of Neriman.

Now when the morning was come, Sohrab put on his armour. Then he went unto a height whence he could look down over the camp of the Iranians. And he took with him Hujir, and spake to him, saying-

"Seek not to deceive me, nor swerve from the paths of truth. For if thou reply unto my questions with sincerity, I will loosen thy bonds and give thee treasures; but if thou deceive me, thou shalt languish till death in thy chains."

And Hujir said, "I will give answer unto thee according to my knowledge."

Then Sohrab said, "I am about to question thee concerning the nobles whose camps are spread beneath our feet, and thou shalt name unto me those whom I point out. Behold yon tent of gold brocade, adorned with skins of leopard, before whose doors stand an hundred elephants of war. Within its gates is a throne of turquoise, and over it floateth a standard of violet with a moon and sun worked in its centre. Tell unto me now whose is this pavilion that standeth thus in the midst of the whole camp?"

And Hujir replied, "It pertaineth unto the Shah of Iran."

Then Sohrab said, "I behold on its right hand yet another tent draped in the colours of mourning, and above it floateth a standard whereon is worked an elephant."

And Hujir said, "It is the tent of Tus, the son of Nuder, for he beareth an elephant as his ensign."

Then Sohrab said, "Whose is the camp in which stand many warriors clad in rich armour? A flag of gold with a lion worked upon it waveth along its field."

And Hujir said, "It belongeth unto Gudarz the brave. And those who stand about it are his sons, for eighty men of might are sprung from his loins."

Then Sohrab said, "To whom belongeth the tent draped with green tissues? Before its doors is planted the flag of Kawah. I see upon its throne a Pehliva, nobler of mien than all his fellows, whose head striketh the stars. And beside him standeth a steed tall as he, and his standard showeth a lion and a writhing dragon."

When Hujir heard this question he thought within himself, "If I tell unto this lion the signs whereby he may know Rustem the Pehliva, surely he will fall upon him and seek to destroy him. It will beseem me better, therefore, to keep silent, and to omit his name from the list of the heroes." So he said unto Sohrab—

"This is some ally who is come unto Kai Kaous from far Cathay, and his name is not known unto me."

And Sohrab when he heard it was downcast, and his heart was sad that he could nowhere discover Rustem; and though it seemed unto him that he beheld the marks whereby his mother said that he would know him, he could not credit the words of his eyes against the words of Hujir. Still he asked yet again the name of the warrior, and yet again Hujir denied it unto him, for it was written that that should come to pass which had been decreed. But Sohrab ceased not from his questionings. And he asked—

"Who dwelleth beneath the standard with the head of a wolf?"

And Hujir said, "It is Gew, the son of Gudarz, who dwelleth within that tent, and men call him Gew the valiant."

Then Sohrab said, "Whose is the seat over which are raised awnings and brocades of Roum, that glisten with gold in the sunlight?"

And Hujir said, "It is the throne of Fraburz, the son of the Shah."

Then Sohrab said, "It beseemeth the son of a Shah to surround himself with such splendour."

And he pointed unto a tent with trappings of yellow that was encircled by flags of many colours. And he questioned of its owner.

And Hujir said, "Guraz the lion-hearted is master therein."

Then Sohrab, when he could not learn the tent of his father, questioned Hujir concerning Rustem, and he asked yet a third time of the green tent. Yet Hujir ever replied that he knew not the name of its master. And when Sohrab pressed him concerning Rustem, he said that Rustem lingered in Zaboulistan, for it was the feast of roses. But Sohrab refused to give ear unto the thought that Kai Kaous should go forth to battle without the aid of Rustem, whose might none could match. So he said unto Hujir—

"An thou show not unto me the tents of Rustem, I will strike thy head from off thy shoulders, and the world shall fade before thine eyes. Choose, therefore, the truth or thy life."

And Hujir thought within himself, "Though five score men cannot withstand Rustem when he be roused to battle-fury, my mind misgiveth me that he may have found his equal in this boy. And, for that the stripling is younger, it might come about that he subdue the Pehliva. What recketh my life against the weal of Iran? I will therefore abandon me into his hands rather than show unto him the marks of Rustem the Pehliva." So he said—

"Why seekest thou to know Rustem the Pehliva? Surely thou wilt know him in battle, and he shall strike thee dumb, and quell thy pride of youth. Yet I will not show him unto thee."

When Sohrab heard these words he raised his sword and smote Hujir, and made an end of him with a great blow. Then he made himself ready for fight, and leaped upon his steed of battle, and he rode till he came unto the camp of the Iranians, and he broke down the barriers with his spear, and fear seized upon all men when they beheld his stalwart form and majesty of mien and action. Then Sohrab opened his mouth, and his voice of thunder was heard even unto the far ends of the camp. And he spake words of pride, and called forth the Shah to do battle with him, and he sware with a loud voice that the blood of Zindeh should be avenged. Now when Sohrab's voice had rung throughout the camp, confusion spread within its borders, and none of those who stood about the throne would accept his challenge for the Shah. And with one accord they said that

Rustem was their sole support, and that his sword alone could cause the sun to weep. And Tus sped him within the courts of Rustem. And Rustem said—

"The hardest tasks doth Kai Kaous ever lay upon me."

But the nobles would not suffer him to linger, neither to waste time in words, and they buckled upon him his armour, and they threw his leopard-skin about him, and they saddled Rakush, and made ready the hero for the strife. And they pushed him forth, and called after him—

"Haste, haste, for no common combat awaiteth thee, for verily Ahriman standeth before us."

Now when Rustem was come before Sohrab, and beheld the youth, brave and strong, with a breast like unto Saum, he said to him—

"Let us go apart from hence, and step forth from out the lines of the armies."

For there was a zone between the two camps that none might pass. And Sohrab assented to the demand of Rustem, and they stepped out into it, and made them ready for single combat. But when Sohrab would have fallen upon him, the soul of Rustem melted with compassion, and he desired to save a boy thus fair and valiant. So he said unto him—

"O young man, the air is warm and soft, but the earth is cold. I have pity upon thee, and would not take from thee the boon of life. Yet if we combat together, surely thou wilt fall by my hands, for none have withstood my power, neither men nor Deevs nor dragons. Desist, therefore, from this enterprise, and quit the ranks of Turan, for Iran hath need of heroes like unto thee."

Now while Rustem spake thus, the heart of Sohrab went out to him. And he looked at him wistfully, and said—

"O hero, I am about to put unto thee a question, and I entreat of thee that thou reply to me according to the truth. Tell unto me thy name, that my heart may rejoice in thy words, for it seemeth unto me that thou art none other than Rustem, the son of Zal, the son of Saum, the son of Neriman."

But Rustem replied, "Thou errest, I am not Rustem, neither am I sprung from the race of Neriman. Rustem is a Pehliva, but I, I am a slave, and own neither a crown nor a throne."

These words spake Rustem that Sohrab might be afraid when he beheld his prowess, and deem that yet greater might was hidden in the camp of his enemy. But Sohrab when he heard these words was sad, and his hopes that were risen so high were shattered, and the day that had looked so bright was made dark unto his eyes. Then he made him ready for the combat, and they fought until their spears were shivered and their swords hacked like unto saws. And when all their weapons were bent, they betook them unto clubs, and they waged war with these until they were broken. Then they strove until their mail was torn and their horses spent with exhaustion, and even then they could not desist, but wrestled with one another with their hands till that the sweat and blood ran down from their bodies. And they contended until their throats were parched and their bodies weary, and to neither was given the victory. Then they stayed them a while to rest, and Rustem thought within his mind how all his days he had not coped with such a hero. And it seemed to him that his contest with the White Deev had been as nought to this.

Now when they had rested a while they fell to again, and they fought with arrows, but still none could surpass the other. Then Rustem strove to hurl Sohrab from his steed, but it availed him nought, and he could shake him no more than the mountain can be moved from its seat. So they betook themselves again unto clubs, and Sohrab aimed at Rustem with might and smote him, and Rustem reeled beneath the stroke, and bit his lips in agony. Then Sohrab vaunted his advantage, and bade Rustem go and measure him with his equals; for though his strength be great, he could not stand against a youth. So they went their ways, and Rustem fell upon the men of Turan, and spread confusion far and wide among their ranks; and Sohrab raged along the lines of Iran, and men and horses fell under his hands. And Rustem was sad in his soul, and he turned with sorrow into his camp. But when he saw the destruction Sohrab had wrought his anger was kindled, and he reproached the youth, and challenged him to come forth yet again to single combat. But because that the day was far spent they resolved to rest until the morrow.

Then Rustem went before Kai Kaous and told him of this boy of valour, and he prayed unto Ormuzd that He would give him strength to vanquish his foe. Yet he made ready also his house lest he should fall in the fight, and he commanded that a tender message be borne unto Rudabeh, and he sent words of comfort unto Zal, his father. And Sohrab, too, in his camp lauded the might of Rustem, and he said how the battle had been sore, and how his mind had misgiven him of the issue. And he spake unto Human, saying-

"My mind is filled with thoughts of this aged man, mine adversary, for it would seem unto me that his stature is like unto mine, and that I behold about him the tokens that my mother recounted unto me. And my heart goeth out towards him, and I muse if it be Rustem, my father. For it behoveth me not to combat him. Wherefore, I beseech thee, tell unto me how this may be."

But Human answered and said, "Oft have I looked upon the face of Rustem in battle, and mine eyes have beheld his deeds of valour; but this man in no wise resembleth him, nor is his manner of wielding his club the same."

These things spake Human in his vileness, because that Afrasiyab had enjoined him to lead Sohrab into destruction. And Sohrab held his peace, but he was not wholly satisfied.

Now when the day had begun to lighten the sky and clear away the shadows, Rustem and Sohrab strode forth unto the midway spot that stretched between the armies. And Sohrab bare in his hands a mighty club, and the garb of battle was upon him; but his mouth was full of smiles, and he asked of Rustem how he had rested, and he said-

"Wherefore hast thou prepared thy heart for battle? Cast from thee, I beg, this mace and sword of vengeance, and let us doff our armour, and seat ourselves together in amity, and let wine soften our angry deeds. For it seemeth unto me that this conflict is impure. And if thou wilt listen to my desires, my heart shall speak to thee of love, and I will make the tears of shame spring up into thine eyes. And for this cause I ask thee yet again, tell me thy name, neither hide it any longer, for I behold that thou art of noble race. And it would seem unto me that thou art Rustem, the chosen one, the Lord of Zaboulistan, the son of Zal, the son of Saum the hero."

But Rustem answered, "O hero of tender age, we are not come forth to parley but to combat, and mine ears are sealed against thy words of lure. I am an old man, and thou art young, but we are girded for battle, and the Master of the world shall decide between us."

Then Sohrab said, "O man of many years, wherefore wilt thou not listen to the counsel of a stripling? I desired that thy soul should leave thee upon thy bed, but thou hast elected to perish in the combat. That which is ordained it must be done, therefore let us make ready for the conflict."

So they made them ready, and when they had bound their steeds they fell upon each other, and the crash of their encounter was heard like thunder throughout the camps. And they measured their strength from the morning until the setting of the sun. And when the day was about to vanish, Sohrab seized upon Rustem by the girdle and threw him upon the ground, and kneeled upon him, and drew forth his sword from his scabbard, and would have severed his head from his trunk. Then Rustem knew that only wile could save him. So he opened his mouth and said-

"O young man, thou knowest not the customs of the combat. It is written in the laws of honour that he who overthroweth a brave man for the first time should not destroy him, but preserve him for fight a second time, then only is it given unto him to kill his adversary."

And Sohrab listened to Rustem's words of craft and stayed his hand, and he let the warrior go, and because that the day was ended he sought to fight no more, but turned him aside and chased the deer until the night was spent. Then came to him Human, and asked of the adventures of the day. And Sohrab told him how he had vanquished the tall man, and how he had granted him freedom. And Human reproached him with his folly, and said-

"Alas, young man, thou didst fall into a snare, for this is not the custom among the brave. And now perchance thou wilt yet fall under the hands of this warrior."

Sohrab was abashed when he heard the words of Human, but he said-

"Be not grieved, for in an hour we meet again in battle, and verily he will not stand a third time against my youthful strength."

Now while Sohrab was thus doing, Rustem was gone beside a running brook, and laved his limbs, and prayed to God in his distress. And he entreated of Ormuzd that He would grant him such strength that the victory must be his. And Ormuzd heard him, and gave to him such strength that the rock whereon Rustem stood gave way under his feet, because it had not the power to bear him. Then Rustem saw it was too much, and he prayed yet again that part thereof be taken from him. And once more Ormuzd listened to his voice. Then when the time for combat was come, Rustem turned him to the meeting-place, and his heart was full of cares and his face of fears. But Sohrab came forth like a giant refreshed, and he ran at Rustem like to a mad elephant, and he cried with a voice of thunder-

"O thou who didst flee from battle, wherefore art thou come out once more against me? But I say unto thee, this time shall thy words of guile avail thee nought."

And Rustem, when he heard him, and looked upon him, was seized with misgiving, and he learned to know fear. So he prayed to Ormuzd that He would restore to him the power He had taken back. But he suffered not Sohrab to behold his fears, and they made them ready for the fight. And he closed upon Sohrab with all his new-found might, and shook him terribly, and though Sohrab returned his attacks with vigour, the hour of his overthrow was come. For Rustem took him by the girdle and hurled him unto the earth, and he broke his back like to a reed, and he drew forth his sword to sever his body. Then Sohrab knew it was the end, and he gave a great sigh, and writhed in his agony, and he said-

"That which is come about, it is my fault, and henceforward will my youth be a theme of derision among the people. But I sped not forth for empty glory, but I went out to seek my father; for my mother had told me by what tokens I should know him, and I perish for longing after him. And now have my pains been fruitless, for it hath not been given unto me to look upon his face. Yet I say unto thee, if thou shouldest become a fish that swimmeth in the depths of the ocean, if thou shouldest change into a star that is concealed in the farthest heaven, my father would draw thee forth from thy hiding-place, and avenge my death upon thee when he shall learn that the earth is become my bed. For my father is Rustem the Pehliva, and it shall be told unto him how that Sohrab his son perished in the quest after his face."

When Rustem heard these words his sword fell from out of his grasp, and he was shaken with dismay. And there broke from his heart a groan as of one whose heart was racked with anguish. And the earth became dark before his eyes, and he sank down lifeless beside his son. But when he had opened his eyes once more, he cried unto Sohrab in the agony of his spirit. And he said-

"Bearest thou about thee a token of Rustem, that I may know that the words which thou speakest are true? For I am Rustem the unhappy, and may my name be struck from the lists of men!"

When Sohrab heard these words his misery was boundless, and he cried-

"If thou art indeed my father, then hast thou stained thy sword in the life-blood of thy son. And thou didst it of thine obstinacy. For I sought to turn thee unto love, and I implored of thee thy name, for I thought to behold in thee the tokens recounted of my mother. But I appealed unto thy heart in vain, and now is the time gone by for meeting. Yet open, I beseech thee, mine armour, and regard the jewel upon mine arm. For it is an onyx given unto me by my father, as a token whereby he should know me."

Then Rustem did as Sohrab bade him, and he opened his mail and saw the onyx; and when he had seen it he tore his clothes in his distress, and he covered his head with ashes. And the tears of penitence ran from his eyes, and he roared aloud in his sorrow. But Sohrab said-

"It is in vain, there is no remedy. Weep not, therefore, for doubtless it was written that this should be."

Now when the sun was set, and Rustem returned not to the camp, the nobles of Iran were afraid, and they went forth to seek him. And when they were gone but a little way they came upon Rakush, and when they saw that he was alone they raised a wailing, for they deemed that of a surety Rustem was perished. And they went and told Kai Kaous thereof, and he said-

"Let Tus go forth and see if this indeed be so, and if Rustem be truly fallen, let the drums call men unto battle that we may avenge him upon this Turk."

Now Sohrab, when he beheld afar off the men that were come out to seek Rustem, turned to his father and said-

"I entreat of thee that thou do unto me an act of love. Let not the Shah fall upon the men of Turan, for they came not forth in enmity to him but to do my desire, and on my head alone resteth this expedition. Wherefore I desire not that they should perish when I can defend them no longer. As for me, I came like the thunder and I vanish like the wind, but perchance it is given unto us to meet again above."

Then Rustem promised to do the desires of Sohrab. And he went before the men of Iran, and when they beheld him yet alive they set up a great shout, but when they saw that his clothes were torn, and that he bare about him the marks of sorrow, they asked of him what was come to pass. Then he told them how he had caused a noble son to perish. And they were grieved for him, and joined in his wailing. Then he bade one among them go forth into the camp of Turan, and deliver this message unto Human. And he sent word unto him, saying-

"The sword of vengeance must slumber in the scabbard. Thou art now leader of the host, return, therefore, whence thou camest, and depart across the river ere many days be fallen. As for me, I will fight no more, yet neither will I speak unto thee again, for thou didst hide from my son the tokens of his father, of thine iniquity thou didst lead him into this pit."

Then when he had thus spoken, Rustem turned him yet again unto his son. And the nobles went with him, and they beheld Sohrab, and heard his groans of pain. And Rustem, when he saw the agony of the boy, was beside himself, and would have made an end of his own life, but the nobles suffered it not, and stayed his hand. Then Rustem remembered him that Kai Kaous had a balm mighty to heal. And he prayed Gudarz go before the Shah, and bear unto him a message of entreaty from Rustem his servant. And he said-

"O Shah, if ever I have done that which was good in thy sight, if ever my hand have been of avail unto thee, recall now my benefits in the hour of my need, and have pity upon my dire distress. Send unto me, I pray thee, of the balm that is among thy treasures, that my son may be healed by thy grace."

And Gudarz outstripped the whirlwind in his speed to bear unto the Shah this message. But the heart of Kai Kaous was hardened, and he remembered not the benefits he had received from Rustem, and he recalled only the proud words that he had spoken before him. And he was afraid lest the might of Sohrab be joined to that of his father, and that together they prove mightier than he, and turn upon him. So he shut his ear unto the cry of his Pehliva. And Gudarz bore back the answer of the Shah, and he said-

"The heart of Kai Kaous is flinty, and his evil nature is like to a bitter gourd that ceaseth never to bear fruit. Yet I counsel thee, go before him thyself, and see if peradventure thou soften this rock."

And Rustem in his grief did as Gudarz counselled, and turned to go before the Shah, but he was not come before him ere a messenger overtook him, and told unto him that Sohrab was departed from the world. Then Rustem set up a wailing such as the earth hath not heard the like of, and he heaped reproaches upon himself, and he could not cease from plaining the son that was fallen by his hands. And he cried continually-

"I that am old have killed my son. I that am strong have uprooted this mighty boy. I have torn the heart of my child, I have laid low the head of a Pehliva."

Then he made a great fire, and flung into it his tent of many colours, and his trappings of Roum, his saddle, and his leopard-skin, his armour well tried in battle, and all the appurtenances of his throne. And he stood by and looked on to see his pride laid in the dust. And he tore his flesh, and cried aloud-

"My heart is sick unto death."

Then he commanded that Sohrab be swathed in rich brocades of gold worthy of his body. And when they had enfolded him, and Rustem learned that the Turanians had quitted the borders, he made ready his army to return unto Zaboulistan. And the nobles marched before the bier, and their heads were covered with ashes, and their garments were torn. And the drums of the war-elephants were shattered, and the cymbals broken, and the tails of the horses were shorn to the root, and all the signs of mourning were abroad.

Now Zal, when he saw the host returning thus in sorrow, marvelled what was come about; for he beheld Rustem at their head, wherefore he knew that the wailing was not for his son. And he came before Rustem and questioned him. And Rustem led him unto the bier and showed unto him the youth that was like in feature and in might unto Saum the son of Neriman, and he told him all that was come to pass, and how this was his son, who in years was but an infant, but a hero in battle. And Rudabeh too came out to behold the child, and she joined her lamentations unto theirs. Then they built for Sohrab a tomb like to a horse's hoof, and Rustem laid him therein in a chamber of gold perfumed with ambergris. And he covered him with brocades of gold. And when it was done, the house of Rustem grew like to a grave, and its courts were filled with the voice of sorrow. And no joy would enter into the heart of Rustem, and it was long before he held high his head.

Meantime the news spread even unto Turan, and there too did all men grieve and weep for the child of prowess that was fallen in his bloom. And the King of Samengan tore his vestments, but when his daughter learned it she was beside herself with affliction. And Tahmineh cried after her son, and bewailed the evil fate that had befallen him, and she heaped black earth upon her head, and tore her hair, and wrung her hands, and rolled on the ground in her agony. And her mouth was never weary of plaining. Then she caused the garments of Sohrab to be brought unto her, and his throne and his steed. And she regarded them, and stroked the courser and poured tears upon his hoofs, and she cherished the robes as though they yet contained her boy, and she pressed the head of the palfrey unto her breast, and she kissed the helmet that Sohrab had worn. Then with his sword she cut off the tail of his steed and set fire unto the house of Sohrab, and she gave his gold and jewels unto the poor. And when a year had thus rolled over her bitterness, the breath departed from out her body, and her spirit went forth after Sohrab her son.

SAIAWUSH

On a certain day it came about that Tus, Gew, Gudarz, and other brave knights of Iran went forth to chase wild asses in the forests of Daghoui. Now when they were come into the wood, they found therein a woman of surpassing beauty, and the hearts of Tus and Gew burned towards her in love. And when they had questioned her of her lineage, and learned that she was of the race of Feridoun, each desired to take her to wife. But none would give way unto the other, and hot words were bandied, and they were like to come unto blows. Then one spake, and said-

"I counsel you, let Kai Kaous decide between you." And they listened to the voice of the counsellor, and they took with them the Peri-faced, and led her before Kai Kaous, and recounted to him all that was come about. But Kai Kaous, when he beheld the beauty of the maid, longed after her for himself, and he said that she was worthy of the throne; and he took her and led her into the house of his women.

Now after many days there was born to her a son, and he was of goodly mien, tall and strong, and the name that was given to him was Saiawush. And Kai Kaous rejoiced in this son of his race, but he was grieved also because of the message of the stars concerning him. For it was written that the heavens were hostile unto this infant; neither would his virtues avail him aught, for these above all would lead him into destruction.

In the meantime the news that a son had been born unto the Shah spread even unto the land of Rustem. And the Pehliva, when he learned thereof, aroused him from his sorrow for Sohrab, and he came forth out of Zaboulistan, and asked for the babe at the hands of its father, that he might rear it unto Iran. And Kai Kaous suffered it, and Rustem bare the child unto his kingdom, and trained him in the arts of war and of the banquet. And Saiawush increased in might and beauty, and you would have said that the world held not his like.

Now when Saiawush was become strong (so that he could ensnare a lion), he came before Rustem, bearing high his head. And he spake, saying-

"I desire to go before the Shah, that my father may behold me, and see what manner of man thou hast made of me."

And Rustem deemed that he spake well. So he made great preparations, and marched unto Iran with a mighty host, and Saiawush rode with him at their head. And the land rejoiced when it looked on the face of Saiawush, and there was great joy in the courts of the King, and jewels and gold and precious things past the telling rained upon Rustem and Saiawush his charge. And Kai Kaous was glad when he beheld the boy, and gave rich rewards unto Rustem; but Saiawush did he place beside him on the throne. And all men spake his praises, and there was a feast given, such as the world hath not seen the like.

Then Saiawush stayed in the courts of his father, and seven years did he prove his spirit; but in the eighth, when he had found him worthy, he gave unto him a throne and a crown. And all was well, and men had forgotten the evil message of the stars. But that which is written in the heavens, it is surely accomplished, and the day of ill fortune drew nigh. For it came about that Sudaveh beheld the youth of Saiawush, and her eyes were filled with his beauty, and her soul burned after him. So she sent unto him a messenger, and invited him to enter the house of the women. But he sent in answer words of excuse, for he trusted her not. Then Sudaveh made complaint before Kai Kaous that Saiawush had deafened his ear unto her request, and she bade the Shah send him behind the curtains of the women's house, that his son might become acquainted with his sisters. And Kai Kaous did that which Sudaveh asked of him, and Saiawush obeyed his commands.

But Sudaveh, when she had so far accomplished her longing that she had gotten him within the house, desired that he should speak with her alone. But Saiawush resisted her wish. And three times did Sudaveh entice him behind the curtains of the house, and three times was Saiawush cold unto her yearning. Then Sudaveh was wroth, and she made complaint unto the Shah, and she slandered the fair fame of Saiawush, and she spread evil reports of him throughout the land, and she inflamed the heart of Kai Kaous against his son. Now the Shah was angered beyond measure, and it availed nought unto Saiawush to defend himself, for Kai Kaous was filled with the love of Sudaveh, and he listened only unto her voice. And he remembered how she had borne his captivity in Hamaveran, and he knew not of her evil deceits. And when she said that Saiawush had done her great wrong, Kai Kaous was troubled in his spirit, and he resolved how he should act, for his heart went out also unto his son, and he feared that guile lurked in these things. And he could not decide between them. So he caused dromedaries to be sent forth, even unto the borders of the land, and bring forth wood from the forests. And they did so, and there was reared a mighty heap of logs, so that the eye could behold it at a distance of two farsangs. And it was piled so that a path ran through its midst such as a mounted knight could traverse. And the Shah commanded that naphtha be poured upon the wood; and when it was done he bade that it be lighted, and there were needed two hundred men to light the pyre, so great was its width and height. And the flames and smoke overspread the heavens, and men shouted for fear when they beheld the tongues of fire, and the heat thereof was felt in the far corners of the land.

Now when all was ready, Kai Kaous bade Saiawush his son ride into the midst of the burning mount, that he might prove his innocence. And Saiawush did as the King commanded, and he came before Kai Kaous, and saluted him, and made him ready for the ordeal. And when he came nigh unto the burning wood, he commended his soul unto God, and prayed that He would make him pure before his father. And when he had done so, he gave rein unto his horse, and entered into the flame. And a great cry of sorrow arose from all men in the plains and in the city, for they held that no man could come forth alive from this furnace. And Sudaveh heard the cry, and came forth upon the roof of her house that she might behold the sight, and she prayed that ill might befall unto Saiawush, and she held her eyes fastened upon the pyre. But the nobles gazed on the face of Kai Kaous, and their mouths were filled with execrations, and their lips trembled with wrath at this deed.

And Saiawush rode on undaunted, and his white robes and ebon steed shone forth between the flames, and their anger was reflected upon his helmet of gold. And he rode until he was come unto the end of the pathway, and when he came forth there was not singed a hair of his head, neither had the smoke blackened his garments.

Now when the people beheld that he was come forth alive, they rent the welkin with their shouting. And the nobles came forth to greet him, and, save only Sudaveh, there was joy in all hearts. Now Saiawush rode till he came before the Shah, and then he got him off his horse, and did homage before his father. And when Kai Kaous beheld him, and saw that there were no signs of fire about him, he knew that he was innocent. So he raised his son from off the ground, and placed Saiawush beside him on the throne, and asked his forgiveness for that which was come to pass. And Saiawush granted it. Then Kai Kaous feasted his son with wine and song, and three days did they spend in revels, and the door of the King's treasury was opened.

But on the fourth day Kai Kaous mounted the throne of the Kaianides. He took in his hand the ox-headed mace, and he commanded that Sudaveh be led before him. Then he reproached her with her evil deeds, and he bade her make ready to depart the world, for verily death was decreed unto her. And in vain did Sudaveh ask for pardon at the hands of the King, for she continued to speak ill of Saiawush, and she said that by the arts of magic alone had he escaped the fire, and she ceased not to cry against him. So the King gave orders that she be led forth unto death, and the nobles approved his resolve, and invoked the blessings of Heaven upon the head of the Shah. But Saiawush, when he learned it, was grieved, for he knew that the woman was beloved of his father. And he went before Kai Kaous, and craved her pardon. And Kai Kaous granted it with gladness, for his heart yearned after Sudaveh. So Saiawush led her back, and the curtains of the house of the women hid her once more behind them, and the Shah was glad again in her sight.

Then it came about that the love of Kai Kaous for Sudaveh grew yet mightier, and he was as wax under her hands. And when she saw that her empire over him was strengthened, she filled his ear with plaints of Saiawush, and she darkened the mind of the Shah till that his spirit was troubled, and he knew not where he should turn for truth.

Now while Kai Kaous thus dallied behind the curtains of his house, Afrasiyab made him ready with three thousand chosen men to fall upon the land of Iran. And Kai Kaous, when he learned it, was sad, for he knew that he must exchange the banquet for the battle; and he was angered also with Afrasiyab, and he poured out words of reproof against him because he had broken his covenant and had once more attacked his land. Yet he made him ready to lead forth his army. Then a Mubid prayed him that he would not go forth himself, and he recalled unto Kai Kaous how twice already he had endangered his kingdom. But Kai Kaous was wroth when he heard these words, and he bade the Mubid depart from his presence, and he sware that he alone could turn the army unto good issue.

But Saiawush, when he heard it, took heart of grace, for he thought within his spirit, "If the King grant unto me to lead forth his army, perchance I may win unto myself a name of valour, and be delivered from the wiles of Sudaveh." So he girded himself with the armour of battle and came before the King his father, and made known to him his request. And he recalled unto Kai Kaous how that he was his son, and how he was sprung from a worthy race, and how his rank permitted him to lead forth a host; and Kai Kaous listened to his words with gladness, and assented to his desires. Then messengers were sent unto Rustem to bid him go forth to battle with his charge and guard him. And Kai Kaous said unto his Pehliva-

"If thou watchest over him, I can slumber; but if thou reposest, then doth it beseem me to act."

And Rustem answered and said, "O King, I am thy servant, and it behoveth me to do thy will. As for Saiawush, he is the light of my heart and the joy of my soul; I rejoice to lead him forth before his enemies."

So the trumpets of war were sounded, and the clang of armour and the tramp of horsemen and of foot filled the air. And five Mubids bare aloft the standard of Kawah, and the army followed after them. And they passed in order before Kai Kaous, and he blessed the troops and his son, who rode at their head. And he spake, saying-

"May thy good star shine down upon thee, and mayst thou come back to me victorious and glad."

Then Kai Kaous returned him unto his house, and Saiawush gave the signal to depart. And they marched until they came unto the land of Zaboulistan.

Now when they were come there they rested them a while, and feasted in the house of Zal. And while they revelled there came out to join them riders from Cabul and from Ind, and wherever there was a king of might he sent over his army to aid them. Then when a month had rolled above their heads they took their leave of Zal and of Zaboulistan, and went forward till they came unto Balkh. And at Balkh the men of Turan met them, and Gersiwaz, the brother of Afrasiyab, was at their head. Now when he saw the hosts of Iran, he knew that the hour to fight was come. So the two armies made them in order, and they waged battle hot and sore, and for three days the fighting raged without ceasing, but on the fourth victory passed over to Iran. Then Saiawush called before him a scribe, and wrote a letter, perfumed with musk, unto Kai Kaous his father. And when he had invoked the blessings of Heaven upon his head, he told him all that was come to pass, and how he had conquered the foes of Iran. And Kai Kaous, when he had read the letter, rejoiced, and wrote an answer unto his son, and his gladness shone in his words, and you would have said it was a letter like to the tender green of spring.

But Afrasiyab, when he learned the news, was discomfited, and that which Gersiwaz told unto him was bitter to his taste, and he was beside himself for anger. Now when he had heard his brother to an end, Afrasiyab laid him down to slumber. Yet ere the night was spent there came out one to the house of Gersiwaz and told unto him that Afrasiyab was shouting like to a man bereft of reason. Then Gersiwaz went in unto the King, and he beheld him lying upon the floor of his chamber roaring in agony of spirit. Then he raised him, and questioned him wherefore he cried out thus. But Afrasiyab said-

"Question me not until I have recovered my wits, for I am like to one possessed."

Then he desired that torches be brought within to light up the darkness, and he gathered his robes about him and mounted upon his throne. And when he had done so he called for the Mubids, and he recounted to them the dream that had visited his slumber. And he told how that he had seen the earth filled with serpents, and the Iranians were fallen upon him, and evil was come to him from Kai Kaous and a boy that stood beside him on the throne. And he trembled as he related his dream, and he would take no comfort from the words of Gersiwaz.

Now the Mubids as they listened were afraid, and when Afrasiyab bade them open their lips, they dared not for fear. Then the King said that he would cleave open their heads if they spake not, and he sware unto them a great oath that he would spare them, even though the words they should utter be evil. Then they revealed to him how it was written that Saiawush would bring destruction upon Turan, and how he would be victorious over the Turks, and how, even though he should fall by the hands of Afrasiyab, this evil could not be stayed. And they counselled Afrasiyab to contend no longer against the son of Kai Kaous, for surely if he stayed not his hand this evil could not be turned aside.

When Afrasiyab heard this message, he took counsel with Gersiwaz, and he said—

"If I cease from warring against Saiawush surely none of these things can come about. It beseemeth me to seek after peace. I will send therefore silver and jewels and rich gifts unto Saiawush, and will bind up with gold the eye of war."

So he bade Gersiwaz take from his treasures rich brocades of Roum, and jewels of price, and bear them across the Jihun to the camp of Saiawush. And he sent a message unto him, saying—

"The world is disturbed since the days of Silim and Tur, the valiant, since the times of Irij, who was killed unjustly. But now, let us forget these things, let us conclude an alliance together, and let peace reign in our borders."

And Gersiwaz did as Afrasiyab bade, and he went forth, and a train of camels bearing rich presents followed after him. And he marched till he came within the tents of Saiawush.

Now when he had delivered his message unto Saiawush, the young King marvelled thereat; and he took counsel with Rustem how they should act, for he trusted not in the words of Afrasiyab, and he deemed that poison was hidden under these flowers. And Rustem counselled him that they should entertain Gersiwaz the space of seven days, and that joy and feasting should resound throughout the camp, and in the mean season they would ponder their deeds. And it was done as Rustem said, and the sounds of revelry were abroad, and Gersiwaz rejoiced in the presence of Saiawush. But on the eighth day Gersiwaz presented himself before Saiawush in audience, and demanded a reply. And Saiawush said—

"We have pondered thy message, and we yield to thy request, for we desire not bloodshed but peace. Yet since it behoveth us to know that poison be not hidden under thy words, we desire of thee that thou send over to us as hostages an hundred chosen men of Turan, allied unto Afrasiyab by blood, that we may guard them as a pledge of thy words."

When Gersiwaz heard this answer, he sent it unto Afrasiyab by a messenger quick as the wind. And Afrasiyab, when he heard it, was troubled, for he said—

"If I give way to this demand I bereave the land of its choicest warriors; yet if I refuse, Saiawush will deny belief unto my words, and the evils foretold will fall upon me."

So he chose out from among his army men allied to him by blood, and he sent them forth unto Saiawush. Then he caused the trumpets to sound, and retreated with his army unto Turan, and restored unto Iran the lands he had seized.

Now when Rustem beheld the warriors, and that Afrasiyab had spoken that which was true, he suffered Gersiwaz to depart; and he held counsel with Saiawush how they should acquaint Kai Kaous with that which was come to pass, for Saiawush said-

"If Kai Kaous desire vengeance rather than peace, he will be angered and commit a deed of folly. Who shall bear unto him these tidings?"

And Rustem said, "Suffer that I go forth to tell them unto Kai Kaous, for verily he will listen unto that which I shall speak, and honour will fall upon Saiawush for this adventure."

Wherefore Rustem went before the King, and told him they had conquered Afrasiyab, and how he was become afraid, and how there was concluded a peace between them. And he vaunted the wisdom of Saiawush that was quick to act and quick to refrain, and he craved the Shah to confirm what they had done. But Kai Kaous was angered when he heard it, and he said that Saiawush had done like to an infant. And he loaded reproaches upon Rustem, and said that his counsels were vile, and he sware that he would be avenged upon Turan. Then he recalled all they had suffered in the days that were past at the hands of Afrasiyab, and he said the tree of vengeance could not be uprooted. And he desired Rustem that he turn him back unto Balkh, and say unto Saiawush that he should destroy these hostages of Turan, and that he should fall again upon Afrasiyab, nor cease from fighting. But Rustem, when he had heard him to an end, opened his mouth and said unto the Shah-

"O King, listen to my voice, and do not that which is evil! Verily I say unto thee that Saiawush will not break his oath unto Afrasiyab, neither will he destroy these men of Turan that were delivered into his hands."

When Kai Kaous heard his speech his anger was kindled, and he upbraided Rustem, and said that his evil counsels had caused Saiawush to swerve from the straight path; and he taunted him and bade him go back unto Seistan, and he said that Tus should go forth as Pehliva unto his son. Then Rustem too was angered, and he gave back the reproaches of the Shah, and he turned him and quitted the courts and sped him back unto his kingdom. But Kai Kaous sent Tus unto the army at his borders, and he bade him speak his desires unto Saiawush his son.

Now Saiawush, when he learned what was come about, was sore

discomfited, and he pondered how he should act. For he said, "How can I come before Ormuzd if I depart from mine oath? Yet, however I shall act, I see around me but perdition."

Then he called for Bahram and Zengueh, and confided to them his troubles. And he said how that Kai Kaous was a king who knew not good from evil, and how he had accomplished that wherefore the army went forth, yet how the Shah desired that vengeance should not cease. And he said-

"If I listen to the commands of the King, I do that which is evil; yet if I listen not, surely he will destroy me. Wherefore I will send back unto Afrasiyab the men he hath placed within my hands, and then hide me from sight."

Then he sent Zengueh before Afrasiyab with a writing. And he told therein all that was come about, and how that discord was sprouted out of their peace. And he recalled unto Afrasiyab how he had not broken their treaty though Kai Kaous had bidden him do it, and he said how he could not return unto the King his father. Then he prayed Afrasiyab that he would make a passage for him through his dominions, that he might hide him wheresoever God desired. For he said-

"I seek a spot where my name shall be lost unto Kai Kaous, and where I may not know of his woeful deeds."

And Zengueh set forth and did as Saiawush desired, and he took with him the hundred men of Turan, and all the gold and jewels that Afrasiyab had sent. And when he was come within the gates Afrasiyab received him right kindly, but when he had heard his message he was downcast in his spirit. Then he called for Piran, the leader of his hosts, and he took counsel with him how he should act. And Piran said-

"O King, live for ever! There is but one road open unto thee. For this Prince is noble, and he hath done that which is right, for he would not give ear unto the evil designs of Kai Kaous, his father. Wherefore I counsel thee, receive him within thy courts, and give unto him a daughter in marriage, and let him be to thee a son; for verily, when Kai Kaous shall die, he will mount upon the throne of Iran, and thus may the hate of old be quenched in love."

Now Afrasiyab, when he had listened to the words of Piran, knew that they were good. So he sent for a scribe, and dictated a writing unto Saiawush. And he said unto him how the land was open to receive him, and how he would be to him a father, and how he should find in Turan the love that was denied of Kai Kaous. And he said-

"I will demand of thee nought but what is good, neither will I suffer suspicion against thee to enter my soul."

Then he sealed the letter with his royal seal, and gave it unto Zengueh the messenger, and bade him depart there with speed. And Saiawush, when he had read it, was glad, and yet he was also troubled in his spirit, for his heart was sore because he was forced to make a friend of the foe of his land. Yet he saw that it could in nowise be altered. So he wrote a letter to Kai Kaous, and he told him therein how it seemed that he could not do that which was right in his eyes, and he recalled unto him the troubles that were come upon him from Sudaveh, and he said how he could not break an oath he had made. Then he confided this writing unto Bahram, and he bade him take the lead of the army till that Tus should be come forth from Iran. And when he had chosen out an hundred warriors of renown from out the host, he departed with them across the border.

Now when Tus arrived and learned what was come to pass, he was confounded; and when tidings thereof reached Kai Kaous, he was struck down with dismay. He cried out against Afrasiyab, and against Saiawush his son, and his anger was kindled. Yet he refrained from combat, and his mouth was silent of war.

In the meantime Saiawush was come into Turan, and all the land had decked itself to do him honour. And Piran came forth to greet him, and there followed after him elephants, white of hue, richly caparisoned, laden with gifts. And these he poured before Saiawush, and gave him welcome. And he told him how Afrasiyab yearned to look upon his face, and he said-

"Turn thee in amity unto the King, and let not thy mind be troubled concerning that which thou hast heard about him. For Afrasiyab hath an ill fame, but he deserveth it not, for he is good."

Then Piran led Saiawush before Afrasiyab. And when Afrasiyab saw him, he rejoiced at his strength and his beauty, and his heart went out towards him, and he embraced him, and spake, saying-

"The evil that hath disturbed the world is quieted, and the lamb and the leopard can feed together, for now is there friendship between our lands."

Then he called down blessings upon the head of Saiawush, and he took him by the hand and seated him beside him on the throne. And he turned to Piran, and said-

"Kai Kaous is a man void of sense, or surely he would not suffer a son like unto this to depart from out his sight."

And Afrasiyab could not cease from gazing upon Saiawush, and all that he had he placed it at his command. He gave to him a palace, and rich brocades, and jewels and gold past the counting; and he prepared for him a feast, and there were played the games of skill, and Saiawush showed his prowess before Afrasiyab. And the sight of Saiawush became a light to the eyes of the King of Turan and a joy unto his heart, and he loved him like to a father. And Saiawush abode within his courts many days, and in gladness and in sorrow, in gaiety or in sadness, Afrasiyab would have none other about him. And the name of Saiawush abode ever upon his lips. And in this wise there rolled twelve moons over their heads, and in the end Saiawush took unto himself to wife the daughter of Piran the Pehliva. And yet again the heavens revolved above his head, and he continued to abide within the house of Afrasiyab. Then Piran gave counsel unto Saiawush that he should ask of Afrasiyab the hand of his daughter to wife. For he said-

"Thy home is now in Turan, wherefore it behoveth thee to establish thy might; and if Afrasiyab be thy father indeed, there can no hurt come near to thee. And peradventure, if a son be born unto thee of the daughter of Afrasiyab, he will bind up for ever the enmity of the lands."

And Saiawush listened to the counsel of Piran, for he knew that it was good, and he asked the hand of Ferangis of her father, and Afrasiyab gave it to him with great joy. Then a mighty feast was made for the bridal, and Afrasiyab poured gifts upon Saiawush past the telling, and he bestowed on him a kingdom and a throne, and he blessed him as his son; and when at length he suffered him to go forth unto his realm, he sorrowed sore at his loss.

Now the space of one year did Saiawush abide in his province, and at the end thereof, when he had visited its breadth, he builded for himself a city in the midst. And he named it Gangdis, and it was a place of beauty, such as the world hath not seen the like. And Saiawush built houses and planted trees without number, and he also caused an open space to be made wherein men could rejoice in the game of ball. And he was glad in the possession of this city, and all men around him rejoiced, and the earth was the happier for his presence, and there was no cloud upon the heaven of his life. Yet the Mubids told unto him that Gangdis would lead to his ill-fortune, and Saiawush was afflicted thereat. But when a little time was sped and he beheld no evil, he put from him their words, and he rejoiced in the time that was; and he was glad in the house of his women, and he put his trust in Afrasiyab.

. . .

But that which is written in the stars, surely it must be accomplished! So it came about after many years that Gersiwaz was jealous of the love which Afrasiyab his brother bare unto Saiawush, and of the power that was his; and he pondered in his heart how he might destroy him. Then he came before Afrasiyab, and prayed the King that he would suffer him to go forth and visit the city that Saiawush had builded, whereof the mouths of men ran over in praises. And Afrasiyab granted his request, and bade him bear words of love unto Saiawush his son. So Gersiwaz sped forth unto the city of Gangdis, and the master thereof received him kindly, and asked him tidings of the King. And he feasted him many days within his house, and he showed freely unto him all that was his; and when he departed he heaped gifts upon his head, for he knew not that Gersiwaz came in enmity unto him, and that these things but fanned his envy.

Now when Gersiwaz returned unto Afrasiyab, the King questioned him concerning his darling. Then Gersiwaz answered and said-

"O King, he is no longer the man whom thou knewest. His spirit is uplifted in pride of might, and his heart goeth out towards Iran. And but that I should make my name to be infamous unto the nations, I would have hidden from thee this grief. But it behoveth me to tell unto thee that which I have seen and which mine ears have heard. For it hath been made known unto me that Saiawush is in treaty with his father, and that they seek to destroy thee utterly."

When Afrasiyab heard these words he would not let them take root in his spirit, yet he could not refuse countenance to the testimony of his brother. And he was sad, and spake not, and Gersiwaz knew not whether the seeds he had strewn had taken root. So when a few days were gone by he came again before the King and repeated unto him the charges that he had made, and he urged him to act, and suffer not Turan to be disgraced. Then Afrasiyab was caught in the meshes of the net that Gersiwaz had spread. And he bade Gersiwaz go forth and summon Saiawush unto his courts, and invite him to bring the daughter of Afrasiyab to feast with her father. And Gersiwaz sped forth with gladness, and delivered the message of Afrasiyab unto the young King. Then Saiawush said-

"I am ready to do the will of Afrasiyab, and the bridle of my horse is tied unto thy charger."

Then Gersiwaz thought within him, "If Saiawush come into the presence of Afrasiyab, his courage and open spirit will give the lie unto my words."

So he feigned before Saiawush a great sorrow, and when the King questioned him thereof he consented to pour out before him the griefs of his spirit. And he said to him how that he loved him tenderly, and how he was in sorrow for his sake, because that the ear of Afrasiyab had been poisoned against him, and he counselled him that he should not seek the courts of the King. And he said-

"Suffer me to return alone, and I will soften the heart of Afrasiyab towards thee; and when he shall be returned unto a right spirit, I will summon thee forth unto his house."

Now Saiawush, who was true and void of guile, listened unto these words, for he knew not that they were false. So he sent words of greeting and of excuse unto Afrasiyab, and he said that he could not quit the chamber of Ferangis, for she was sick and chained unto her couch. And Gersiwaz rode forth bearing the letter, and he sware unto Saiawush that he would cement the peace that was broken. But when he came unto Afrasiyab he delivered not the writing, but spake evil things of Saiawush, and maligned him. And he fed the anger of Afrasiyab, until the King commanded that the army be led forth to go against Saiawush his friend, and he took the lead thereof himself.

Now when the men of Turan came nigh unto the city that Saiawush had builded, Gersiwaz sent an envoy unto Saiawush, saying-

"Flee, I counsel thee, for my words have availed nought, and Afrasiyab cometh forth in enmity against thee."

When Saiawush learned this he was sore downcast in his spirit, and he went unto Ferangis and charged her how she should act when he should be fallen by the hands of Afrasiyab, for he held it vile to go forth in combat with one who had been to him a father. So he made ready his house for death. Now when he came to his steed of battle he pressed its head unto his breast, and he wept over it and spake into its ear. And he said-

"Listen, O my horse, and be brave and prudent; neither attach thyself unto any man until the day that Kai Khosrau, my son, shall arise to avenge me. From him alone receive the saddle and the rein."

Then he bade the men of Iran that were about him go back unto their land, and when all was ready he went forth beyond the gates. But even yet he hoped to turn from him the suspicions of Afrasiyab, and he would not suffer his men to offer combat unto the men of Turan. So he went before Afrasiyab, and questioned him wherefore he was come out in anger against him. Now Gersiwaz suffered not Afrasiyab to reply, but heaped reproaches upon Saiawush, and said that he had received him vilely, and that he had slandered his benefactor. And Saiawush, when he had listened, was confounded, and in vain did he strive to bear down the upbraiding of his foe. For the heart of Afrasiyab was angered yet the more, now that his eyes rested yet again upon the face of Saiawush, whom he loved, because he deemed that he must give credit unto the words of his brother, and because distrust of Iran was graven in his soul. So he hardened himself against the speech of Saiawush, and he bade the army fall upon his beloved. But Saiawush remembered his oath, and he stretched not forth his hand against Afrasiyab, neither did he defend himself from the assaults of his men, and he bade the warriors that were with him that they unsheathe not the sword. So speedily were they mown down, and their bodies lay round about Saiawush their King. And when all were slain a knight stretched out his hand against Saiawush, yet he slew him not, but bound him with cords, and led him before Afrasiyab the King. And Afrasiyab commanded that Saiawush be led forth into a desert place, and that his head be severed from off his trunk. Now the army murmured when they heard this command, and beheld the beauty of Saiawush and his face of truth, and there stepped forth one from among the nobles to plead for him. But Gersiwaz would not suffer the heart of Afrasiyab to be softened.

Now while Gersiwaz yet spake evil of the young King, there came forth from the house of the women Ferangis, the daughter of Afrasiyab, and she demanded audience of her father. And when he would have denied it, she forced herself into his presence, and she pleaded for her lord, and she sware that evil tongues had maligned him, and she entreated of her father that he would not destroy the joy he had given to her. And she said-

"Listen, O King! if thou destroyest Saiawush, thou becomest a foe unto thyself. Deliver not by thy folly the land of Turan unto the winds, and remember the deeds that have been done of Iran in the days that are gone by. An avenger will arise from out the midst of the Kaianides. Mayest thou never recall my counsel too late."

But the world grew dark before the eyes of Afrasiyab with anger. And he spake, and said-

"Go hence, and trouble not again my face; for how canst thou judge of that which is right?"

Then he commanded that she should be bound, and cast into a dungeon.

Now Gersiwaz, when he beheld the anger of the King, deemed that the time was ripe. He therefore gave a sign unto the men that held Saiawush in bondage, and desired that they should slay him. And by the hairs of his head they dragged him unto a desert place, and the sword of Gersiwaz was planted in the breast of the royal cedar. But when it was done, and they had severed the head from the trunk, a mighty storm arose over the earth, and the heavens were darkened. Then they trembled and were sore afraid, and repented them of their deed. And clamour arose in the house of Saiawush, and the cries of Ferangis reached even unto Afrasiyab her father. Then the King commanded that she should be killed also. But Piran spake, and said—

"Not so, wicked and foolish man. Wouldst thou lift thine hand against thine offspring, and hast thou not done enough that is evil? Shed not, I counsel thee, the blood of yet another innocent. But if thou desire to look no more upon Ferangis, I pray thee confide her unto me, that she may be to me a daughter in my house, and I will guard her from sorrow."

Then Afrasiyab said, "Do that which seemeth best in thy sight."

And he was glad in his heart, for he desired not to look upon the face that should recall to him the friend that he had loved. So Piran took Ferangis unto his house beyond the mountains, and Afrasiyab returned unto his courts. But the King was sorrowful in his spirit and unquiet in his heart, and he could not cease from thinking of Saiawush, and he repented of that which he had done.

THE RETURN OF KAI KHOSRAU

In a little time it came about that there was born unto Ferangis, in the house of Piran, a son of the race of Saiawush. And Piran, when he had seen the babe, goodly of mien, who already in his cradle was like unto a king, sware a great oath that Afrasiyab should not destroy it. And when he went before the King to tell unto him the tidings, he pleaded for him with his lips. Now the heart of Afrasiyab had been softened in his sorrow for Saiawush, wherefore he shut his ear unto the evil counsellors that bade him destroy the babe which should bring vengeance upon Turan. And he said—

" I repent me of mine evil deed unto Saiawush, and though it be written that much evil shall come upon me from this child sprung from the loins of Tur and Kai Kobad, I will strive no more to hinder the decree of the stars; let him, therefore, be reared unto manhood. Yet I pray that he be brought up among shepherds in the mountains far from the haunts of men, and that his birth be hidden from him, that he may not learn of his father or of the cruel things I did unto Saiawush."

And Piran consented unto the desires of Afrasiyab, and he rejoiced because he had spared the babe. Then he took the infant from its mother and bare it unto the mountains of Kalun, and confided the boy unto the shepherds of the flocks. And he said—

"Guard this child even as your souls, so that neither rain nor dust come near him."

Thus it came about that no man knew of the babe, neither did Ferangis know whither it was vanished. But oftentimes was Piran sore disturbed in his spirit, for he knew that the beginning of strife was yet to come, and that much evil must befall Turan from this infant. Yet he forgot not his promise of protection given unto Saiawush his friend, whom he had led to put his trust in Afrasiyab. So he quieted his spirit from thinking, for he knew that no man can change the course of the stars.

Now when some time was passed the shepherds came out to Piran and told him how they could not restrain this boy, whose valour was like to that of a king. Then Piran went forth to visit Kai Khosrau, and he was amazed when he looked upon him and beheld his beauty and his strength, and he pressed him unto his heart with tenderness. Then Kai Khosrau said-

"O thou that bearest high thy head, art thou not ashamed to press unto thee the son of a shepherd? "

But Piran was inflamed with love for the boy, so he pondered not his words, but said-

"O heir of kings, thou art not the son of a shepherd." Then he told him of his birth, and clad him in robes befitting his station, and took him back with him unto his house. And henceforward was Kai Khosrau reared in the bosom of Piran and of Ferangis his mother. And the days rolled above their heads in happiness.

Then it came about one night that Piran was awakened by a messenger from Afrasiyab the King. And the King bade Piran come before him. And when he was come unto him, he said-

"My heart is disquieted because of the child of Saiawush, and I repent me of my weakness which kept him alive; for in my dreams I have beheld that he will do much evil unto Turan. Wherefore I would now slay him to avert calamity."

Then Piran, wise in counsel, opened his mouth before Afrasiyab and spake, saying-

"O King, disquiet not thyself because of this boy, for he is devoid of wit; and though his face be like unto that of a Peri, his head, which should bear a crown, is empty of reason. Commit, therefore, no violence, but suffer that this innocent continue to dwell among the flocks."

Afrasiyab, when he had listened to these words of wile, was comforted; yet he said-

"Send Kai Khosrau before me, that I may behold with mine eyes his simplicity."

And Piran assented to his request, because he ventured not to gainsay it. So he returned him unto his house and sought out the boy, and told him how he should disguise his wit before the King. Then he led him unto the court mounted upon a goodly charger, and all the people shouted when they beheld his beauty and his kingly mien. And Afrasiyab too was confounded at his aspect, and he gazed with wonder at his limbs of power, and he strove to remember the promise that he had given unto Piran that he would not hurt a hair of the head of this boy. Then he began to question him that he might search his spirit. And he said-

"Young shepherd, how knowest thou the day from the night? What doest thou with thy flocks? How countest thou thy sheep and thy goats?"

And Kai Khosrau replied-

"There is no game, and I have neither cords nor bow and arrows."

Then the King questioned him concerning the milk that was given of the herds. And Kai Khosrau said-

"The tiger-cats are dangerous and have mighty claws."

Then Afrasiyab put to him yet a third question, and he asked of him-

"What is the name of thy mother?"

And Kai Khosrau answered and said-"

"The dog ventureth not to bark when a lion threateneth him."

Then Afrasiyab asked him yet again whether he desired to go forth into the land of Iran and be avenged upon his enemies. And Kai Khosrau answered and said-

"When a leopard appeareth, the heart of a brave man is torn with fear."

And Afrasiyab smiled at these answers and questioned him no further. And he said unto Piran-

"Restore the boy unto his mother, and let him be reared with kindness in the city that Saiawush hath builded, for I behold that from him can no harm alight upon Turan."

When Piran heard these words he hastened to remove Kai Khosrau from the court, and his heart was glad because of the danger that had passed by. So Kai Khosrau was reared in the house of his father, and Ferangis spake unto him of Saiawush and of the vengeance that was due. And she instructed him concerning the heroes of Iran and their deeds of prowess, as she had learned them from Saiawush her lord.

In the mean season Kai Kaous had learned of the death of Saiawush his son, and a mighty wailing went forth throughout the land of Iran, so that even the nightingale in the cypress was silent of her song, and the leaves of the pomegranate tree in the forest were withered for sorrow. And the heroes that stood about the throne of Kai Kaous clad themselves in the garb of woe, and bare dust upon their heads in place of helmets. And Rustem, when he learned of it, was bowed to the earth with agony, and for seven days he stirred not from the ground, neither would he let food or comfort come near him. But on the eighth he roused him from the earth, and caused the trumpets of brass to be sounded into the air. And he assembled his warriors, and marched with them into Iran, and he came before Kai Kaous and demanded audience.

Now when he was come into the presence-chamber he found the Shah seated upon his throne. He was clothed in dust from his head unto his feet, because of his grief. But Rustem regarded it not, and straightway reproached him, and said-

"O King of evil nature, behold the harvest that is sprung from the seed that thou didst sow! The love of Sudaveh and her vile intents have torn from off thy head the diadem of kings, and Iran hath suffered cruel loss because of thy folly and thy suspicions. It is better for a king that he be laid within his shroud than that he be given over to the dominion of a woman. Alas for Saiawush! Was ever hero like unto him? And henceforward I will know neither rest nor joy until his cruel death be avenged."

When Kai Kaous had listened to the words of his Pehliva, the colour of shame mounted into his cheek, but he held his peace, for he knew that the words spoken of Rustem were deserved. Then Rustem, when he saw that the King answered him not, strode out from his presence. And he went into the house of the women, and sought for Sudaveh, who had given over Saiawush unto death. And when he had found her, he tore her from off her throne, and he plunged his dagger into her heart, and he quitted her not until the life was gone from her. And Kai Kaous, when he learned it, trembled and was afraid, for he dared not oppose himself unto Rustem. Then Rustem commanded that the army of vengeance be made ready. And he said-

"I will make the earth to tremble before my mace, as it shall tremble on the day of judgment."

And when all was prepared they made them haste to be gone, and the air was full of the gleaming of armour, and the rattling of drums was heard on all sides.

Now when Afrasiyab learned that a great army was come forth from Iran to avenge the death of Saiawush, he bade Sarkha, the best beloved of his sons, lead forth the hosts of Turan against them. But he craved Sarkha have a care that Rustem, the son of Zal, put not his life in danger. And Sarkha set forth, bearing aloft the black banner of Turan, and he went towards the plains where Rustem was encamped. Now when the armies beheld one another, their hearts were inflamed, and the battle raged sore, and many were the brave heads laid low on that day. And Sarkha fell into the hands of Rustem, and he spared him not, because he was the best beloved son of Afrasiyab. So he gave orders that Sarkha be slain, even as Saiawush was slain, that the heart of his enemy might be rent with anguish.

And when Afrasiyab learned it he was beside himself with grief. And when he had torn his hair and wailed in the dust for his son, he arose to go forth unto the army, that he might avenge his death. And he said unto his knights-

"Henceforth ye must not think of sleep or hunger, neither must ye breathe aught but vengeance, for I will never stay my hand until this murder be avenged."

Now when the army that was with Afrasiyab came nigh unto Rustem, Pilsam, that was brother to Piran, a warrior valiant and true, challenged Rustem unto single combat. Then Piran sought to stay him because of his youth, but Pilsam listened not unto his counsel. So Rustem came forth against him, and he was armed with a stout lance, and he was wrapped about with his anger. And he fell upon Pilsam with fury, and he lifted him from his saddle, and he took him by the girdle and flung him, as a thing that is vile, into the midst of the camp of the Turanians. Then he shouted with a voice of thunder-

"I counsel you, wrap ye this man in robes of gold, for my mace hath made him blue."

Now when the Turanians beheld that Pilsam was dead, they wept sore, and their courage departed from out of them. And in vain did Afrasiyab pray them to keep their hearts. Yet he said within himself-

"The good fortune that watched over me is asleep."

And when they were met in battle yet again, and the army of Rustem had beaten down once more that of Afrasiyab, the King bethought him of flight. And the hosts of Turan vanished like to the wind, but they left behind them much riches and goodly treasure.

Now while they were flying from the face of Rustem, Afrasiyab said unto Piran-

"Counsel me how I shall act concerning this child of Saiawush."

And Piran said, "Haste not to put him to death, for he shall in nowise do thee hurt. But if thou wilt listen unto my voice, send him far into

Khoten, that he be hidden from sight, and that the men of Iran learn not of his being."

And Afrasiyab did as Piran counselled, and a messenger was sent forth to lead out the young King and his mother unto the land of Cathay. And Afrasiyab himself fled until that he came within the borders of China, and no man knew where he was hidden. And the land of Turan was given over to plunder, and the Iranians scathed it with fire and sword because of Saiawush, whom Afrasiyab had foully slain. And Rustem seated himself in the seat of Afrasiyab, and for the space of seven years did he rule over the land. But in the eighth messengers came out to him, and said how that Kai Kaous was without a guide in Iran, and how they feared lest folly might result from his deeds. So Rustem went forth to stand beside his Shah.

Now when Afrasiyab learned that Rustem was departed out of the land of Turan, his fears forsook him, and he gathered together a mighty army, and he fell upon his borders, and he regained them unto himself. And he wept when he beheld the havoc that was come upon Turan, and he incited his army to be avenged. So they fell into Iran, and shattered its host, and they suffered not that repose come near unto their foes. And they pursued them with fire and sword, and laid waste their fields. And during seven years the heavens withheld their rains, and good fortune was turned away from Iran, and the prosperity of the land was quenched. And men groaned sore under these misfortunes, neither did Rustem come forth from Zaboulistan unto their aid.

Then it came about one night that Gudarz, who was descended from Kawah the smith, dreamed a dream. He beheld a cloud heavy with rain, and on the cloud was seated the Serosch the blessed. And the angel of God said unto Gudarz-

"Open thine ears, if thou wilt deliver thy land from anguish, and from Afrasiyab the Turk. There abideth in Turan the son of a noble race, an issue sprung from the loins of Saiawush, who is brave, and beareth high his head. And he is sprung from Kai Kobad and from Tur, and from him alone can deliverance come to Iran. Suffer, therefore, that Gew, thy son, go forth in search of Kai Khosrau, and bid him remain in his saddle until he shall have found this boy. For such is the will of Ormuzd."

When Gudarz awoke, he thanked God for his dream, and touched the ground with his white beard. And when the sun was risen and had chased away the ravens of night, he called before him his son, and he spake to him of his dream. And he commanded him that he go forth to do the behests of God.

And Gew said, "I will obey thine orders while I live."

Then Gudarz said, "What companions wilt thou take with thee?"

And Gew said, "My cord and my horse will suffice unto me for company, for it is best to take none with me into Turan. For behold, if I lead out an host, men will ask what I am, and wherefore I come forth; but if I go alone, their doubts will slumber."

Then Gudarz said, "Go, and peace be upon thee."

So Gew made ready his steed, and when he had bidden farewell unto the old man his father, he set out upon his travels. And wherever he met a man walking alone, he questioned him concerning Kai Khosrau; and if the man knew not the name, he struck off his head, that none might learn his secret or wherefore he was come forth.

Now Gew wandered thus many days throughout the length of Turan, like to a man distraught, and he could learn nought concerning Kai Khosrau, the young king. And seven years rolled thus above his head, and he grew lean and sorrowful. And for house he had nought save only his saddle, and for nourishment and clothing the flesh and skin of the wild ass, and in place of wine he had only bad water. And he began to be downcast in his spirit, and afraid lest the dream dreamed of his father had been sent unto him by a Deev. Now it came about one day that while he pondered thus he entered a forest, and when he was come into its midst, he beheld therein a fountain, and a young man, slim as a cypress, seated beside it. And the youth held in his hand a wine-cup, and on his head was a crown of flowers, and his mien was such that the soul of Gew rejoiced thereat, and the door of his cares was loosened. And he said within himself-

"If this be not the King, then must I abandon my search, for I think to behold in him the face of Saiawush."

Then he went nigh unto him.

Now when Kai Khosrau beheld the warrior, he smiled and said-

"O Gew, thou art welcome unto my sight, since thou art come hither at the behest of God. Tell unto me now, I pray thee, tidings of Tus and Gudarz, of Rustem, and of Kai Kaous the King. Are they happy? Do they know of Kai Khosrau?"

When Gew heard this speech, he was confounded; and when he had returned thanks unto God, he opened his mouth and spake, saying-

"O young King, who bearest high thy head, reveal unto me who hath told thee of Gudarz and of Tus, of Rustem and of Kai Kaous, and how knowest thou my name and aspect."

Then Kai Khosrau said, "My mother hath told me of the things which she learned of my father. For I am son unto Saiawush, and before he entered upon death he foretold unto Ferangis how Gew would come forth from Iran to lead me unto the throne."

Then Gew said, "Prove unto me thy words. Suffer that mine eyes behold the mark of the Kaianides which thou bearest about thy body."

Then Kai Khosrau uncovered his arm, and when Gew looked upon the mark that was borne of all the royal house since the time of Kai Kobad, he fell down upon the ground and did homage before this youth. But Kai Khosrau raised him from the dust and embraced him, and questioned him concerning his journey and the hardships he had passed through. Then Gew mounted the young King upon his charger, and he walked before him bearing an Indian sword unsheathed in his hand. And they journeyed until they came to the city that Saiawush had builded.

Now when Ferangis saw them she received them joyfully, for her quick spirit divined what was come to pass. But she counselled them to tarry not in whatsoever they would do. For she said-

"When Afrasiyab shall learn of this he will neither eat nor sleep, he will send out an army against us. Let us flee, therefore, before he cometh. And listen now unto the words that I shall speak. Go forth unto the mountain that is raised unto the clouds, and take with thee a saddle and a bridle. And when thou shalt have scaled its crest thou wilt behold a meadow green as a paradise, and browsing upon it the flocks of Saiawush. And in their midst will be Behzah the steed of battle. Go nigh unto him, my son, and embrace him, and whisper thy name into his ear; and when he shall have heard it he will suffer thee to mount him, and seated upon him thou shalt escape from the slayer of thy father."

Then Gew and Kai Khosrau went out and did as Ferangis told unto them; and they found the steed, and when Behzah beheld the saddle of Saiawush and the leopard-skin he had worn, he sighed, and his eyes were filled with tears. Then he suffered Kai Khosrau to mount him, and they turned back unto Ferangis. And she chose forth the armour of Saiawush from among her treasures and gave it to her son, and she clad herself in mail of Roum like unto a warrior, and she sprang upon a horse of battle, and when all was done they set forth to fly from the land of Afrasiyab.

Now one brought tidings unto Piran of these things, and he was dismayed thereat, for he said-

"Now will be accomplished the fears of Afrasiyab, and mine honour will be tarnished in his eyes."

So he bade Kelbad and three hundred valiant knights pursue Kai Khosrau and bind him and bring him back in chains.

Now Ferangis and her son slept for weariness by the roadside, but Gew held guard over them. And when he beheld Kelbad and the men that were with him, he knew that they were come in pursuit; yet he awakened not Kai Khosrau, but of his strength alone put them to flight. But when they were gone he roused the sleepers, and he urged haste upon them.

But Piran, when he beheld that Kelbad returned unto him defeated at the hand of one man, was loath to credit it, and he was angered against him, and said that he would go forth himself. So Piran made him ready, and a thousand brave warriors went with him. For Piran was afraid of the anger of Afrasiyab, and that he would put this flight unto his account, and not unto that of the rotation of the stars. Now when he was come unto the fugitives Gew and the young King slumbered, but Ferangis was keeping watch. And when she beheld the army she woke them and bade them prepare for combat; but Gew suffered not that Kai Khosrau should go forth, for he said-

"If I fall, what mattereth that? my father hath seventy and eight sons like unto me; but thou art alone, and if thy head shall fall, what other is worthy of the crown?"

And Kai Khosrau did as Gew desired. Then Gew gave combat unto Piran, and by his courage he overcame the army; and he caught the old man Piran in the meshes of his cord. Then he brought him bound before Ferangis and Kai Khosrau her son.

Now Piran, when he beheld Kai Khosrau, demanded not mercy at his hands, but invoked the blessings of Heaven upon his head, and he mourned the fate of Saiawush. And he said-

"O King, had thy slave been nigh unto Afrasiyab, surely the head of thy father would not have fallen at his hands. And it was I who preserved thee and Ferangis thy mother, yet now is it given unto me to fall under thy hands."

When Kai Khosrau heard these words his heart went out unto Piran, and when he looked towards his mother he saw that her eyes were filled with tears. Then she opened her mouth and poured forth curses upon Afrasiyab her father, and she wailed the fate of Saiawush, and she pleaded for the life of this good old man. For she said-

"His tenderness hath been an asylum unto our sorrow, and now is it given unto us to remember the benefits we have received at his hands."

But Gew, when he heard it, said-

"O Queen, I pray thee speak not thus, for I have sworn a great oath that I would stain the earth with the blood of Piran, and how can I depart from my vow?"

Then Kai Khosrau said, "O hero like unto a lion, thou shalt not break the oath that thou hast made before God. Satisfy thy heart and accomplish thy vow. Pierce with thy dagger the ear of Piran, and let his blood fall on the earth, that thy vengeance and my clemency may both be satisfied."

Then Gew did as Kai Khosrau bade, and when he had crimsoned the earth with the blood of Piran, they mounted him upon a charger fleet of foot and bound him thereon, and caused him to swear unto them that none other but Gulshehr his wife should release him from these bonds. And Piran sware it and went forth, and his mouth poured blessings upon Kai Khosrau.

Now while these things were passing Afrasiyab grew impatient, and set forth himself at the head of a great army that he might learn tidings of Kai Khosrau. And when he heard that the armies had been beaten at the hand of one man, his cheeks grew pale with fear; but when he met Piran his Pehliva tied upon his charger, his anger knew no bounds, so that he cried aloud, and commanded Piran that he depart from out his presence. Then he sware that he would himself destroy this Gew, and lay low the head of Kai Khosrau and of his mother. And he made great haste after them, and he urged upon his men that they must find Kai Khosrau before he should have crossed the Jihun and have entered upon the land of Iran; yet before ever he was come nigh to them, the three were come unto its banks.

Now, a boat was lying ready, and a boatman slumbered beside it; and Gew roused him, and said that he should bear them across the river. But the man was greedy of gain, and beheld that Gew was in haste. So he said-

"Why should I carry thee across? Yet, if thou desire it, I demand that thou give unto me one of four things: thy coat of mail, or thy black horse, yon woman, or the crown of gold worn by this young man."

Then Gew was angry, and said-

"Thou speakest like a fool; thou knowest not what thou dost ask."

Then he turned unto Kai Khosrau, and said-

"If thou be Kai Khosrau indeed, thou wilt not fear to enter this river and cross it, even as it was crossed by Feridoun thy sire."

Now the river was swollen with the rains, but the young King regarded it not. He entered upon its surge with Behzah his steed, and the horse of his father bare him across the boiling waters. And Ferangis followed after him and Gew the bold. And when Kai Khosrau was come unto the other side, he dismounted and knelt and kissed the ground of Iran, and gave thanks unto God the mighty.

Yet scarce were they come to the other side than Afrasiyab came up with his army. And Afrasiyab demanded of the boatman wherefore he had borne them across, and when the man told him how it was come to pass, the King was bowed down with anguish, for he knew now that that which was written would be accomplished. So he returned him right sorrowful unto his house.

Now when Kai Khosrau came nigh unto the courts of the Shah, Gew sent a writing unto Kai Kaous and told him all that was come to pass. And Kai Kaous sent forth riders to lead before him his son; and the city was decked to give him welcome, and all the nobles received him joyfully, and Kai Kaous was glad at the sight of him, and all men regarded Kai Khosrau as the heir, and only Tus was sorrowful at that which was come to pass. But Tus was angered, and said that he would pay homage only unto Friburz, and to none other. And he came before Kai Kaous and said-

"Friburz is thy son also, why therefore wilt thou give the crown unto one who is sprung from the race of Afrasiyab?

Then Gew said, "It is fitting that the son of Saiawush should succeed unto the throne."

But Tus listened not, and refused allegiance unto Kai Khosrau, and there was strife among the nobles of Iran.

Then one came before Kai Kaous and begged of him that he would declare himself, for he said-

"If we are divided among ourselves we shall fall a prey into the hands of Afrasiyab. Let the Shah, therefore, bind up this quarrel."

Then Kai Kaous said, "Ye ask of me that which is hard, for both my sons are dear unto me, and how should I choose between them? Yet I will bethink me of a means to quiet this dissension. Let Kai Khosrau and Friburz go forth unto Bahman, the fortress that is upon my borders which no man hath conquered, for it is an abode of Deevs, and fire issueth thence continually. And let them take with them an army, and I will bestow my crown and my treasures upon him at whose hands the castle shall be subdued."

So Friburz and Kai Khosrau set forth, and Kai Khosrau suffered that his elder take the lead. But in vain did Friburz strive against the Deevs that were hidden behind the walls, and when seven days had passed he returned discomfited from his emprise. Then Kai Khosrau set forth, and he wrote a letter, amber-perfumed, and in it he desired the evil Deevs that they give place unto him in the name of Ormuzd. And he affixed the letter unto the point of his lance, and when he was come nigh unto the burning fort he flung it beyond the walls. Then a great noise rent the air like thunder, and the world became darkened, and when the light returned unto the sky the castle was vanished from off the face of the earth.

Now when Kai Kaous heard it, he knew that the son of Saiawush was learned in the arts of magic, as was fitting unto a king; and he beheld also that he was wise and brave. And because that he was weary he surrendered the throne unto him, and Kai Khosrau wore the crown of the Kaianides in his stead.

FIROUD

*B*ut a little while had Kai Khosrau sat upon the throne of Iran, yet the world resounded with his fame, and all men bare upon their lips the praises of his wisdom. He cleansed the earth of the rust of care, and the power of Afrasiyab was chained up. And men from all parts of the earth came forth to do homage before him; and Rustem also, and Zal the aged, did obeisance at his footstool. And there came with them an army that made the plains black like to ebony, and the sounds of their war trumpets made the heart to tremble. Then Kai Kaous made ready a great feast to do honour to his Pehliva. And when they were seated thereat his mouth ran over with praises of Saiawush, and he lamented the evil that he had done, and he poured maledictions upon the head of Afrasiyab. And he spake unto Kai Khosrau his son, and said-

"I demand of thee that thou swear before me a great oath, and that thou keep it carefully. Swear unto me that thy heart shall be ever filled with hatred of Afrasiyab, and that thou wilt not let this flame be quenched by the waters of forgetfulness, and that thou regard him not as the father of thy mother, and that thou think only of Saiawush thy sire, whom he hath slain. And swear unto me further that there shall be no other mediator between you save only the sword and the mace."

Then Kai Khosrau turned him towards the fire and sware the oath demanded of his sire, and he vowed to keep it in the name of God the Most High. And Kai Kaous caused the oath to be written on a royal scroll, and he confided it to the care of Rustem his Pehliva. And when it was done they feasted seven days without ceasing, but on the eighth Kai Khosrau mounted his throne. Then he called about him his nobles, and he said unto them that the time was ripe to avenge the death of his father, and he bade them make ready their armies, and he told them how on a certain day they should lead them out before him.

Now when the day was come Kai Khosrau descended into the plains to receive them. And he was seated upon an elephant of war, and on his head he wore the crown of might, and about his neck the chain of supremacy; and in his hand he bare a mace of might, and on his arms were bracelets of great worth, and precious stones were strewn about his garments. Now when he was come into the midst of the camp he threw a ball of silver into a cup of gold. And when the army heard the sound thereof they knew it to be the signal, and they arose and passed before the Shah. And the first to come forth was the army of Friburz. And Friburz was seated upon a horse of saffron hue, and he wore shoes of gold upon his feet, and in his hands were a sword and a mace; and around his saddle was rolled a cord of might, and over his head floated a banner the colour of the sun. And Kai Khosrau, when he saw him, invoked blessings upon his head. And there came after Friburz Gudarz the wise in counsel, and behind him was borne a standard whereon was broidered a lion. And at his right hand and his left marched his mighty sons, and a brave army followed after them. And they did homage before the Shah, and Kai Khosrau regarded them kindly. Then there came after them yet many other noble knights, eager for battle as a bull whom no man hath put to flight, and the sounds of cymbals and the bells of war-elephants filled the air, and lances and targets gleamed in the sun, and banners of many hues streamed upon the breeze. And Kai Khosrau blessed his heroes every one. Then he caused his treasurer to bring forth rich gifts of gold and jewels and slaves, and brocades of Roum, and cloth of gold, and skins of beaver. And they placed them before him, and he divided them into portions, and he said they should be owned of those who should do feats of valour in the war against Afrasiyab. Then he bade them to a great feast, and they made merry in the house of the Shah.

But when the sun had unsheathed its sword of light and the sombre night was fled in fear, Kai Khosrau commanded that the trumpets of departure sound. Then the army came before the Shah, and he gave into the keeping of Tus the standard of Kawah, and he bade him lead forth the hosts. And he said unto Tus-

"Be obedient unto my will and lead mine army aright. I desire of thee that thou avenge the death of my father, but I desire also that thou molest none but those that fight. Have mercy upon the labourer and spare the helpless. And furthermore, I charge thee that thou pass not through the land of Kelat, but that thou leave it on one side and take thy course through the desert. For in Kelat abideth Firoud my brother, who was born of the daughter of Piran, and he dwelleth in happiness, and I would not that sorrow come nigh unto him. And he knoweth no man in Iran, not even by name, and unto no man hath he done hurt, and I desire that no harm come to him."

And Tus said, "I will remember thy will and take the road that thou commandest."

Then the army set forth towards Turan, and they marched many days until they came to a spot where the roads parted. And the one led unto the desert, arid and devoid of water, and the other led unto Kelat. Now when they were come to the parting of the roads the army halted until Tus should have told unto them which road they should follow. And when Tus came up he said unto Gudarz-

"The desert is void of water, and what shall we do deprived thereof, for the army sore needeth refreshment after its march of weariness? It is better, therefore, that we should take the road that leadeth to Kelat, and abide there a while that our men may be rested."

And Gudarz said, "The King hath set thee at the head of his army, but I counsel thee choose the path that he hath named, lest sorrow come upon thee."

But Tus laughed, and said, "O noble hero, disquiet not thyself, for what I do is pleasing in. the sight of the King."

Then he commanded the army that they march into Kelat, and he remembered not the desires of Kai Khosrau.

Now when Firoud saw that the sky was darkened with dust from the feet of dromedaries and elephants of battle, he called before him Tokhareh his counsellor, and questioned him concerning these things. And Tokhareh said-

"O young man, thou knowest not what is come to pass. This army pertaineth unto thy brother, and he hath sent it forth into Turan that the death of thy father be avenged; and it marcheth right upon Kelat, and I know not where the battle may take place."

Now Firoud, who was void of experience, was troubled when he learned this; and he made safe his castle that was upon a high hill, and he gathered in his flocks. Then he seated himself upon the ramparts and looked down over the sea of armour that approached him. And when he had done so he went in before his mother, who had never ceased from weeping for Saiawush her spouse. And he told her what was come about, and he asked of her how he should act. Then she said unto him-

"Listen, O my son ! There is a new Shah in Iran, and he is brother unto thee, for ye are sprung from one father. Now, since thy brother sendeth forth an host to avenge his murder, it beseemeth thee not to remain aloof, but rather shouldst thou serve as vanguard unto the host. Wherefore call together thy knights, and then go forth and seek out the leader of this host, and make thyself known to him. For it behoveth not a stranger to reap this glory or usurp the place that is due unto thy rank."

Then Firoud said, "Who shall be my stay in battle among the heroes who carry high their heads?"

And his mother said, "Seek out Bahram, for he was a friend unto thy father. And listen also to the words of Tokhareh, and go not out at once with thine army until thou hast made thyself known unto the men of Iran."

Then Firoud said, "O my mother, I will faithfully observe thy counsel."

And he went forth unto a high place on the mountain, and he took with him Tokhareh, and they looked down upon the mighty army that was spread at their feet. Then Firoud questioned of the warriors, and Tokhareh answered him according to his knowledge. And he counted up the standards of the heroes, and he made Firoud acquainted with the names of might in Iran.

Now, while they were so doing, Tus beheld them upon the heights, and he was angered at the sight of them, and said-

"Let a wary knight go forth unto those two seated aloft, and search out what manner of men they be. And if they be of the army, let them be lashed two hundred times about the head; but if they be Turks and spies, bind them, and bring them before me that I may destroy them."

Then Bahram, the son of Gudarz, said, "I will search into this matter."

And he rode forth towards the mountain. Now Firoud, beholding him, said unto Tokhareh, "Who is he that cometh out with so haughty an air? By his bearing it would seem that he holdeth me of light esteem, and that he would mount hither by force."

Then Tokhareh said, "O Prince, be not angered thus easily. I know not his name, but I seem to behold the device of Gudarz, and perchance this is one of his sons."

Now Bahram, when he had neared the summit, lifted up his voice, that was like unto thunder, and cried, saying-

"Who art thou that seatest thyself upon the heights and lookest down upon the army? Fearest thou not Tus the Pehliva? "

Then Firoud answered and said-

"Speak not unto me thus haughtily, for I have given thee no cause. Thinkest thou, perchance, that I am but a wild ass of the desert, and that thou art a lion, great of might? It behoveth a man of sense to put a bridle on his tongue. For I say unto thee, that thou art in nowise my better, neither in courage nor in might. Look upon me, and judge whether I have not head and heart and brain, and when thou shalt have seen that I possess them, threaten me not with empty words. I counsel this unto thee in friendship. And if thou wilt listen to reason, I will put some questions unto thee."

Then Bahram replied, "Speak; thou art in the sky, and I am on the ground."

Then Firoud asked of him who were the chiefs of this army, and wherefore they were come forth. And Bahram named unto him the names of might. Then Firoud said unto him-

"Why hast thou not spoken the name of Bahram? There is none among all the host of Iran that mine eyes would rather look upon."

Then Bahram said, "O youth, say unto me who hath spoken unto thee thus of Bahram, and who hath made thee acquainted with Gudarz and Gew."

Then Firoud said, "My mother hath made them known unto me, and she bade me seek out Bahram from among this host, because that he was foster-brother unto my father."

Then Bahram spake, and said, "Verily thou are Firoud, of the seed of Saiawush."

And Firoud answered, "Thou hast said. I am a branch of the cypress that was struck down."

Then Bahram said, "Uncover thine arm, that I may behold the mark of the Kaianides."

And Firoud did so, and Bahram beheld the mark. Then he knew that Firoud was of the race of Kai Kobad, and he did homage before him, and he drew nigh unto him on the mountain. Then Firoud laid bare before Bahram his desires, and he said how that he would make a great feast unto the army in his house, and how, when this was done, he desired to take the lead and march with it into Turan, and he craved Bahram to bear his words of greeting unto Tus. And Bahram said-

"O Prince, brave and young, I will bear thy message unto Tus, and I will implore of him that he listen to thy voice. Yet because he is a man easily angered, I fear the answer he may return. For though he be valiant, yet is he also vain, and he cannot forget that he is sprung from the race of the Kaianides, and he deemeth ever that the first place pertaineth unto him."

Then Bahram told Firoud wherefore he had been sent forth by Tus, and he departed from him, saying-

"If Tus hearken unto my voice, I will return unto thee; but if thou beholdest another, confide not thyself to him."

Then he departed, and came before Tus, and related to him all that he had heard. And Tus was beside himself with anger, and he cried out against this young man, and questioned wherefore he would usurp his place. And he upbraided Bahram for that which he had done, and he refused to give credit unto his words, and he sware that he would cause this youth to perish. And he called upon his warriors, and bade them go forth and sever the head of this Turk. But Bahram said unto them-

"Ye know not that he sendeth you forth against Firoud, who is brother unto Kai Khosrau, and sprung from the seed of Saiawush. I counsel you have the fear of the Shah before your eyes, and lift not your hands in injustice against his brother."

When the warriors heard these words, they retreated back into the tents. But Tus was angered exceedingly, and he commanded yet again that one should go forth to do his behests. Then Rivniz, who was husband unto the daughter of Tus, said that he would do his desires. So he rode forth unto the mountain.

Now when Firoud beheld a horseman, who brandished aloft his sword in enmity, he said unto Tokhareh-

"Tus despiseth my words, and since Bahram cometh not back, my heart is disquieted. Look, I pray thee, if thou canst tell unto me what noble this may be."

And Tokhareh said, "It is Rivniz, a knight of great cunning, son unto Tus, whose daughter he hath in marriage."

Then Firoud asked, saying, "Since he attacketh me, whom shall I slay-the steed or its rider?"

And Tokhareh said, "Direct thine arms against the man, then perchance, when Tus shall learn of his death, he will repent him that he listened not unto thy words of peace."

So Firoud bent his bow and shot Rivniz through the breast. And he fell dead from off his saddle, and his horse turned him back in terror unto the camp. Now when Tus beheld the horse that was come back without its rider, he knew what was come to pass, and his anger against Firoud burned yet the more. So he called unto him Zerasp his son, and bade him go forth and avenge the blood of Rivniz. And when Firoud saw him approach, he asked yet again the name of his foe, and he prepared his bow, that Tus might learn that he was a man that should not be treated with dishonour. And when Zerasp would have fought with him, he pinned him dead unto his saddle. And the horse sped back with him into the camp, so that Tus saw that which was come about. Then his fury knew no limit, and he sprang upon his charger, and he set forth himself against Firoud.

Now when Tokhareh beheld it, he said unto Firoud-

"Tus himself is come forth to combat thee, and thou canst not stand against this crocodile. Retreat, therefore, I counsel thee, into thy castle, and let us await the decrees of the stars."

But Firoud answered in anger, "Who is Tus, that I should fear him? I will not flee from his presence."

Then Tokhareh said, "If thou be resolved to do battle with this lion, I counsel thee that thou destroy him not, lest thy brother be angered if the leader of his host perish by thy hand. Moreover, the army will come forth to avenge him, and how canst thou stand against an host? Direct thine arrows, therefore, against his charger, for a prince fighteth not on foot. if, therefore, thou kill his horse from Under him, thou wilt have shown unto him thy skill."

Then Firoud did as Tokhareh counselled, and the arrow was faithful to its aim, and he shot the horse of Tus from under him, and laid the charger low upon the ground. And Tus had to turn him back on foot unto his camp, and rage against Firoud burned in his spirit. And the nobles, when they beheld their Pehliva treated thus with contempt,- were angry also, and Gew said-

"Who is this young man, that he despiseth an army, and how may he treat us with disdain? 'Though he be of the race of the Kaianides, and of the seed of Kai Kobad, he hath opened a door, and knoweth not whither it leadeth."

And as he spake he girded his armour about him, and made him ready to go out against Firoud.

Now when Firoud beheld him he sighed, and said, "This army is valiant, but it cannot distinguish good from evil. I fear me that by them will Saiawush not be avenged, for their leader is devoid of sense. Else could he not persist in enmity against me. Tell me now, I pray, who this new foe may be?"

Then Tokhareh said, "It is Gew, the son of Gudarz, a knight of great renown, before whom even the lion trembleth unto his marrow. And he led forth thy brother into Iran, and he is girt with the armour of Saiawush, that no man can pierce with in arrow. Direct thy bow, therefore, yet again unto the charger, or thy strife will be vain."

And Firoud the brave did as Tokhareh said, and he sent forth his arrow, and the horse of Gew sank unto the earth. Now all the nobles rejoiced when Gew returned unto them in safety; but Byzun, his son, was wroth, and he upbraided his father, and he said-

"O thou who fearest not an army, how canst thou turn thee back before a single knight?"

Then he sware a great oath that he would not quit the saddle until the blood of Rivniz and of Zerasp should be avenged.

Now Gew was afraid for his son, who was young, and would have restrained him. But Byzun suffered it not, and when his father saw that he was resolved, he gave unto him the armour of Saiawush, and sent him forth unto the mountain.

Now when Firoud saw that yet another was come out against him, he questioned Tokhareh again of his name. And Tokhareh said-

"It is a youth who hath not his like in Iran. Byzun is he called, and he is only son unto Gew the brave. And because that he is clad in the armour of Saiawush, thy father, strike at his horse, or thy bow will avail thee nought."

So Firoud shot his arrows at the horse, and he laid it low, as he had done the others. Then Byzun cried, saying-

"O young man, who aimest thus surely, thou shalt behold how warriors fight on foot."

And he ran up the side of the mountain, that he might come near unto Firoud. But Firoud turned and entered in upon his gates, and he rained down stones from his walls upon the head of his adversary. Then Byzun taunted him, and said-

"O hero of renown, thou fliest before a man on foot, thou who art brave! Alas! whither is vanished thy courage? "

Then he returned unto the camp, and told unto Tus how that this scion of the Kaianides was filled with valour, and how his bow was sure, and he said that he feared no man could stand against him. But Tus said, "I will raze unto the dust his castle, I will destroy this Turk, and avenge the blood that he hath spilled."

. . .

Now when the brilliant sun was vanished and the black night had invaded the earth with her army of stars, Firoud caused his castle to be strengthened. And while he did so, his mother dreamed a dream of evil portent, and she came forth weeping before her son. And she spake, saying-

"O my son, the stars are evil disposed towards us, and I am afraid for thee."

Then Firoud answered her, saying, "Woe unto thee, my mother, for I know it is not given unto thee to cease from shedding tears of sorrow. For verily I shall perish like unto my father, in the flower of my youth. Yet will I not crave mercy of these Iranians."

And he bade her go back unto the chamber of the women, and pray God for his soul.

Now when the sun returned and lifted his glorious face above the vault of heaven, there was heard the sound of armour on all sides, and Firoud beheld that the host of Iran was come forth against him. So he went out beyond the gates, leading his warriors. And since there was no plain whereon they could give battle, they fought upon the mountain-side, and many were the Turkish heads that were felled. But Firoud made great havoc among his enemies, and they beheld that he was a lion in the fight. But the stars of the young hero were waning, for even a brave man cannot contend alone against an host. For when he would have ridden back unto his castle, Rehham and Byzun lay in ambush against him, and they closed unto him the two ends of the path. But Firoud was not dismayed thereat. He fell upon the son of Gew, and would have slain him; but Rehham came upon him from behind, and struck him down with a mighty club. Then Firoud knew that his hour was come, and he returned unto his mother. Now when she saw him she raised a great cry, but he bade her keep silence, and he spake, saying-

"Weep not, for the time suffereth it not. For the Iranians follow fast upon me, and they will enter and take this house, and do violence unto thee and to thy women. Go out, therefore, and cast you from off the walls into the abyss, that death may come upon you, and that Byzun when he entereth find none alive. As for me, my moments are but few, for the heroes of Iran have murdered the days of my youth."

And the women did as he commanded, save only his mother, who abode beside him until the breath was gone out from his body. Then she made a great fire, and threw therein all his treasures, and she went out into the stables and laid low the horses that were therein. And when she had made the place a desert unto the Iranians, she returned unto the feet of her son, and pierced her body with a sword.

Now when the Iranians had broken down the bars of the gates and entered into the castle, they came unto the chamber and beheld the bodies of Firoud and of his mother. And when they saw them, they could not withhold their tears, and they sorrowed for the anger of Tus, and the fear of Kai Khosrau came upon them. And Gudarz said unto Tus-

"Thou hast sown hatred, and thou wilt reap war. It beseemeth not a leader to be quick to ire. Thy haste hath brought to death a youth of the race of the Kaianides, and hath caused the blood of thy sons to be spilled."

When Tus heard these words he wept in his sorrow, and said-

"Evil fortune is come upon me."

Then he caused a royal tomb to be made, and seated Firoud therein upon a throne of gold, and he decked him with all the signs of kingship. And when he had so done he returned with his army unto the plains, and three days they halted in their grief. But on the fourth the trumpets were sounded for departure, and Tus led forth the army towards Turan.

Now when Afrasiyab learned that a host was come forth against him from out of Iran, he bade Piran make ready his army. For he said-

"Kai Khosrau hath unveiled unto us the secrets of his heart, and we know now that forgiveness is not hidden in his soul."

Now while they made them in order, there came a great storm of snow that covered the earth like to a carpet, and the water became hard, and for many days no man beheld the earth or the sun. And food was lacking unto the Iranians, and they were fain to devour their steeds of battle. And when at last the sun came back, the earth was changed into a lake, and the Iranians suffered yet again. Then Tus said-

"Let us return whence we came forth."

But his army said, "Not so. Shall we flee before the face of Afrasiyab?"

So they made them ready to meet their foes. And they fought right valiantly, and many were the heads of Turan that were laid in the dust by their hands, and the victory inclined towards them. Then Tus was glad, and made a great feast and invited thereto his warriors. And he darkened their heads with wine, so that they laid aside their armour, neither did they set watches in the camp. Now Piran, when he learned of this, saw that the time served him, and when the night was fallen he went out against the camp of Iran. And all the nobles were drunk save only Gudarz the wise.

Now when he heard that the Turanians were come into the camp, he ran to the tents of Tus and cried, saying-

"Is this the hour to hold the wine-cup?"

Then he called together his sons, and he set his army in order; but the Turanians routed them utterly, for the men of Iran were heavy with wine, and they knew not whither they sent their blows. And the carnage was great, and when the sun had brought back the day the ground was strewn thick with the bodies of the Iranians. And cries of agony were heard around, and there were none to heal the hurts, for those that were whole were captive. And Tus was beside himself for sorrow, and Gudarz alone was not defraught of reason. So the old man sent forth a messenger to bear the tidings of woe unto the Shah. Now he was a messenger that made the earth disappear beneath his feet, and speedily did he stand within the courts of the King. And Kai Khosrau, when he had listened to his words, was angered, and his tongue called down curses on the head of Tus. Then he pondered all night how he should act, but when the cock crew he wrote a letter unto Friburz the son of Kai Kaous. And he bade him take unto him the flag of Kawah and the golden boots, and lead the army in the place of Tus. And he bade him in all things be obedient to the counsels of Gudarz the wise, and he recalled how Tus had disobeyed his commandments, and he said-

"I know no longer who is my friend or my foe."

Then he put his seal to the letter and gave it unto the messenger. And the man sped forth and brought it into the camp. Then Friburz read it out before the army. And when he had heard it Tus did that which the Shah desired, and when he had given over unto Friburz the command he turned him to go back unto Iran.

Now when he was come before Kai Khosrau, he fell upon the earth before his throne, and the Shah raised him not, neither did he give him words of greeting. And when he parted his lips, it was to let forth words of anger. And he made known to him his sore displeasure, and he reproached him with the death of Firoud, and he said-

"But that thou art sprung from Minuchihr, and that thy beard is white, I would sever thy head from off thy body for this deed. Yet, as it is, a dungeon shall be thy dwelling, and thine evil nature thy gaoler."

And when he had thus spoken he drove him from his presence, and gave orders that he should be put into chains.

Now while these things passed in Iran, Friburz craved of Piran that he would grant unto him a truce. And Piran said—

"It is ye who have broken into our land; yet I will listen unto your desires and grant unto you this truce, and it shall be of the length of one moon. But I counsel unto you that ye quit the land of Turan in its course."

But Friburz would not Lead back the army thus discomfited, and he spent the time accorded to him in preparation, and when it was at an end he offered battle again to the Turanians. And there was waged a combat s sun hath not looked upon its like, and the army of the Iranians was overthrown. And the slaughter was terrible, neither did the men of Turan escape, and many were the great ones of the land that perished. And the men of Iran fought till that their strength was departed. They had sought the conflict and found defeat. And they that were not slain fled from the battlefield, and it is they that saved their lives in this manner whom thou must bewail.

Now when another day was risen upon the world, Piran sent for his guards to bring him news of the Iranians. And when they told him that their tents were vanished from off the plains, he sent the news of victory to Afrasiyab. And the King rejoiced thereat, and all the land prepared a great feast unto the army. And when Piran entered into the city the terraces thereof were decked with carpets of gay hue, and the houses were clothed with arras of Roum, and pieces of silver rained down upon the warriors. And the King poured upon Piran gifts of such number that you would not have patience to hear me recount them. And he sent him back unto Khoten with much honour and many counsels. And he said—

"Let not thine army slumber, and trust not thy foe because he is drawn back. I charge thee keep thine eyes fixed upon the land of Rustem, for if thy vigilance slumber he will surely come forth and destroy thee, for he alone is to be feared of the men of Iran. Therefore be brave and watchful, and may Heaven preserve thee unto my throne."

And Piran listened unto the words spoken of Afrasiyab, as it beseemed him. And when he was returned unto his kingdom, he set watchers upon all sides, that they might acquaint him concerning Rustem the Pehliva.

THE VENGEANCE OF KAI KHOSRAU

*D*ire was the wailing among the army of Iran at their sore defeat, and they turned them back discomfited. And they came before the Shah, their hearts torn with anguish. And their hands were crossed upon their breasts, and they were humble as slaves. And Kai Khosrau was angry when he beheld them, and he remembered Firoud, and he railed against Tus, from whom was sprung this evil. And he said-

"Cursed be he and his elephants and his cymbals." And the Shah withdrew from his courts, and he withheld his countenance from the land. So the nobles went out unto Rustem, and entreated of him that he would intercede for them with the Shah. And Rustem did as they desired, and he pleaded for the army and its leaders, and he spake good even of Tus. And Kai Khosrau inclined his ear unto his Pehliva, and he let the light of his countenance shine again upon his army, and he confided unto Tus once more the standard of Kawah, but he made Gew march beside him and restrain his haste.

So they set forth again unto Turan, and Afrasiyab, when he learned of their approach, made ready his army also. And there were joined unto him the hosts of the Khakan of China, and of the Kamous of Kushan, men mighty in the battlefield. And from Ind and all the highlands of Asia there came forth troops unto the aid of Afrasiyab, King of Turan. And he rejoiced thereat, for he was assured that if Rustem came not forth to aid them, the men of Iran could not stand against his host.

. . .

FERDOWSI

Now when the two armies met, many and fierce were the combats waged between them, and blows were given and received, and swords flashed and showers of arrows descended on all sides. And the blood of brave men was shed like unto the shedding of rain from a black cloud. And day by day were the Iranians weakened, for they were smitten with great slaughter, and the number of their dead was past the counting. But Afrasiyab rejoiced in his victory, and his heart shouted within him when he learned after many days that the Iranians were drawn back into the mountains. But Kai Khosrau, when he learned it, was afflicted, and wept sore. Then he sent greeting unto Rustem, his Pehliva, and he craved of him that he would come forth to aid the army, for in him alone could he put his trust. And Rustem said-

"O Shah, since the day that mine arm could wield a mace, I have ever fought the battles of Iran, and it would seem that rest may never come nigh unto me. Yet since I am thy slave, it behoveth me to obey. I am ready to do thy desires."

So he made ready an host to go unto the succour of Iran. And while he did so the army was defeated yet again, and all heart went from the Iranians, and they would have given them over unto their foes. But while they pondered it, there came tidings unto Gudarz that Rustem was drawing nigh. Yet they feared to give way unto belief. But Piran when he heard it was sore discomfited, for he remembered of old the might of Rustem, and he knew that none could stand before it. But the Khakan and the Kamous scoffed at his fears, and they made loud boastings that Rustem should fall by their hands.

Now when some days had passed in this disquietude, it came about one night that, when the moon showed her face above the mountains, like unto a victorious king seated upon a throne of turquoise, a watchman of Iran set up a great cry. And he said-

"The plain is filled with dust, and the night resoundeth with noise. And I behold a mighty army drawing nigh, and they bear torches, and in their midst rideth Rustem the mighty."

When the men of Iran heard this, they set up a great shout, and their hearts seemed to come back into their bodies, and their courage, that had been as dead, returned. And glad was the greeting that they gave unto Rustem the Pehliva. And Rustem mustered them and put them into battle order, and when the sun had wearied of the black veil, and had torn the night asunder, and reappeared unto the world, the men of Iran called upon the host of Turan to come forth in combat. And they defied them unto battle, and they fought with new valour, and they made great havoc in their ranks. And when the evening was come, the day belonged unto Iran.

Then Piran called before him Human the brave, and said unto him-

"The nobles of Iran have found again their courage, since an army is come to their aid. Yet I would know if Rustem be their leader, for him alone do I fear."

And when he learned it his spirit was troubled. But the Kamous mocked him, and sware a great oath that, ere the sun should be set once more, he would have broken the might of Rustem. For he said-

"There is none, not even a mad elephant, that is mine equal in the fight."

So when the day was come, the Kamous challenged Rustem unto single combat. And Rustem strode forth from the camp, and the Kamous met him upon the plain. Then they struggled sore, and wrestled one with another, but in the end Rustem caught the Kamous in the meshes of his cord. And he showed him unto the army, and he asked of them, saying-

"What death desire ye that the Kamous should die, for his hour is come?"

Then he threw him among the nobles, and they made an end of him with their spears, and they flung his body to the vultures.

Now when the Khakan heard of the death of the Kamous, he sware that he would avenge him, and he sent forth a messenger to defy Rustem. But Rustem said unto the messenger-

"I seek no quarrel with the Khakan, and in all your army I desire only to look upon the face of Piran. And I beg of him that he will come forth to greet me, for my heart burneth towards him, because he was afflicted for the death of Saiawush, my foster-son, and because of the good he did unto Kai Khosrau and unto his mother."

So the messenger bare these words unto Piran. And Piran, when he had taken counsel, listened unto the desires of Rustem, and came into his tents. And he said-

"I am Piran, leader of the hosts of Turan. Speak unto me thy name."

And Rustem said, "I am Rustem of Zaboulistan, and I am armed with a mace and a sword of Cabul."

Then he gave him greeting from Kai Khosrau, and he lauded him for the good deeds that he had done unto Saiawush and to his son, and he entreated him that he would turn away from Afrasiyab, and go with him unto Kai Khosrau. And he said-

"Iran desireth not to destroy the innocent. Therefore deliver over unto me the men upon whose head resteth the blood of Saiawush, and we will withdraw our hosts, and there shall be peace in the land."

Then Piran said, "That which thou askest, verily it can never be, for the slayers of Saiawush are near kinsfolk unto Afrasiyab. And because he hath named me the leader of his hosts, it may not be that I abandon them. But I say unto thee, that it would be sweeter unto me to die than to conduct this warfare, and that my heart is torn because I must lift up the sword of enmity against Kai Khosrau, my son."

And Rustem saw that the words that Piran spake were true, and he sorrowed for him. And when they parted it was in friendship, although they knew that battle must rage between them. Then they drew up their armies, and for forty days there was waged a battle, mighty and terrible. And great ravages were committed, and Rustem did deeds of valour, and the strong and the weak were alike impotent before him. And the plains were strewn with the bodies of the slain, until that an ant could not have found a road to pass between them, and the blood of the wounded streamed on all sides, and heads without bodies and bodies without heads covered the ground. For neither the claw of the leopard nor the trunk of the elephant, neither the high mountains nor the waters of the earth, could prevail against Rustem when he fought at the head of his hosts. And he slew the mightiest among the Turanians, and only Piran was he mindful to spare. And the Khakan of China was enmeshed in his cord, and he sent him bound unto Kai Khosrau with news of the victory. And when the Turanians fled before his face, he followed after them and pursued them unto the mountains.

Then Piran made haste to come before Afrasiyab, and he spake to him and said-

"The land is changed into a sea of blood, for Rustem is come forth, and who can stand against him? And he followeth after me close. Wherefore I counsel thee, flee; for how canst thou stand alone against him? Alas for the woe that thou hast brought upon Turan! Thou hast wounded our hearts with the iron of the arrow wherewith thou didst slay Saiawush the noble."

Then he urged upon him that he tarry not. So Afrasiyab fled from before the face of Rustem and hid himself in the mountains. And when Rustem came into his courts and found that the King was fled, he seized upon much booty and divided it among his men, and he feasted them many days in the house of Afrasiyab, and he suffered them to enjoy repose. Then he destroyed with fire the palace, and when he had done so he turned him to go back unto Kai Khosrau.

Now when he was come within the city of the Shah, glad cries rang through all the air, and the sound of drums filled the land of Iran, and there was joy throughout its breadth because the destroyer of Turan was returned. And the heart of Kai Khosrau rejoiced like a paradise, and he came out to meet his Pehliva mounted upon an elephant gaily caparisoned, and music and singers went before him. And he invited him to a great feast, and he poured rich gifts upon him. And for a month Rustem abode in the presence of his Shah, making merry with wine. And the singers chanted of his great deeds, and the sounds of flutes and stringed instruments went with their words. But when that time was over Rustem asked of Kai Khosrau that he would suffer him to return unto Zal his father, for his heart yearned to look upon his face. And Kai Khosrau suffered it.

Now Rustem was not returned long unto Zaboulistan before there came into the courts of the Shah a shepherd who desired to speak with Kai Khosrau. And the Shah granted his request, and the man opened his mouth before him, and he said-

"A wild ass is broken in among my horses, and he doeth great mischief, for his breath is like unto a lion. Send forth, therefore, I entreat of thee, O King of Kings, a warrior of thine host that he may slay him."

Now Kai Khosrau, when he had listened, knew that this was not a wild ass but the Deev Akwan, who had taken this disguise upon him. So he cast about whom he should send forth to meet him, and he knew there was none other but Rustem, the son of Zal, to whom he could turn in this strait. So he sent a messenger swift as a cloud before a storm to summon him forth yet again. And Rustem obeyed the voice of his Shah, and he set forth in search of the Deev, and he was mounted upon Rakush his steed. And in his hand was a mighty mace, and round his wrist was rolled a cord of length. And he went in search of the wild ass, and when he had found him he threw his cord about him. But the ass vanished under his hands. Then Rustem knew that it was a Deev, and that he fought against the arts of magic. Yet was he not dismayed. And after a while the ass came forth again, and Rustem threw his cord once more about him. And yet again the Deev vanished under his hand. And thus did the Deev three days and three nights without ceasing, so that weariness came upon Rustem and he was heavy with slumber. So he sought

FERDOWSI

out a spot of safety and he laid him down to rest, and he bade Rakush browse beside him.

Now when the Deev saw that Rustem was sleeping, he drew nigh and loosened the earth whereon he lay, and lifted it and placed it upon his head, that he might cast it away and destroy Rustem. But as he carried him Rustem awoke, and when he saw what was come to pass he feared that his hour was come. And the Deev, when he beheld that Rustem was awakened, spake, and said unto him—

"O hero, which death dost thou covet? Shall I fling thee down upon the mountain or cast thee into the sea?"

Now Rustem knew that the Deev questioned him in wile, and he bethought him that he would of a surety do that which Rustem desired not, so he said—

"I have heard it said that it is not given to those that perish in the waters to look upon the face of the Serosch or to find rest in the life that is beyond."

Then the Deev said, "I desire that thou know not repose."

And he flung him into the sea at a spot where hungry crocodiles would devour him.

Now Rustem, when he felt the water beneath him, forthwith drew out his sword and combated the crocodiles with his right hand, and with his left he swam towards the shore. And long did he struggle and sore, but when the night was fallen he put his foot upon the dry land. Then, when he had given thanks unto God and rested him, he returned unto the spot where he had found the Deev. And he sought after Rakush his steed, and his eye beheld him not. Then fear filled his spirit, and he roamed around to seek him. And he found him at last among the horses of Afrasiyab, that grazed in a spot hard by, for the keepers had ensnared him. But when Rakush heard the voice of Rustem he neighed aloud, and brake from the keepers and ran towards his master. And Rustem put the saddle upon him and mounted him. Then he slew the keepers and took their herds unto himself.

Now while he was so doing Afrasiyab came forth from his hiding-place, for his heart yearned to look upon his horses. And when he beheld Rustem in their midst he was dismayed, and knew not whither he should turn, for he deemed that the Pehliva had discovered his hiding-place and was come forth against him. So he offered battle unto him with the men that were with him. And Rustem accepted the challenge, although he was alone; and he fought with might and overcame the men, and slew sixty of them with his sword and forty with his mace. And Afrasiyab fled once more from before him.

Now when it was done the Deev came forth again, for he thought he could quell Rustem now that he was weary. But Rustem sprang on him and crushed him, and he was slain at his hands. Then the Pehliva returned unto Kai Khosrau. And when the Shah had learned of all his deeds, and beheld the booty that he had brought back, his mouth could not cease from praising the prowess of Rustem, and he would have kept his Pehliva beside him for ever. But Rustem said-

"Suffer thy servant to go forth. For I would make ready an host, since it behoveth us not to cease from the vengeance that is due unto Saiawush, for his murderers yet cumber the ground."

Wherefore Rustem departed yet again from out the courts of the Shah.

BYZUN AND MANIJEH

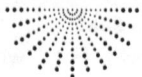

*P*eace reigned again within the borders of Iran, and P the sword slept in its scabbard, and Kai Khosrau ordered the world with wisdom. And men rejoiced that the glory of Turan had been brought low, and the Shah feasted his nobles in lightness of heart.

Now it came about one day that while they were shortening the hours with wine there entered in unto them the keeper of the curtains of the door. And he said that men from Arman stood without and craved an audience. Then Kai Khosrau bade that they be let in. So the men came before him, and they uttered cries of lamentation, and they fell down at his feet and implored his aid. And Kai Khosrau said-

"Who hath done you wrong?"

Then the men answered, "Our wrong cometh unto us from the borders of Turan, for there issue forth thence wild boars that break into our fields and do destruction to our crops. And our fortunes are entwined with the ground, and no man can overcome these beasts. Wherefore, we pray thee, send forth a Pehliva that he may subdue them, for our land groaneth under this plague."

Then Kai Khosrau said, "It shall be done as you desire," and he dismissed them graciously. Then he called before him his treasurer, and bade him bring forth precious stones, and horses with girdles of gold, and rich brocades of Roum. And when they were placed before him he showed them to his nobles, and he said that whoever would go forth to combat the wild boars should not find him close-handed. But for a while none answered, for no man listed to go forth to battle with wild beasts. Then Byzun, the son of Gew, arose and spake, saying-

"If the Shah will grant leave unto me, I will go forth and slay these foes."

Now Gew was grieved thereat, because that Byzun was his only son, and he feared for his youth. Therefore he sought to restrain him. But Byzun suffered it not, and he said-

"O King, listen unto my desires; for though I be young in years, yet am I old in prudence, and I will do nought that is not fitting unto thy slave."

And Kai Khosrau granted his request, but he bade him take forth with him Girgin, the wise in counsel, that he should guide him aright. And Byzun did as the Shah desired, and they set forth unto the land of Arman.

Now when they were come unto the wood they rested them, and made a great fire, and drank wine until they were refreshed. Then Girgin would have laid him down to slumber. But Byzun said-

"Not so, let us go forth and seek the wild boars."

Then Girgin said, "Go thou alone, for it is thou who hast engaged in this combat, and who hast taken to thyself the gifts of the Shah. Therefore it behoveth me only to look on."

When Byzun heard these words he was amazed, but he regarded them not, and he entered in upon the forest. And after a while he came upon the wild boars, and they fell upon him. But he slew them with his mace, and he reddened the ground with their gore, and he went after them, even unto their lairs, and not one of them did he suffer to escape. Then when he had done thus, he parted their mighty teeth from off their heads and hung them about his saddle, that the men of Iran might behold them. And after this he turned him back unto Girgin.

Now Girgin, when he beheld him mounted upon his horse, and bearing round his saddle the tokens of his triumph, was envious thereat. And with his mouth he gave him joy, but Ahriman took hold of his spirit. So he pondered all night long how he could lay a snare for Byzun. And when the morning was come he praised his prowess, and they quaffed wine together, and fair words were exchanged between them. Then Girgin said-

"This land is known unto me, for I sojourned here with Rustem. And I know that at the distance of two farsangs lies the garden of Afrasiyab, where his women go forth to keep the feast of spring. And I bethink me that the time is at hand. Wherefore, I say unto thee, let us go hence, and

FERDOWSI

behold with our eyes the fair ones whom the King of Turan hideth behind his curtains."

Now these words inflamed the blood of Byzun, and he gave ear unto Girgin, for he was young, and he acted like a young man. So they set forth upon the road, and Girgin filled the mind of Byzun with feasts and with sounds of music. And when they were come unto the spot, Byzun burned with impatience to look upon the women of Afrasiyab. And Girgin feigned as though he would restrain his foot within the skirt of patience, but he rejoiced in secret, for he hoped that from this deed evil would arise. So Byzun sped forth unto the garden, and he hid himself beneath the shade of a tall cypress, and he feasted his eyes upon the beauty of the women. And the garden was clad in its robes of spring, and the world was green and fair, and all the air was filled with the sweet sounds of music and of song. And there moved amid the rose-bushes maidens of Peri face, and in stature they were like to the cypress-trees, and one was exalted above them all. And she was daughter unto Afrasiyab, and Manijeh was she named.

Now it came about that as Manijeh stood at the door of her tent she beheld Byzun where he was hid. And she marvelled at his beauty, and her heart was captive unto him. So she called about her her maidens, and said-

"Go forth and question the stranger who regardeth us, for I bethink me that he is a Peri, or that Saiawush is come back unto the earth, for no mortal can own such beauty, neither can any man enter here."

Then one went forth and bare unto Byzun this message. And his heart leaped thereat, and he said-

"Say unto your mistress that I am come forth from Iran to slay the wild boars of Arman. And I came hither that perchance I might gaze upon the face of the daughter of Afrasiyab, for tidings of her beauty were told unto me, and reached even unto Iran. Go, therefore, and ask if I may speak with her."

Then the handmaidens did as Byzun desired, and Manijeh said, "Let him come forth."

So Byzun entered into the tents of Manijeh, and she received him with joy, and she caused his feet to be washed with musk and amber, and she poured jewels before him, and prepared for him a feast of sweet meats. And slaves stood around and made soft music, and the heart of Byzun was ensnared in the meshes of the net that had been spread. And three days and three nights did he sojourn beside Manijeh, and his passion for her waxed greater, and he thought not of Iran, neither of the time of departure. And

Manijeh too rejoiced in his presence, and when the time was come for her to quit the garden of spring she would not part with him. So she gave unto him a cup wherein she had mingled a potion. And the wine caused Byzun to sleep, and while he slept the maidens bare him in a litter even into the house of Afrasiyab. And Manijeh hid him behind the curtains of the women, and none, save only her handmaidens, were aware of his presence.

Now when Byzun awoke he asked whither he was come, and when he learned that he was in the house of Afrasiyab he was afraid, and desired to return unto Iran. But Manijeh quieted his distrust, and he forgot his fears in her love. And she made the earth glad about him, and the hours fled on the wings of wine and of joy. And many days sped thus, and none knew what passed in the house of the women.

Then it came about that a guardian of the door learned thereof, and he came before Afrasiyab, and told unto him that his daughter hid within her house a man of the race of Iran. And Afrasiyab, when he learned it, was beside himself with anger, and he cursed Manijeh, and he said-

"The hour is come unto this man."

Then he called for Gersiwaz, his brother, and bade him go forth with a band of armed men unto the house of the women. And Gersiwaz did as Afrasiyab commanded, and he put guards at all the doors. Then the sounds of lutes and of rejoicing fell upon his ear, for none were aware of the vengeance that was come upon them. And when Gersiwaz was come unto the house of Manijeh, the daughter of Afrasiyab, he brake open the doors, and stood in the midst of the revels. And he beheld within the chamber many slaves playing on lutes of gold, and fair women that handed the wine-cups. And Manijeh was seated upon a throne of gold, and beside her was Byzun, the son of Gew, the Iranian, and joy was painted on his visage.

Now when Gersiwaz beheld Byzun, he cried, "O vile man, thou art fallen into my hands! How wilt thou now save thy life?"

And Byzun was dismayed, for he had neither sword nor armour, and he thought within himself-

"I fear me that my life will end this day."

But he drew forth from his boot a dagger that was hidden therein, and he threatened Gersiwaz, and he said that he would plunge it into his breast if he led him not before Afrasiyab.

Now Gersiwaz knew that Byzun was quick to act, and would do that which he spake, so he held back from combat, and he seized Byzun and

FERDOWSI

bound him, and led him before Afrasiyab. And when Afrasiyab saw him in such plight, he said-

"O man of evil, wherefore didst thou come into my land?"

Then Byzun told him how he was gone forth to slay the boars, and how he was come into the garden of Afrasiyab, and he said that a Peri had borne him unto the palace, for he would not do hurt unto Manijeh. But Afrasiyab refused belief unto his words, and he commanded that a gibbet should be raised without his court, and that Byzun be hung thereon, because he had dishonoured the house of the women, and had stolen like a thief in the night into the house of the King. And in vain did Byzun invoke mercy at the hands of Afrasiyab, and he was led forth beyond the courts. And the men of Afrasiyab made ready the gallows, and Byzun stood bound beneath. And he wept sore in his distress, and he prayed to the winds that they would bear tidings of him unto the Shah of Iran, and he sware that his death should be avenged upon Turan.

Now while he waited thus there passed by Piran, the Pehliva, who was come forth to do homage unto the King. And when he beheld the gibbet he questioned concerning it, and when he learned that it was for Byzun he was troubled. So he got him from his horse and came near unto the youth, and questioned him of this adventure. And Byzun told him all that was come about, and how his evil comrade had laid for him a snare. Then Piran commanded that punishment be stayed until he should have spoken unto Afrasiyab. And he went in and stood before the King as a suppliant. Then Afrasiyab bade him make known his desires. And Piran opened his mouth and spake words of wisdom unto Afrasiyab, his King. And he reminded him of the death of Saiawush, and how Byzun was of much account in his own country, and how surely his blood would be avenged. And he said how the land of Turan was not ready to stand again in a new war, and he prayed Afrasiyab to content him with a dungeon. And he said-

"Heap chains upon Byzun, and let the earth hide him, that Iran may not know whither he is vanished."

Now Afrasiyab knew that the words of Piran were wise, and he gave ear unto them. So Byzun was led forth unto a desert place and he was laden with chains of iron and his tender flesh was bound and he was thrown into a deep hole. And the opening thereof was closed with a mighty stone that the Deev Akwan had torn from the nethermost sea, and neither sun nor moon could be seen by Byzun, and Afrasiyab trusted that his reason would forsake him in this pit. And when he had done thus unto

Byzun, he bade Gersiwaz go in unto the house of the daughter that had dishonoured him, and tear off her costly robes, and her crown, and her veil. And he said-

"Let her be cast forth also into the desert, that she may behold the dungeon wherein Byzun is hid. And say unto her, 'Thou hast been his Spring, be now his comforter, and wait upon him in his narrow prison.'"

And Gersiwaz did as Afrasiyab commanded, and he tore the veil from off Manijeh, and he caused her to walk barefooted unto the spot where Byzun was hid.

Now Manijeh was bowed down with sorrow, and she wept sore, and she wandered through the desert day and night bewailing her fate. And ever did she return unto the pit, and she sought how she might enter therein. But she could not move the mighty stone that closed its mouth. Yet after some days were gone by she found an opening where she could thrust in her hand. Now when she had found it she rejoiced, and daily she went forth unto the city and begged of men that they would give her bread. And none knew her for the daughter of Afrasiyab, but all had pity upon her sorry plight, and they gave her freely of that which they had. And she returned with it unto Byzun, and she fed him through the hole that she had made. And she spake unto him sweet words of comfort, and she kept his heart alive within him.

Now while these things were passing in Turan, Girgin was returned unto Iran much discomfited. And he pondered how he should come before the Shah, and what he should say unto Gew. And he told them that they had of their combined strength overcome the boars, and he boasted that he had done deeds of great prowess, and he said that a wild ass was come forth out of the forest and had borne away Byzun from before his eyes, and verily he held that it must be a Deev. Then Kai Khosrau questioned him closely, and when he had done so he saw that Girgin held not unto his story. So his mind misgave him, and he commanded that Girgin be put in chains. And he said-

"I will guard thee until I have learned tidings of Byzun."

Now Gew was beside himself with grief because of his only son, whom he loved, but Kai Khosrau spake comfort unto his soul. And he bade riders go forth unto all corners of the wind to seek tidings of Byzun, and he said-

"If I learn nought concerning him until the feast of Neurouz be come, I will search for him in the crystal globe wherein I can behold the world, and read the secrets of destiny."

Now when the horsemen had sought Byzun in vain throughout the plains of Iran and in the gorges of the land of Arman, they returned them unto the courts of the Shah. So when the feast of Neurouz was come, Kai Khosrau clothed himself in a robe of Roum, and he took from off his head the crown of the Kaianides, and he presented himself in humility before Ormuzd. Then he took in his hand the globe of crystal, and he prayed to God that He would grant unto him to behold the seven zones of the world. And God granted it. And Kai Khosrau surveyed all the lands of the earth, and nowhere upon them could he behold Byzun. And he was downcast and sad in his spirit, for he deemed that Byzun was departed from the world. Then Ormuzd showed unto him where he was hidden in a pit, and Kai Khosrau beheld him, and the damsel that watched beside him. So he called before him Gew, and said-

"Let thy heart cease from sorrow, for thy son liveth, and he is tended by a maiden of noble birth. But he is bound, and a mighty stone is laid above his prison, and Rustem alone can deliver him. Wherefore I counsel thee, speed forth unto Zaboulistan and entreat the son of Zal that he come unto our aid yet again."

Then Kai Khosrau wrote a letter unto Rustem, wherein he told him all that was come about, and he gave the writing unto Gew. And Gew sped forth therewith unto Zaboulistan.

Now when he was come within the courts of Rustem, Zal beheld him from afar, and he feared that evil was come upon Iran since the Shah sent forth a man of might like unto Gew to be his messenger. So he came forth in haste and questioned him. And when he learned his mission he bade him come within, and he told him how Rustem was gone forth to chase the wild ass, and he made a feast for him, and entertained him until his son was returned within the courts. Now when Rustem learned the tidings, his eyes were filled with tears, but he spake comfort unto Gew, and he said-

"Be not disquieted, for verily Rustem shall not remove the saddle from Rakush until he hath grasped the hand of Byzun, and broken his chains and his prison."

And when he had read the letter of the Shah, he made him ready to go, before Kai Khosrau. And when he was come into his presence, he did obeisance before him, and he said-

"O King of kings, I am ready to do thy commandments, for my mother brought me into the world that I might weary myself for thee, and unto thee pertaineth rest and joy, and unto me combat everlasting."

Then he chose forth from among the warriors men of renown, that they should go out with him to deliver Byzun. And Girgin sent greeting unto Rustem, and craved of him that he would plead for him with the Shah. And he bewailed his fault, and he entreated that he might go out to succour Byzun. And Rustem asked his forgiveness of Kai Khosrau, and when the Shah would have refused his suit, he pressed him hard. So Kai Khosrau listened to the desires of his Pehliva. Then he said unto him-

"Tell me what men and treasures thou desirest to bear with thee into Turan."

And Rustem said, "I desire not a large army, for I think to regain Byzun by the arts of wile. Give unto me, therefore, jewels and rich brocades, and carpets, and stuffs of value, for I purpose to go forth in the garb of a merchant."

Then Kai Khosrau gave him the key to all his treasures, and Rustem chose forth rich stuffs, and loaded them upon an hundred camels. And he desired seven valiant knights that they should go forth with him clad in the dress of merchants, and that an army be posted in secret upon the borders. And when all was ready the caravan went forth. And they journeyed until they came into the town of Khoten, and all the people came forth to gaze upon their merchandise. Then Rustem, in his disguise, went unto the house of Piran, and he poured gifts before him, and he asked leave of him that he might remain within the borders to sell his wares. And Piran granted his request. So Rustem took for himself a house, and showed his goods unto the people, and bartered them, and it was noised through all the land that a caravan was come out from Iran, and all who had need of aught flocked into the city. And the news spread even unto the ears of Manijeh. And when she learned that it was men of Iran who were come forth, she made her way unto the city, and came before Rustem and questioned him, saying-

"What news is there abroad in Iran concerning Byzun, the son of Gew, and doth no army come forth to save him? O noble merchant, I entreat of thee when thou goest back to thy land, to seek out Gew, and Kai Khosrau, and Rustem the mighty, and bring unto them tidings of Byzun, lest he perish in his chains."

Now Rustem, when he heard her words, was afraid for his secret, for he knew not who she was. Wherefore he spoke roughly unto her, and he said-

"I am a man of peace and of ignoble birth, a merchant, and I know nought of Gew, or of Byzun, or of the Shah. Get thee hence, maiden, thou dost but hinder my business, and this alone concerneth me."

When he had thus spoken, Manijeh looked on him with sorrow, and wept, saying-

"Do the men of Iran refuse tidings unto the poor?"

Then Rustem repented him of his harshness, and said-

"Woman, who art thou, and how do these things regard thee?"

And he caused food to be put before her, and he comforted her with kind words. Then Manijeh said-

"I am daughter unto Afrasiyab, and my father hath cast me forth because of Byzun."

And she told him all that was come about, and how she had tended her beloved, and how she had kept him alive. And she related unto Rustem how he languished in his chains, and how they put their trust alone in Rustem the Pehliva. And she said-

"When it was told unto me that men from Iran were come forth, I sped hither unto thee, for I hoped that tidings of Byzun might come thus unto the mighty warrior."

When Rustem heard her words he was moved with compassion. And when he had spoken softly unto her, he gave to her savoury meats, and he bade her bear them unto Byzun. Now within the body of a fowl he had hidden a ring whereon was graven his seal. And when Byzun came upon it, and felt the ring, and that it bare the name of Rustem, his heart laughed within him, for he knew that the end of his ills was come. And his lips laughed also, and his laughter shook the walls of the pit.

Now when Manijeh heard his laughter she was amazed, and she feared lest his wits were distraught, and she leaned over the mouth of the pit and spake, saying-

"O man of ill fortune, wherefore is thy heart thus light, thou who seest neither sun, nor moon, nor stars?"

Then Byzun answered and said, "Hope is sprung up in my breast."

And Manijeh said, "Whence dost thou behold the rays of hope?"

And Byzun answered, "I know not whether I can confide it unto thee, for a woman cannot keep a secret."

Now Manijeh was pained at these words, and she upbraided Byzun, and recalled to him all she had suffered for his sake. And Byzun repented him of his hasty speech, for he knew that she was prudent and strong of spirit. So he said-

"Swear unto me a great oath, and I will tell it unto thee."

And Manijeh sware. Then Byzun said-

"I know that the merchant who is come forth from Iran is come out because of me. Go therefore again into his presence, and say unto him, 'O Pehliva of the King of kings, tell unto me, art thou the master of Rakush?'"

Now Manijeh, when she had heard these words, sped forth to do the bidding of Byzun. And she came before Rustem, and spake to him the words that had been told her. And he answered and said-

"Go say unto thy friend, verily I am the master of Rakush, and that I am come forth to deliver him."

Then he bade her gather together wood into a pyre, and set light thereto when the night should be come, that he might know where Byzun was laid. And Manijeh did as Rustem commanded, and she wearied not to scour the land, and she stripped the trees of their branches, and her tender body was torn of thorns; but she bare all gladly for the sake of Byzun, whom she loved. And when the night was fallen she set light unto the wood, and Rustem came forth unto the spot, and his seven comrades came with him. And each strove in turn to lift the stone that closed the pit, but none could roll it aside. Then Rustem prayed to God that He would grant him strength, and he came unto the mouth of the pit, and he bent down his body, and he spake unto Byzun, and questioned him how he was come into these straits. Then he said-

"I would ask of thee a boon. Grant thy forgiveness unto Girgin, if it be given unto me to move this stone, and to free thee from out of this pit. For verily he repenteth him of his evil deed, and because he is valiant I would that there should be peace between you."

But Byzun said, "Thou knowest not all the evil that Girgin hath brought upon me. I cannot give ear unto thy request, for I desire to take vengeance upon him."

Then Rustem said, "If thy mind be thus evil that thou wilt not listen to my desires, nor remember how I am come forth in friendship to succour thee, I shall mount upon Rakush and leave thee to perish in thy chains."

When Byzun heard these words he gave a loud cry, and bewailed his evil plight. And he said, "Be it as thou desirest."

Then Rustem laid hold of the stone, and he put forth all his strength, and he lifted it from off the mouth of the pit and threw it far into the desert. Then he let down his cord and enmeshed Byzun therein, and drew him forth from his dungeon. And he was a sorry sight to see, for the earth had withered his body, and his skin hung about his bones.

. . .

Now Rustem, when he had broken the chains of Byzun, covered him with a cloak and set him upon a horse, and he took Manijeh also, and led them unto his house in the city. Then when he had refreshed them with water, and covered them with new robes, he desired that they be led unto the spot where the army was hidden. And he said unto Byzun-

"I desire to fall upon Turan, but thou art too wasted to fight."

But Byzun said, "Not so; let Manijeh go forth into shelter, but it behoveth not a man to be guarded like a woman."

And he refused ear to the desires of Rustem, and he clad him in a coat of mail, and he girded him to ride beside the Pehliva. And they went forth in the darkness until they were come unto the house of Afrasiyab. And when they were come there, Rustem lifted the doors from off their hinges and entered into the precincts, and he slew the guards that kept the curtains, and he made him a passage unto the chamber of Afrasiyab. And when he stood therein he lifted up his voice of thunder, and he cried-

"Sleep, man of folly, and may thy slumbers be deep. Thou hast rested upon thy throne while Byzun was hidden in a pit. But thou hast forgotten that a road leadeth from Iran into Turan, and thou didst think in thine evil heart that none would come forth to avenge him. Listen, therefore, unto my voice; for I am Rustem, the son of Zal, the Pehliva, and I have broken down thy doors, and released Byzun from his chains, and I am come to do vengeance upon thee."

When Afrasiyab heard these words he awoke, and cried out in his fear. And he called upon the names of his guards. But no man came forth, because they had been laid low by the hands of Rustem. Then Afrasiyab made his way unto the door, and because it was dark he escaped thence, and he fled before the face of Rustem, and left his house between his hands. Then Rustem took much rich booty of slaves, and horses, and jewels, and when he had done so he sped back unto his army, for he knew that with the day Afrasiyab would come forth with an host to assail him. And it came about as he foresaw, and when the day was risen the watchers cried out that an army marched forth from Turan. Then Rustem set his men in battle order, and he sent Manijeh and the slaves and the booty into Iran, and he placed himself at the head of the host, and Byzun rode beside him. And there was fought a mighty battle, and great was the slaughter, and the bodies of the slain and the broken armour covered the earth. And the banner of Turan sank, and Afrasiyab fled before his enemies.

Then Rustem returned with joy unto Kai Khosrau, and the Shah was glad also. And he came forth to greet his Pehliva, and there rode with him Gew and Gudarz, his warriors. And when Kai Khosrau saw Rustem he embraced him, and said-

"O stay of my soul, and man of valour, thou resemblest the sun, for wheresoever men may look they behold the traces of thy mighty deeds. Happy is Zal who owneth a son such as thou!"

Then he blessed him, and showered rich gifts upon him; and Gew blessed him also, and Gudarz, because he had brought back Byzun into their midst. Then Kai Khosrau gave orders that a great feast be prepared, and the heroes drank until their heads were heavy with wine. But in the morning Rustem came before the Shah in audience, and opened his mouth and said-

"May it please the King to lend his ear unto his slave. I desire to return unto Zal, my father."

And Kai Khosrau listened to the just desires of Rustem, though he would fain have kept him in his courts.

Now when Rustem was departed, Kai Khosrau called before him Byzun, and he spake to him of that which was come about, and he poured pity upon the daughter of Afrasiyab when he learned all she had suffered for the sake of Byzun; and he gave him rich gifts, and bade him bear them unto her, and he said-

"Cherish this woman in thy bosom, and suffer not that grief come nigh unto her, neither speak to her cold words, for she hath endured much for thee. And may thy life beside her be happy."

And when the Shah had thus spoken he dismissed Byzun from his presence.

Thus endeth the history of Byzun and Manijeh.

THE DEFEAT OF AFRASIYAB

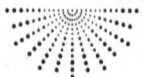

Mourning and sorrow filled the heart of Afrasiyab because of his defeat, and he pondered in his spirit how the fortunes of Iran might be retrieved. So he sent messengers unto all his vassals that they should unsheathe the sword of strife and make ready an army. And the nobles did as Afrasiyab bade them, and they got together an host that covered the ground, and sent it forth before the King. And the King placed Schideh his son at the head thereof, and he said unto him—

"Open not the door of peace, neither treat Kai Khosrau other than as an enemy."

Now when the Shah heard tidings of the army that Afrasiyab had made ready against him, he commanded that no man who could use the bridle and the stirrup should stay within the borders of Iran. And when the army was ready he placed at its head Gudarz the wise. But Kai Khosrau bade yet again that Gudarz should seek to win Piran the Pehliva unto Iran ere the hosts met in battle. For the Shah remembered the benefits he had received at his hands, and it grieved him sore to go out against him in enmity. And Gudarz did as the Shah desired, and when he had crossed the Jihun he sent Gew, his son, unto Piran that he might speak with him. But Piran shut ear unto the voice of Gew, and he said that he had led forth his army to battle, and that it behoved him to do that which was commanded of Afrasiyab.

So the two armies were drawn up in order of battle, and each desired that the other should fall upon them the first. And for three days and three nights they faced each other, and you would have said that no man so much as moved his lips. And Gudarz was posted before his men, and day and night he searched the stars and the sun and moon for augury. And he demanded of them whether he should advance or whether he should stay. And Piran also waited that he might behold what the Iranians would do.

But Byzun was angry thereat, and he went before his father and entreated him to urge his grandsire unto action. "For surely," he said, "Gudarz hath lost his wits that he thus regardeth the sun and stars, and thinketh not of the enemy." And Gew strove in vain to quiet him.

And in the ranks of Turan also Human grew impatient, and he asked permission of his brother to challenge the nobles of Iran to single fight. And Piran sought to dissuade him in vain. So he got ready his steed of battle, and rode until he came within the lines of Iran. And when he was come thither he sought out Rehham, the son of Gudarz, and challenged him to measure his strength. But Rehham said-

"My soul thirsteth after the combat, yet since my father hath commanded that the army advance not, it beseemeth me not to forget his behests. And remember, O valiant Turk, that he who ventureth first upon the battlefield hath no need to seek the pathway to return."

Then Human said, "Men had told unto me that Rehham was a knight of courage, but now I know that he is afraid." And he turned away his steed and rode until he came nigh unto Friburz, and he challenged him also in words of pride, and he said-

"Thou art brother unto Saiawush, show now if there live within thee aught of valour."

But Friburz answered, "Go forth before Gudarz and demand of him that I may fight, and verily if he listen unto thy voice, it will be a joy unto my soul."

Then Human said, "I see that thou art a hero only in words." And he turned his back upon him also, and he rode till that he came before Gudarz the Pehliva. And he raised his voice and spake unto him words of insolence, and he defied him to lead forth his army. But Gudarz would not listen unto his voice. Then Human turned him back unto the camp of Turan, and he said unto the army how that the men of Iran were craven. And when the army heard it they raised shouts of great joy.

Now the shouting of the men of Turan pierced even unto the cars of the Iranians, and they were sore hurt thereat; and the nobles came before Gudarz and laid before him their complaints, and they entreated of him that he would lead them forth that they might prove their valour. And Byzun, when he heard what had been done, came before his grandsire like to a lion in his fury, and he craved that he would grant unto him that he might reply unto the challenge of Human. Now when Gudarz beheld that all the nobles were against him, he listened unto the ardour of Byzun, and he gave to him leave to go forth, and he accorded to him the armour of Saiawush, and he blessed him and bade him be victorious. Then Byzun sent a messenger unto Human, and the place of combat was chosen. And when the sun was risen they met upon the field, and Human cried unto his adversary, and he said-

"O Byzun, thine hour is come, for I will send thee back unto Gew in such guise that his heart shall be torn with anguish."

But Byzun answered and said, "Why waste we our time in words, let us fall upon one another."

Then they did as Byzun desired. And they fought with swords and with arrows, with maces also and with fists, and sore was the struggle and weary, and the victory leaned unto neither side. And they strove thus from the time of dawn until the sun had lengthened the shadows, and Byzun was afraid lest the day should end in doubt. Then he sent up a prayer unto Ormuzd that He would lend unto him strength. And Ormuzd listened unto the petition of His servant. Then Byzun caught Human in his arms and flung him upon the ground, and he beat out his brains, and he severed his head from off his trunk, that the murder of Saiawush might be avenged. Then he gave thanks unto God, and turned him back unto the camp, and he bore aloft the head of Human. And the army of Iran, when they beheld it, set up a great shout, but from the ranks of Turan there came the noise of wailing. And Piran was bowed down with grief and anger, and he commanded the army should go forth and fall upon the Iranians.

Now there was fought a battle such as men have not seen the like. And the earth was covered with steel, and arrows fell from the clouds like hail, and the ground was torn with hoofs, and blood flowed like water upon the plains. And the dead lay around in masses, and the feet of the horses could not stir because of them. Then the chiefs of the army said among themselves-

"If we part not these heroes upon the field of vengeance, there will remain nought when the night is come save only the earth that turns, and God, the Master of the world."

Yet they withdrew not from the combat until the darkness had thrown a mantle over the earth, and they could no longer look upon their foes.

. . .

Now when the earth was become like unto ebony, the leaders of the hosts met in conference. And it was decided between them that they should choose forth valiant men from their midst, and that on the morrow the fate of the lands should be decided by them. For they grieved for the blood that had been spilled, and they desired that the hand of destruction be stayed. So when the morning was come they chose forth their champions, and ten men of valour were picked from each host, and Piran and Gudarz led them out unto the plain. Now on each side of the plain uprose a mountain. So Gudarz said unto his comrades-

"Whosoever among you hath laid low his adversary, let him mount this hill and plant the flag that he hath won upon its crest, that the army may learn whom we have vanquished."

And Piran spake unto his men in like manner. Then the ten drew up and faced one another, and each man stood opposed to the adversary that he had chosen. Now Friburz was the first to begin combat, and he was opposed unto Kelbad, the kinsman of Piran. And he rode at him with fury, and he laid him low with his bow, and he galloped with joy unto the mountain and planted the standard of Kelbad upon its crest. Then when it was done, Gew came forward to meet his adversary, and he was placed over against Zereh, the man whom Kai Khosrau hated because he had severed the head of Saiawush from its trunk. And Gew was careful not to slay him, but he threw his cord about him and caught him in the snares and bound him. Then he took from him his standard, and led him bound unto the mountain. And there followed after him Gourazeh, and he too laid low his foe and planted his flag upon the crest of the hill. And likewise did all the champions of Iran; and when the ninth hour was ended there waved nine standards from off the hill, and none remained to fight save only Piran and Gudarz the aged. Then Gudarz girded him for the combat, and for a mighty space they wrestled sore, but in the end Gudarz laid low the power of Piran.

Now when the Iranians beheld the standard of Piran planted aloft amid those of his champions, they were beside themselves for joy, and they called down the blessings of Heaven upon the knight. Then a messenger was sent to bear the tidings unto Kai Khosrau, and he took with him Zereh that the Shah might with his own hand sever that vile head from off its trunk. And Kai Khosrau rejoiced at the news, and he rode forth that he might visit his army. But when he beheld the body of Piran he wept sore, and he remembered his kindness of old, and he grieved for the man that had been to him a father. Then he commanded that a royal tomb be raised unto Piran, and he seated him therein upon a throne of gold, and he did unto him all reverence. But when it was done he aided his army to beat back the men of Turan yet again, and he caused them to sue for peace. And when they had brought forth their armour and piled it at the feet of Kai Khosrau, he bade them depart in peace. Then he returned with joy unto his own land, and he gave thanks unto God for the victory that was his. But he knew also that the time of peace could not be long, and that Afrasiyab would dream of vengeance.

THE PASSING OF KAI KHOSRAU

*N*ow it came to pass as Kai Khosrau foretold. For Afrasiyab, when he learned the death of Piran, was beside himself with grief. And he lifted up his voice in wailing, and he spake, saying-

"I will no longer taste the joys of life, nor live like unto a man that weareth a crown, until I be avenged upon Kai Khosrau, the offspring of an accursed race. May the seed of Saiawush perish from off the face of the earth!

"And when he had so spoken he made ready for yet another war, and from all corners of the earth the kings came forth to aid him. And Kai Khosrau, when he learned thereof, got ready his army also, and he sware that he would lead this war of vengeance unto a good end. So he sent greeting unto Rustem his Pehliva, and prayed of him that he would aid him in his resolve. And Rustem listened to the voice of his Shah, and came forth from Zaboulistan with a mighty army to aid him. Then the Shah confided his hosts unto Tur and Rustem, and the valleys, and the hills, and the deserts, and the plains were filled with the dust that uprose from their footsteps. And they were warriors that bare high their heads, and they knew neither weariness nor fear.

Now when the armies met, Afrasiyab called before him Pescheng, his son, and bade him bear a writing unto the Shah of Iran. And he wrote, saying-

"That which thou hast done, it is contrary to custom; for a son may not lift his hand against his father, and the head of a grandson that goeth out in enmity against his grandsire is filled with evil. And I say unto thee, Saiawush was not slain without just cause, for he turned him away from his ruler. And if thou sayest unto me that I am an evil man, and issue of the race of Ahriman, remember that thou too art sprung from my loins, and that thy insults fall back upon thyself. Renounce, therefore, this strife, and let a treaty be made between us, and the blood of Saiawush be forgotten. And if thou wilt listen unto my voice, I will cover thee with jewels, and gold and precious things will I give unto thee, and joy shall reign throughout the land."

But Kai Khosrau, when he had read this message, knew that Afrasiyab sought only to beguile him. So he sent a writing unto the King of Turan, and he said-

"The cause of strife between us is not sprung from Saiawush alone, but for that which thou didst aforetime, and which thy fathers did unto Irij. Yet that which thou hast done hath caused the measure of wrath to overflow. Wherefore the sword alone can decide between us."

Then he challenged the nobles of Turan to come forth in combat. And he himself strove with Schideh, the son of Afrasiyab, and he laid him low after the manner in which Afrasiyab had laid low the head of Saiawush. And when he had done so, the army of Turan came forth to avenge their king, but the men of Iran overcame them. And Afrasiyab was constrained to fly from before the face of Kai Khosrau, and it was as gall and wormwood unto his spirit. And Kai Khosrau followed after him, and he would not suffer him to hide himself from his sight; and he made him come forth yet again in battle, and yet again he routed him utterly. And the men of Iran slew the men of Turan until the field of battle was like unto a sea of blood, and they fought until the night covered the heavens, and the eyes of the warriors were darkened with sleep. And Afrasiyab fled yet again beyond the borders of Turan, and he craved of his vassals that they would hide him from the wrath of Kai Khosrau. But the nobles were afraid of the Shah, and of Rustem, who went with him; and they refused shelter unto Afrasiyab, and he was hunted over the face of the earth. Then he sought out the King of China, and asked of him that he would shelter him. And the King gave him shelter for a while. But when Kai Khosrau learned where Afrasiyab was hid, he followed after him, and he bade the King of China render to him his enemy, and he menaced him with fire and sword if he did not listen to his behest. So the King bade Afrasiyab depart from out his borders. And Afrasiyab fled yet again, but wheresoever he hid himself he was found of Kai Khosrau, and his life was a weariness unto him.

. . .

Now for the space of two years Kai Khosrau did thus unto Afrasiyab, and the glory of Turan was eclipsed, and Rustem reigned within the land. And when the second year was ended the power of Afrasiyab was broken, and Kai Khosrau bethought him to return unto Iran and seek out Kai Kaous, his sire. And the old Shah, when he learned it, was young again for joy. He caused his house to be decked worthy a guest, and he made ready great feasts, and he called forth all his nobles to do honour unto Kai Khosrau, his son. And all the land was decked in festal garb, and the world resembled cloth of gold, and musk and amber perfumed the air, and jewels were strewn about the streets like unto vile dust.

Now when the Shah came nigh unto the city, Kai Kaous went forth to meet him, and he prostrated him in the dust before his son. But Kai Khosrau suffered it not, but raised him, and he kissed him upon his cheeks, and he took his hand, and he told unto him of all the wonders that he had beheld upon his travels, and of the mighty deeds that had been done of Rustem and his men. And Kai Kaous was filled with marvel at his grandson, and he could not cease from praising him and pouring gifts before his face. And when they had feasted the army, and were sated with speech, they went in unto the temple of Ormuzd and gave thanks unto God for all His blessings.

Now while these things were passing in the land of Iran, Afrasiyab wandered over the earth, and he knew neither rest nor nourishment. And his soul was unquiet, and his body was weary, and he feared danger on all sides. And he roamed till that he found a cavern in the side of a mountain, and he crept into it for rest. And he remained a while within the cave pondering his evil deeds, and his heart was filled with repentance. And he prayed aloud unto God that He would grant him forgiveness of his sins, and the cries of his sorrow rent the air.

Now the sound thereof pierced even unto the ears of Houm, a hermit of the race of Feridoun, who had taken up his abode in the mountains. And Houm, when he heard the cries, said within himself, "These are lamentations of Afrasiyab." So he sought out the spot whence they came forth, and when he had found Afrasiyab he wrestled with him and caught him in his snare. Then he bound him, and led him even into Iran before the face of Kai Khosrau, that the Shah might deal with him according to his desire.

Now when Afrasiyab was come before the Shah, Kai Khosrau reproached him yet again with his vile deeds. And when he had done speaking, he lifted up his sword and he smote with it the neck of

Afrasiyab, and he severed his head from off his trunk, even as Afrasiyab had done unto Saiawush, his father. And thus was the throne of Turan made void of Afrasiyab, and his evil deeds had in the end brought evil upon himself. And Gersiwaz, whom the Shah had taken captive in the battle, was witness of the fate of his brother. And when he had looked upon the end of Afrasiyab, Kai Khosrau lifted up the sword against him also, and caused him to perish in like manner as he had slain Saiawush.

And when it was done, and the vengeance was complete, the Shah caused a writing to be sent unto all his lands, and to every noble therein and every vassal, even from the west unto the east. And he told unto them therein how that the war of vengeance was ended, and how that the earth was delivered of the serpent brood. And he bade them think on the arts of peace and deliver up their hearts to gladness. And when it was done Kai Kaous made him ready to depart from the world. So he gave thanks unto God that He had suffered him to see the avenging of Saiawush accomplished, and he said-

"I have beheld my grandson, the light of mine eyes, avenge me and himself. And now am I ready to go forth unto Thee, for thrice fifty years have rolled above my head, and my hair is white and my heart is weary."

And after he had thus spoken Kai Kaous passed away, and there remained of him in the world but the memory of his name. Then Kai Khosrau mourned for his grandsire as was fitting. But when the days of mourning were ended he mounted again the throne of the Kaianides, and for sixty years did Kai Khosrau rule the world in equity, and wisdom flourished under his hands. And wheresoever the Shah looked he beheld that his hand was stretched out in gladness, and there was peace in all the lands. Then he gave praise unto God that He had suffered him to do these things. And when he had done so he pondered within himself, and he grew afraid lest Ahriman should get possession of his soul, and lest he should grow uplifted in pride like unto Jemshid, that forgot whence came his weal and the source of his blessings. So he said within himself-

"It behoveth me to be careful, for I am sprung from the race of Zohak, and perchance I may become a curse unto the earth, like to him. Wherefore I will entreat of Ormuzd that He take me unto Himself before this evil befall me, since there is no longer work for me to do on earth."

Then he gave commandment to the keepers of the curtains that they suffer no man to enter in upon him, but he bade them refuse it with all kindness. And when it was done Kai Khosrau withdrew him into the inner courts, and he ungirded him of his sash of might, and he laved his limbs in a running stream, and he presented himself in prayer before God his Maker. And for seven days the Shah stood in the presence of Ormuzd, neither did he weary to importune Him in prayer.

Now while he did so many great ones of Iran came unto the courts of the Shah and demanded audience. And it was refused them. Then they murmured among themselves, and they marvelled why the thoughts of the King should have grown dark in a time of good fortune. And when they found that their importunity availed them nought, they consulted among themselves what they should do. Then Gudarz said-

"Let us send tidings of these things even unto Zal and Rustem, and entreat of them that they come unto our aid, for perchance Kai Khosrau will listen unto their voice."

So Gew was sent forth into Zaboulistan.

Now when he was gone, it came about that on a certain day, when the sun had lifted his shield of gold above the world, Kai Khosrau ordained that the curtains of the audience-chamber be lifted. So there came in unto him his Mubids and the nobles, and they stood about his throne, and their hands were crossed in supplication. Then Kai Khosrau, when he saw it, asked of them what they desired. So they opened their mouths and said-

"May it please the Shah to tell unto us wherein we have failed that we are shut out from his presence."

Then Kai Khosrau answered and said, "The fault is not with you, and the sight of my nobles is a feast unto mine eyes. But my heart hath conceived a desire that will not be quieted, and it giveth me rest neither by day nor by night and I know not how it will end. Yet the time is not ripe to tell unto you my secrets, but verily I will speak when the hour is come. Return, therefore, unto your homes, and be glad in your spirits, and rejoice in the wine-cup, for no foe troubleth the land, and prosperity hangeth over Iran."

Then when he had so spoken, Kai Khosrau dismissed them graciously. But when they were departed he gave commandment that the curtains be closed, and that no man be suffered to enter his courts. And he presented him yet again before God, and he prayed in the fervour of his spirit, and he entreated of Ormuzd that He would suffer him to depart from the world now that his task therein was ended. For he beheld that this life is but vanity, and he yearned to go hence unto his Maker. And for the space of five weeks did Kai Khosrau stand thus before his God, and he could neither eat nor sleep, and his heart was disquieted.

Now it came about one night that Kai Khosrau fell asleep for weariness. And there appeared unto him a vision, and the Serosch, the angel of God, stood before him. And he spake words of comfort to Kai Khosrau, and he said that the Shah had done that which was right in the sight of God, and he bade him prepare for his end, and he said-
"Before thou goest hence choose from amongst thy nobles a king that is worthy the throne. And let him be a man that hath a care of all things that are created, even unto the tiny emmet that creepeth along the ground. And when thou hast ordered all things, the moment of thy departure shall be come."
When Kai Khosrau awoke from his dream he rejoiced, and poured out his thanks before God. Then he went unto his throne and seated himself thereon, and got together his treasures. And he ordered the world for his departure.
Now while he did so, Zal and Rustem, his son, were come unto the city, and their hearts were filled with sore displeasure because of that which the nobles had told unto them. And the army came forth to greet them, and they wept sore, and prayed of Zal that he would turn back unto them the heart of Kai Khosrau. And they said, "A Deev hath led him astray." Then Zal and Rustem went in before the Shah. And Kai Khosrau, when he saw them, was amazed, but he was glad also, and he gave them his hand in greeting. And he accorded to them seats of honour, as was their due, and when he had done so, he asked of them wherefore they were come forth. Then Zal opened his mouth and spake, saying-
"I have heard, even in Zaboulistan, that the curtains of the Shah are closed unto his servants. And the people cry out thereat, and men say that Kai Khosrau is departed from the path that is right. Wherefore I am come forth to entreat of thee, if thou have a secret care, that thou confide it to thy servant, and surely a device may be found. For since the days of Minuchihr there is no Shah like to thee, but thy nobles are afraid lest thou stumble in the paths of Zohak and Afrasiyab. Wherefore they entreat of me that I admonish thee."
Now when Kai Khosrau had listened unto the voice of Zal the aged, he was not angered, but he answered, saying-
"O Zal, thou knowest not that whereof thou speakest. For I have withdrawn myself from men that I might do no evil, and I have prayed unto

God that He take me unto Himself. And now is the Serosch come unto me, and I know that Ormuzd hath listened unto my voice."

When the nobles heard this they were afflicted, but Zal was angered, and he deemed that the wits of Kai Khosrau were distraught. And he said-

"Since I have stood before the throne of the Kaianides no Shah hath spoken words like to thine. And I fear that a Deev hath led thee astray, and I implore of thee that thou listen not unto his voice, and that thou give ear unto the words of an aged man, and that thou turn thee back into the path that is right."

And when Zal had done speaking, the nobles cried with one accord that he had spoken for them also. Then Kai Khosrau was sorrowful, but he would not suffer anger to come into his spirit. And when he had pondered, he opened his mouth and spake, saying-

"O Zal, I have given ear unto the words which thou hast spoken, give ear now unto the answer. For I have not departed from the paths of Ormuzd, and no Deev hath led me astray. And I swear it unto thee, even by God the Most High. But because I am sprung from Afrasiyab the evil one, and am linked unto the race of Zohak, I am afraid, and I fear to grow like to Jemshid and Tur, who wearied the world with their oppressions. And, behold, I have avenged my father, and have made the world submissive unto my will; and I have established justice in the realm, and the earth is glad, wherefore there is no longer aught for me to do, for the power of the wicked is broken. Therefore, lest I grow uplifted in my soul, I have entreated of Ormuzd that He suffer me now to go hence, even unto Himself. For I am weary of the throne and of my majesty, and my soul crieth for rest."

When Zal heard these words he was confounded, for he knew that they were true. And he fell in the dust before the Shah, and he craved his forgiveness for the hard speech that he had spoken, and he wept, saying-

"O Kai Khosrau, we desire not that thou go hence."

And the Shah accorded forgiveness unto the old man, because of the great love he bare him; and he lifted him from the ground and kissed him. And when he had done so, he bade him go forth with Rustem. And he commanded that the nobles and all their armies should camp upon the plains. And Zal did as the Shah desired, and the hosts were encamped without the doors.

Now when it was done, Kai Khosrau mounted upon the crystal throne, and he held in his hand the ox-headed mace, and he bare on his head the crown of the Kaianides, and a sash of might was girded round his loins. And on his right hand stood Rustem the Pehliva, and on his left Zal the aged. And he lifted up his voice and spake words of wisdom unto his army; and he said unto them that the sojourn of man was brief upon the earth, and that it became him to remember his end. And he said how he had also bethought him of his death. And he spake, saying-

"I have made me ready to depart, and my testament will I speak before you. I will give richly unto those that have wearied themselves in my service, and of those to whom I owe gratitude I will speak unto God, and implore of Him that He reward them according to their deserts. And I give unto the Iranians my gold, and my armour, and my jewels, and whosoever is great among you to him do I give a province."

Thus for the space of seven days did the Shah sit upon his throne and order his treasurer how he should act. Then on the eighth he called before him Gudarz the wise, and he gave to him instructions. And he bade him be kind unto the poor, and the widowed, and the fatherless, and he entreated him to dry the eye of care. Then he gave unto him much treasure, and rendered unto him thanks for the services that he had done before him. And he gave rich gifts also unto Zal, and Gew, and Rustem, and to all his nobles, according to their degree. And he desired of them that they should ask a boon at his hands, and whatsoever it was he gave it. And he spake, saying-

"May my memory be hateful unto none."

Then he called before him Rustem, and praised the mighty deeds that he had done, and he invoked the blessings of Heaven upon his Pehliva. And after many days, when all these things were accomplished, the Shah was weary, but his task was not yet fulfilled. For there was one among the nobles whose name he had not named. And the others knew thereof, but they ventured not again to admonish Kai Khosrau, for they were amazed at his wisdom and his justice, and they saw that he did that which was right.

Now after some time the Shah opened his mouth and called before him Byzun, and he said-

"Lead forth before me Lohurasp, who is sprung from the seed of Husheng, the Shah."

And Byzun did as Kai Khosrau commanded.

Now when he had brought Lohurasp before the throne, Kai Khosrau descended from its height, and he gave his hand unto Lohurasp and blessed him. Then he put upon his head the crown of the Kaianides and saluted him Shah, and he said-

"May the world be submissive to thy will."

But the nobles, when they saw it, were confounded, and they murmured among themselves that Lohurasp should have the kingdom, and they questioned wherefore they should pay allegiance unto him. Then Kai Khosrau was angered, and he opened his lips, saying-

"Ye speak of that ye know not, and haste hath unbridled your tongues. For I say unto you that which I have done I have done justly, and in the sight of God, and I know that Lohurasp is a man worthy the throne, and that Iran will prosper under his hands. And I desire that ye salute him Shah, and whosoever regardeth not this, my last desire, I hold him a rebel unto God, and judgment shall fall upon him."

Now Zal, when he heard these words, knew that they were just. So he stepped out from among the nobles and came before Lohurasp, and did obeisance unto him as to the Shah. And the army, when they saw it, shouted their homage also, and all the land of Iran was made acquainted with the tidings.

Now when it was done, Kai Khosrau turned him to his nobles, saying-

"I go now to prepare my spirit for death." And when he had so spoken he entered behind the curtains of his house. And he called before him his women, and he told unto them how he should depart. And they wept sore at the tidings. Then Kai Khosrau confided them unto Lohurasp, and he gave to him safe counsels, and he said-

"Be thou the woof and the warp of justice."

And when all was ready, he gat him upon his horse to go forth into the mountains. And Lohurasp would have gone also, but Kai Khosrau suffered it not. But there went with him Zal and Rustem, Gudarz also, and Gustahem and Gew, and Byzun the valiant, and Friburz, the son of Kai Kaous, and Tus the Pehliva. And they followed after him from the plains unto the crest of the mountains. And they ceased not from mourning that which was done of Kai Khosrau, and they said among themselves that never had Shah done like unto him. And they strove to change his purpose. But Kai Khosrau said unto them-

"All is well, wherefore weep ye and trouble my spirit?"

Now when they were gone with him the space of seven days, Kai Khosrau turned unto his nobles and spake, saying-

"Return now upon the road that ye are come, for I am about to enter in upon a path where neither herb nor water can be found. Wherefore I entreat of you that ye spare yourselves this weariness."

Then Zal and Rustem, and Gudarz the aged, listened unto the voice of the Shah, for they knew that he spake that which it became them to obey. But the others refused ear unto his voice, and they followed after him yet another day, but their force was spent in the desert. Now when the evening of that day was come they found a running stream. Then Kai Khosrau said, "Let us halt in this spot." And when they were encamped he spake unto them of the things that were past, and he said unto them that when the sun should have lifted up its face anew they should behold him no longer in their midst, for the time of his departure was at hand. And when the night was fallen he drew aside and bathed his body in the water, and prayed unto God his Maker. Then he came yet again before his nobles, and he awakened them from their slumbers, and he spake unto them words of parting. And he said—

"When the daylight shall be come back, I say unto you, return upon your path, neither linger in this place, though it should rain musk and amber, for out of the mountains a great storm will arise that shall uproot the trees and strip the leaves from off their branches. And there shall come a fall of snow such as Iran hath not seen the like. But if ye do not as I say unto you, verily ye shall never find the path of return."

Now the nobles were troubled when they heard these words, and the slumber that fell upon their eyelids was fined with sorrow. But when the raven of night flew upwards, and the glory of the world flooded the earth with its light, Kai Khosrau was vanished from among them, and they sought out his traces in vain. Now when they beheld that he was gone, they wept in the bitterness of their hearts, and Friburz spake, saying—

"O my friends, listen to the words that I shall speak. I pray of you, let us linger yet a while in this spot, lest peradventure Kai Khosrau should return. And since it is good to be here, I know not wherefore we should haste to depart."

And the nobles listened to his voice, and they encamped them on this spot, and they spake continually of Kai Khosrau, and wept for him, but they forgot the commandment that he had spoken. Now while they slept there arose a mighty wind, and it brought forth clouds, and the sky grew dark, and before the daylight was come back unto the world the earth was wrapped in snow like to a shroud, and none could tell the valleys and the hills asunder. And the nobles, when they awoke, knew not whither they should turn, and they sought after their path in vain. And the snow fell down upon them, and they could not free them of its might, and though they strove against it, it rose above their heads and buried them, and after a little the life departed out of their bodies.

Now after many days, when Zal, and Rustem, and Gudarz beheld that the nobles returned not, they grew afraid and sent forth riders to seek them. And the men searched long, but in the end they found the bodies, and they bare them down into the plains. And sore was the wailing in the army when they beheld it, and a noble tomb was raised above their heads. But Lohurasp, when he learned that Kai Khosrau was vanished, mounted the throne of the Kaianides. And he called before him his people that they should do allegiance unto him. And they did so, and the place of Kai Khosrau knew him no more.

ISFENDIYAR

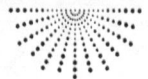

Lohurasp reigned in wisdom upon the crystal throne, and Iran was as wax under his hands. And men were content under his sway, save only Gushtasp, his son, who was rebellious of spirit. And Gushtasp was angered because his father would not abandon unto him the sovereignty. Wherefore, when he beheld that his pleading was vain, he stole away from Iran and sought out the land of Roum, and the city that Silim his forefather had builded. And he did great deeds of prowess in the land, so that the King gave unto him his daughter to wife.

Now Lohurasp, when he learned of the mighty deeds done of his son, strove to win him back unto himself. So he sent forth messengers bearing words of greeting and entreated of Gushtasp that he would return unto the courts of his father. And he sware unto him that if he would listen unto his voice, he would abandon unto him the throne. So Gushtasp listened to the voice of his father, and he returned him unto Iran. And Lohurasp stepped down from off the throne of the Kaianides and gave place unto Gushtasp, his son. And one hundred and twenty years had he reigned in equity, and now that it was done he hid himself within the temples of Balkh, that he might live in the sight of God, and make him ready to meet his end. And Gushtasp, his son, ruled the land worthily, and he administered justice in such wise that sheep could drink at the same brook as the wolves.

. . .

Now when he had sat some while upon the throne, there appeared in the land Zerdusht, the prophet of the Most High. And he came before the Shah and taught him, and he went out in all the land and gave unto the people a new faith. And he purged Iran of the might of Ahriman. He reared throughout the realm a tree of goodly foliage, and men rested beneath its branches. And whosoever ate of the leaves thereof was learned in all that regardeth the life to come, but whosoever ate of the branches was perfect in wisdom and faith. And Zerdusht gave unto men the Zendavesta, and he bade them obey its precepts if they would attain everlasting life.

But tidings concerning Zerdusht were come even unto Arjasp, who sat upon the throne of Afrasiyab, and he said within himself, "This thing is vile." So he refused ear unto the faith, and he sent a writing unto Gushtasp, wherein he bade him return unto the creed of his fathers. And he said—

"If thou turn thee not, make thee ready for combat; for verily I say unto thee, that unless thou cast out Zerdusht, this man of guile, I will overthrow thy kingdom and seat me upon thy throne."

When Gushtasp heard the haughty words that Arjasp had spoken, he marvelled within himself. Then he called before him a scribe, and sent back answer unto Arjasp. And he said that he would deliver up unto the sword whosoever swerved from the paths of Zerdusht, and whosoever would not choose them, him also would he destroy. And he bade him, therefore, get ready to meet Iran in battle. Then when he had sent this writing, Gushtasp got together his hosts and mustered them, and he beheld that they outnumbered the grass upon the fields. And the dust that uprose from their feet darkened the sky, and the neighing of their horses and the clashing of their armour were heard above the music of the cymbals. And the banners pierced the clouds like to trees that grow upon a mountain. And Gushtasp gave the command of this host unto Isfendiyar, his son. And Isfendiyar was a hero of renown, and his tongue was a bright sword, and his heart was bounteous as the ocean, and his hands were like the clouds when rain falls to gladden the earth. And he took the lead of the army, and he led it forth into Turan.

Now when the men of Turan and of Iran met in conflict, a great battle was waged between them, and for the space of twice seven days they did not cease from combat, neither did any of the heroes close their eyes in slumber. And their rage was hot one against another, but in the end the might of Iran overcame, and Arjasp fled before the face of Isfendiyar.

Then Isfendiyar returned him unto Iran, and presented himself before his father, and demanded a blessing at his hands. But Gushtasp said—

"The time is not yet come when thou shouldest mount the throne."

So he sent him forth yet again that he might turn all the lands unto the faith of Zerdusht. And Isfendiyar did as Gushtasp commanded.

Now while he was gone forth there came before the Shah one Gurjam, who was of evil mind and foe unto Isfendiyar. And he spake ill of Isfendiyar unto his father, and he said unto Gushtasp that his son strove to wrest from him the sovereignty. And Gushtasp, when he learned it, was wroth, and he sent forth messengers that they should search out Isfendiyar, and bring him before the Shah in the assembly of the nobles. And when Isfendiyar was come, Gushtasp spake not unto him in greeting, but he turned him to his nobles, and he recounted unto them a parable. Then he told unto them of a son who sought to put to death his father, and he asked of them what punishment this father should mete out unto his child. And the nobles cried with one accord—

"This thing which thou relatest unto us, it is not right, and if there be a son so evil, let him be put into chains and cast in bondage."

Then Gushtasp said, "Let Isfendiyar be put into chains."

And Isfendiyar opened his mouth in vain before his father, for Gushtasp would not listen unto his voice. So they cast him out into a dungeon, and chains of weight were hung upon him, and the daylight came not nigh unto him, neither did joy enter into his heart. And he languished many years, and the heart of the Shah was not softened towards him.

Now when Arjasp learned that the might of Isfendiyar was fettered, and that Gushtasp was given over to pleasures, he gathered together an army to fall into Iran and avenge the defeat that was come upon his hosts. So he fell upon Balkh before any were aware of it and he put to death Lohurasp the Shah and he made captive the daughters of Gushtasp. And Arjasp threw fire into the temples of Zerdusht and did much destruction unto the city and it was some while ere Gushtasp learned that which he had done. But when he had news thereof he was dismayed, and he called together his army and put himself at their head. But the Turanians were mightier than he, and they routed him utterly, and Gushtasp fled before their face. Then the Shah called together his nobles, and consulted with them how he should act in these sore straits. And one among them who was wise above the rest said-

"I counsel thee that thou release Isfendiyar, thy son, and that thou give to him the command, for he alone can deliver the land."

And Gushtasp said, "I will do as thou sayest, and if Isfendiyar shall deliver us from this foe, I will abandon unto him the throne and the crown."

Then he sent messengers unto Isfendiyar that they should unbind his chains. But Isfendiyar, when they came before him, closed ear unto their voice. And he said-

"My father hath kept me in bondage until he hath need of me. Why therefore should I weary me in his cause? I will not go unto his aid."

Then the men reasoned with him, and they told unto him how it had been revealed unto Gushtasp that the words spoken of Gurjam were false, and that he had sworn that he would deliver this man of false words unto the vengeance of his son. But Isfendiyar was deaf yet again to their voice. Then one spake and said-

"Thou knowest not that thy brother is in bondage unto Arjasp. Surely it behoveth thee to deliver him."

When Isfendiyar heard these words he sprang unto his feet, and he commanded that the chains be struck from off his limbs. And because the men were slow, he was angered, and shook himself mightily, so that the fetters fell down at his feet. Then he made haste to go before his father. And peace was made between them on that day, and Gushtasp sware a great oath that he would give the throne unto Isfendiyar when he should return unto him victorious.

So Isfendiyar went out against the foes of Iran, and he mowed them down with the sword and he caused arrows to rain upon them like hail in spring, and the sun was darkened by the flight of the weapons. And he brake the power of Arjasp, King of Turan, and he drove him out from the borders of the realm. And when it was done, and the men of Iran had prevailed over the men of Turan, Isfendiyar presented himself before his father and craved of him the fulfilment of his promises. But Gushtasp, when he beheld that all was well once more, repented him of his resolve, for he desired not to give the throne unto his son. So he pondered in his spirit what he should say in his excuse, and he was ashamed in his soul. But his mouth revealed not the thoughts of his heart, and he spake angrily unto his son, and he said-

"I marvel that thou comest before me with this demand; for while thy sisters languish in the bondage of Arjasp, it beseemeth us not to hold this war as ended, lest men mock us with their tongues. And it hath been told unto me that they are hidden in the brazen fortress, and that Arjasp and all his men are gone in behind its walls. I charge thee, therefore, overthrow the castle and deliver thy sisters who pine. And I swear unto thee, when thou hast done it, I will abandon unto thee the throne, and thy name shall be exalted in the land."

Then Isfendiyar said, "I am the servant of the Shah, let him command his slave what he shall do."

And Gushtasp said, "Go forth."

Then Isfendiyar answered, "I go, but the road is not known unto me."

And Gushtasp said, "A Mubid hath revealed it unto me. Three roads lead unto the fortress of brass, and the one requireth three months to traverse, but it is safe, and much pasture is found on its path. And the second demandeth but two moons, yet it is a desert void of herbs. And the third asketh but seven days, but it is fraught with danger."

Then Isfendiyar said, "No man can die before his time is come. It behoveth a man of valour to choose ever the shortest path."

Now the Mubids and the nobles who knew the dangers that were hidden in this path sought to deter him, but Isfendiyar would not listen to their voice. So he set forth with his army, and they marched until they came to the spot where the roads divided. Now it needed seven stages to reach the fortress of Arjasp, and at each stage there lurked a danger, and never yet had any man overcome them or passed beneath its walls. But Isfendiyar would not give ear to fear, and he set forth upon the road, and each day he overcame a danger, and each danger was greater than the last. And on the first day he slew two raging wolves, and on the second he laid low two evil Deevs that were clothed as lions, and on the third he overcame a dragon whose breath was poison. And on the fourth day Isfendiyar slew a great magician who would have lured him into the paths of evil, and on the fifth he slew a mighty bird whom no man had ever struck down. And weariness was not known of Isfendiyar, neither could he rest from his labours, for there was no camping-place in his road of danger. And on the sixth day he was nigh to have perished with his army in a deep snow that fell upon him through the might of the Deevs. But he prayed unto God in his distress, and by the favour of Heaven the snow vanished from under his feet. Then on the seventh day he came nigh to perish in a flood of waters but Isfendiyar overcame them also, and stood before the castle of Arjasp. Now when he beheld it, his heart failed within him, for he saw that it was compassed by a wall of brass, and the thickness thereof was such that four horsemen could ride thereon abreast. So he sighed and said-

"This place cannot be taken, my pains have been in vain."

Yet he pondered in his spirit how it might be done, and he knew that only wile could avail. Wherefore he disguised himself in the garb of a merchant, and chose forth from his army a hundred camels, and he loaded them with brocades of Roum and much treasure. A hundred and sixty stalwart warriors too did he choose forth, and he seated them in chests, and the chests he bound upon the backs of the camels. And when the caravan was ready he marched at its head unto the doors of the fortress.

Now when he was come thither, he craved permission of Arjasp that he might enter and sell unto them that dwelt therein. And Arjasp granted his request, and gave unto him houseroom, and bade him barter his wares in safety. Then Isfendiyar spread forth his goods and unloaded the treasures of the camels, but the chests wherein were hidden the warriors did he keep from the eyes of men. And after he had sojourned a while in the castle he beheld his sisters, and he saw that they were held as slaves, and his heart went out towards them. So he spake to them tenderly, and they knew his voice, and that help was come out to them, but they held their peace and made no sign. And Isfendiyar, when he saw that he was trusted of Arjasp, came before him and asked of him a boon. And Arjasp said that he would grant it. Then Isfendiyar said-

"Suffer that ere I go hence I may feast thee and thy nobles, that I may show my gratitude."

And it was done as Isfendiyar desired, and he made a great feast and troubled the heads of the nobles with wine. And when their heads were heavy and the moon was seated upon her silver throne, Isfendiyar arose and let forth his warriors from the chests. Then he fell upon the nobles and slew them, and they weltered in their blood. And with his own hand Isfendiyar struck down Arjasp, and he hung up his sons upon high gallows. Then he made signals unto his army that they should come forth to aid him, for there were yet many men hidden in the fort, and Isfendiyar had but a handful wherewith to withstand them. And they did as he desired, and there was a great slaughter within the brazen fort, but Isfendiyar bare off the victory. Then he took with him his sisters and much booty, and made haste to return unto Iran, and come into the presence of Gushtasp, his father. And the Shah rejoiced in his sight, and he made a great feast, and gave gifts richly unto all his servants. And the mouths of men overflowed with the doughty deeds done of Isfendiyar, and there was gladness throughout the land.

RUSTEM AND ISFENDIYAR

When a little while had been passed in feasting, Isfendiyar came before Gushtasp, his father, and demanded the fulfilment of the promises that he had made unto him. And he recalled unto Gushtasp how he had mistrusted him and thrown him into chains. And he spake of the doughty deeds that he had done at his behest, and he craved him to remember that Isfendiyar was his son. And Gushtasp knew that that which was spoken was right, but he desired not to abandon the throne. Wherefore he communed within him what he should do. Then he opened his mouth and spake, saying-

"Verily thou hast done that which thou sayest, and there is none who is thine equal in this world, save only Rustem, the son of Zal. And he acknowledgeth none his like. Now because he is grown proud in his spirit, and hath rendered no homage unto me, neither is come forth to aid me against Arjasp, I desire that thou go forth unto Zaboulistan, and that thou lead out the Pehliva, and bring him bound before me, that he may know that I am the Shah, and that he must do my behests. And when thou shalt have done it, I swear unto thee by Him from whom cometh all strength, and who hath kindled the sun and the stars unto light, that I will step down from the throne, neither withhold it from thee any longer."

Then Isfendiyar said, "O King, I would entreat of thee that thou ponder the words that thou hast spoken. For thine ancestors held this old man, ripe in wisdom, in much honour, and he was a staff unto their throne. Now since thou calledst him not forth, it was not fitting he should aid thee against Turan."

But Gushtasp would not listen unto the words of Isfendiyar, and he said-

"If thou lead not Rustem bound before me, I will not grant unto thee the throne."

Then Isfendiyar said, "Thou sendest me forth in guile on this emprise, for verily no man hath stood against the might of Rustem, wherefore I perceive that thou desirest not to abandon unto me the throne. I say unto thee, therefore, that I desire it no longer; but since I am thy slave, it beseemeth me to obey thy behests. I go forth therefore, and if peradventure I fall before Rustem, thou wilt answer unto God for my blood."

And when he had so spoken, Isfendiyar went out of the presence of the Shah, and he was exceeding sorrowful. Then he gathered together an army, and he set forth upon the road that leadeth to Seistan.

Now when they were gone but a little way, the camel that walked at their head laid him down in the dust. And the drivers struck him, but he would not rise from the earth. Then Isfendiyar said, "The omen is evil." But he commanded the driver that he cut off the head, that the evil might fall upon the beast and tarnish not the glory of the Shah. And it was done as Isfendiyar desired, but he could not rid him of his sadness, and he pondered in his spirit this sign.

Now when they were come unto the land of Zaboulistan, Isfendiyar spake, saying-

"I will send an envoy unto Rustem, a man prudent and wise. And I will entreat of the Pehliva that he come before me with gladness, for I desire no evil unto him, and I come forth only at the behest of the Shah."

Then he called before him Bahman, his son, and he spake long unto him, and he charged him with a message unto Rustem. And he bade him speak unto the son of Zal how Gushtasp was angered because he sought not his courts, wherefore he deemed that Rustem was grown proud in his spirit, and would uplift himself above his Shah. And he said-

"The King hath sent me out that I lead thee before him. I pray thee, therefore, come unto me, and I swear unto thee that no harm shall befall thee at his hands. For when I shall have led thee before him, I will demand as my guerdon that he suffer thee to go unharmed."

So Bahman laid up these words in his spirit, and he went with all speed unto the courts of Rustem. Now, he found therein none but Zal, for

Rustem was gone forth with his warriors to chase the wild ass. And Zal came forth with courtesy to greet Bahman, and he asked of him his desires, and he invited him unto a feast. But Bahman said-

"My mission doth admit of no delay. Isfendiyar hath bidden me not tarry by the road. Tell me, therefore, where I may find thy son."

Then Zal showed unto him the way.

Now when Bahman was come unto the spot, he beheld a man like unto a mountain, who was roasting a wild ass for his supper. And in his hand was a wine-cup, and about him stood brave knights. Then Bahman said within himself, "Surely this is Rustem," and he watched him from where he was hid, and he beheld that Rustem devoured the whole of a wild ass for his meal, and he was amazed at the might and majesty of this man. Then he thought within him, "Peradventure if I cast down a rock upon him, I may slay him, for surely even Isfendiyar, my father, shall not withstand his strength." So he loosened a rock from the mountain-side, and set it rolling unto the spot where Rustem was encamped. Now Zevarah heard the sound thereof, and beheld the rock, and he said unto Rustem-

"Behold a rock that springeth forth from the mountain-side."

But Rustem smiled, and arose not from his seat; and when the rock was upon him, he lifted up his foot and threw it far unto the other side. Then Bahman was amazed, but he was affrighted also, and he dared not come forth at once. Yet when he was come before the Pehliva, Rustem greeted him kindly, and would have entertained him. And Bahman suffered it, and he marvelled yet again when he beheld that which was eaten of Rustem, and he was afraid. Then he delivered unto him the message of Isfendiyar, his father. And Rustem listened unto it, and when it was ended he spake, saying-

"Bear greeting unto the hero of renown, and say unto him that I have longed to look upon his face, and that I rejoice that he is come forth unto Zaboulistan. But his demand is the device of Deevs, and I would counsel him that he depart not from the paths of wisdom. And I say unto him, Count not upon thy strength, for it is given to no man to shut up the winds within a cage, neither can any man stand against my might. And I have ever done that which was right before the Shahs, thy fathers, and no man hath beheld Rustem in chains. Therefore thy demand is foolish, and I bid thee abandon it, and honour my house with thy presence. And when we shall have feasted, I will go forth with thee before Gushtasp, thy father, and the reins of my horse shall be tied unto thine throughout the journey.

FERDOWSI

And when I shall be come before the Shah, and shall have taken counsel with him, I know that his anger against me, which is unjust, will vanish like unto smoke."

Then Rustem sent a messenger unto Rudabeh, his mother, to make ready a great feast in his courts. And Bahman sped back unto his father.

Now Isfendiyar, when he had listened unto the words sent by Rustem, mounted his steed, and rode forth to meet him. And Rustem was come forth also, and they met beside the stream. Then Rakush swam across its breadth, and the hero of the world stood before Isfendiyar, and he greeted him, and did homage unto the son of his Shah. And Rustem rejoiced in the sight of Isfendiyar, and he deemed that he beheld in him the face of Saiawush. And he said unto him-

"O young man, let us commune together concerning the things that divide us."

And Isfendiyar assented unto the desires of Rustem, and he pressed him unto his bosom, and his eyes could not cease from gazing upon his strength. Then Rustem said-

"O hero, I have a prayer to make before thee; I crave that thou enter into my house as my guest."

And Isfendiyar said, "I cannot listen unto thy demand, for the Shah commanded me neither to rest nor tarry until I should have brought thee unto him in chains. But I entreat of thee that thou consider that the chains of the King of kings do not dishonour, and that thou listen willingly unto the desires of the Shah, for I would not lift my hand in anger against thee, and I am grieved that it hath been given unto me to do this thing. But it behoveth me to fulfil the commandments of my father."

Thus spake Isfendiyar in the unquietude of his spirit, for he knew that what was demanded of Rustem was not fitting or right. And Rustem replied, saying-

"It would be counted shame unto me if thou shouldst refuse to enter into my house. I pray thee, therefore, yet again that thou accede to my desires, and when it shall be done I will do that which thou desirest, save only that I cannot submit unto the chains. For no man hath beheld me fettered, neither shall any do so while I draw my breath. I have spoken, and that which I have said, it is true."

And Isfendiyar said, "I may not feast with thee, and if thou listen not to my voice, I must fall upon thee in enmity. But to-day let there be a truce between us, and drink thou with me in my tents."

And Rustem said, "I will do so gladly, suffer only that I go forth and change my robes, for I am clad for the chase. And when thy meal shall be ready, send forth a messenger that he may lead me thither."

And when he had so spoken, Rustem leaped upon Rakush and returned unto his courts. Now when he had arrayed himself for the banquet, he awaited the envoy that Isfendiyar should send. But Isfendiyar was full of cares, and he said unto Bashuntan, his brother-

"We have regarded this affair too lightly, for it is full of danger. Wherefore I have no place in the house of Rustem, neither should he enter into mine, for the sword must decide our strife. For which cause I shall not bid him unto my feast."

Then Bashuntan answered and said, "A Deev hath led thee astray, O my brother, for it is not fitting that men like unto Rustem and Isfendiyar should meet in enmity. Wherefore I counsel thee that thou listen not unto our father, for his desires are evil, and he seeketh but to ensnare thee. Yet thou art wiser than he; abandon, therefore, this device of evil."

But Isfendiyar answered and said, "If I obey not the words of the King, my father, it will be a reproach unto me in this world, and I shall have to render account for it in the next before God, my Maker. And I would not lose both worlds because of Rustem."

Then Bashuntan said, "I have given unto thee counsel according to my wisdom, it resteth with thee to do as thou desirest."

Then Isfendiyar bade the cooks serve before him the banquet, but he sent not forth to call Rustem unto the feast.

Now Rustem, when he had waited a long while and beheld that Isfendiyar sent not to call him forth, was angered, and he said-

"Is this the courtesy of a King?"

And he sprang upon Rakush and rode unto the tents of the prince that he might question him wherefore he regarded Rustem thus lightly. Now the warriors of Iran, when they beheld the Pehliva, murmured among themselves against Gushtasp, and they spake as with the voice of one man, that surely the Shah was bereft of reason or he would not thus send Isfendiyar unto death. And they said-

"Gushtasp loveth yet more his treasures and his throne as age creepeth upon him, and this is but a device to preserve them unto himself."

Now Rustem, when he had presented himself before Isfendiyar, spake and said-

"O young man, it would seem unto me that thou didst not deem thy guest worthy a messenger. Yet I say unto thee that it is I who have made the throne of Iran to shine out unto all the world, and I have ever been the Pehliva of its Shahs, and have endured much pain and toil for their sakes. And I have not passed a day save in doing that which is right, and I have purged the land of its enemies. I am the protector of the Kings of Iran, and the mainstay of the good in all places of the earth. Wherefore it behoveth thee not to treat me thus disdainfully."

Then Isfendiyar said, "O Rustem, be not angered against me, but listen wherefore I sent not forth to call thee. For the day was hot and the road long, and I bethought me that fatigue would come upon thee from this course. Therefore I had resolved to visit thee in the morning. But since thou hast taken upon thee this fatigue, I pray of thee that thou rest within my tents, and that we empty the wine-cup together."

Then he made a place for him at his left hand.

But Rustem said, "This is not my place. It is not fitting that I should sit upon thy left, for my seat hath ever been at the right hand of the Shah."

Then Isfendiyar bade a chair of gold be brought, and he caused it to be placed upon his right, and he bade Rustem be seated upon it. And Rustem sat him down, but he was angered in his spirit because of the dishonour that Isfendiyar had shown unto him.

Now when they had drunk together awhile, Isfendiyar lifted up his voice and said-

"O Rustem, it hath been told unto me that thine origin is evil, for thou art sprung from a Deev whom Saum cast forth from his house. And he was reared of a vile bird, and his nourishment was garbage."

Then Rustem said, "Why speakest thou words that do hurt?" And he told unto him of his father, and Saum, and Neriman who was of the race of Husheng the Shah. And he vaunted the great deeds done of his house, and he hid not that which he had accomplished himself, and he said-

"Six hundred years have passed since I came forth from the loins of Zal, and for that space I have been the Pehliva of the world, and have feared neither that which was manifest, nor that which was hid. And I speak these things that thou mayest know. Thou art the King, and they that carry high their heads are thy subjects, but thou art new unto the world, wherefore thou knowest not the things that are come to pass."

When Isfendiyar had listened unto the words of Rustem, he smiled and spake, saying-

"I have given ear unto thy voice, give ear now also unto the words that I shall speak."

Then he vaunted him of his forefathers, and he recounted unto Rustem how that he had overcome the Turks, and how Gushtasp had cast him into chains, and he told him of the seven stations, and that he had converted the world unto the faith of Zerdusht. And he said-

"We have spoken enough concerning ourselves, let us drink until we be weary."

But Rustem said, "Not so, for thou hast not heard all the deeds that I have done, for they are many, and the ear sufficeth not to hear them, nor the mouth to tell. For if thou knewest them, thou wouldest not exalt thyself above me, or think to cast me into chains."

And he recounted to him yet again of his deeds of might.

But Isfendiyar said, "I entreat of thee that thou apply thyself unto the wine-cup, for verily thou shalt fall tomorrow in the fight, and the days of thy feasting shall be ended."

And Rustem answered, "Boast not thus rashly, thou shalt yet repent thee of thy words. But to-morrow will we meet in conflict since thou desirest it, and when I shall have lifted thee from off thy saddle, I will bear thee unto my house and spread a feast before thee, and pour upon thee my treasures. And when it shall be done, I will return with thee unto the courts of the Shah, thy father, and uproot from his spirit this plant of evil. And when thou shalt be mounted into his seat, I will serve thee with gladness as thy Pehliva."

But Isfendiyar said, "Thy words are idle, and we waste but our breath in talk of combat. Let us therefore apply us to the banquet."

And they did so, and ate and drank until the night was far spent, and all men were amazed at the hunger of Rustem.

Now when it was time for him to depart, he prayed Isfendiyar yet again that he would be his guest, and yet again Isfendiyar refused it to him, and he said-

"Suffer that I put chains about thee, and lead thee forth into Iran, that Gushtasp be satisfied. But if thou wilt not do this thing, I must attack thee with the spear."

Now Rustem, when he heard these words, was sorrowful in his soul. And he thought within him-

"If I suffer these chains it is a stain that cannot be wiped out, and I cannot outlive my dishonour, for men will mock at Rustem, who permitted

a boy to lead him bound. Yet if I slay this youth, I do evil, for he is son unto the Shah, and my glory will be tarnished, for men will say I lifted my hand against a Kaianide. And there can arise no good out of this combat. Wherefore I will strive yet again to win him unto wisdom."

So he lifted up his voice and said, "I pray thee listen not to the counsel of Deevs, and shut thy lips concerning these chains. For it seemeth unto me that Gushtasp desireth evil against thee, that he sendeth thee forth against Rustem, the unvanquished in fight. Dishonour, therefore, not the champion of thy fathers, but feast within my gates, and let us ride forth in friendship unto Iran."

But Isfendiyar said, "I charge thee, old man, that thou waste not words concerning this thing, for I will not disobey the behests of my father. Prepare, therefore, for combat; for to-morrow I will make the world dark unto thine eyes."

Then Rustem said, "O foolish youth! when I grasp my mace, the head of my foe is lost. Prepare thee rather for thine end."

And when he had so spoken, he rode forth from out the tents of Isfendiyar, and he was exceeding sorrowful. But Isfendiyar smiled after him and said-

"The mother that hath borne thee shall weep. I will cast thee down from Rakush, I will lead thee bound into Iran."

But once again did Bashuntan come before Isfendiyar, and he pleaded with him for Rustem, and he bade him remember the great deeds that he had done unto Iran, and he desired him not to lift his hand against the Pehliva.

But Isfendiyar said-

"He is a thorn in my rose-garden, and through him alone can I attain unto the throne. Strive not, therefore, to hinder me, for thy pains will be in vain. For Zerdusht hath spoken that whosoever honoureth not the behests of his king, he shall surely suffer the pains of hell. And my father hath told unto me to do this thing, and though I grieve to do hurt unto Rustem, the desires of the Shah must be accomplished."

Then Bashuntan sighed and said, "Alas! a Deev hath taken possession of thy spirit.'"

Now Rustem, when he was come into his house, commanded that his leopard-skin should be brought before him, and his helmet of Roum, his spear of Ind also, and the war garb of Rakush. And when he saw them, he said-

"O my raiment of battle, ye have rested a long time from strife, yet now must I take you forth again to combat, and it is for the hardest fight that ye have fought. For I must lift my hand against the son of my master, or suffer that he disgrace me in the sight of men."

And Rustem was sad, and all night he spake unto Zal of his end, and what he should do if he fell in battle.

Then when the morning was come he girded on his armour, but he resolved in his spirit that he would strive again with Isfendiyar in words. So he rode forth unto the tents of the young King; and when he was come nigh unto them he shouted with a loud voice. And he said-

"O Isfendiyar, hero of great renown, the man with whom thou wouldst wrestle is come forth; make thee ready, therefore, to meet him."

Then Isfendiyar came out from his tents, and he was armed for battle. Now when they were met, Rustem opened his mouth and prayed him yet again that he would stay his hand from this impiety. And he said-

"If thy soul thirsteth after blood and the tumult of battle, suffer that our hosts meet in combat, that thy desires may be satisfied."

But Isfendiyar said, "Thy talk is folly; thou art armed for the conflict, let not the hours be lost."

Then Rustem sighed and made him ready for combat. And he assailed Isfendiyar with his lance, but with a nimble stroke Isfendiyar resisted his attack. And they fought with their lances until they were bent, and when that was done they betook them unto swords. And ever the heroes parried the strokes that were dealt. And when their swords were broken they seized upon maces, but either hero warded off the blows. And they fought until that their shields were rent and their helmets dinted with the blows, and their armour was pierced in many places. And it was a bitter fight. But the end thereof came not, and they were weary, and neither had gained the upper hand. So they rested them awhile from combat. But when they were rested they fell again one on another, and they fought with arrows and bows. And the arrows of Isfendiyar whizzed through the air and fastened into the body of Rustem and of Rakush his steed; and twice thirty ar-rows did Isfendiyar thus send forth, until that Rakush was like to perish from his wounds. And Rustem also was covered with gore, and no man before this one had ever done harm unto his body. But the arrows of Rustem had done no ill unto Isfendiyar, because Zerdusht had charmed his body against all dangers, so that it was like unto brass.

Now Isfendiyar, when he beheld that Rustem staggered in his seat, called out unto him to surrender himself into his hands and suffer chains to be put about his body. But Rustem said-

"Not so, I will meet thee again in the morning," and he turned and swam across the stream, so that Isfendiyar was amazed, for he knew that the steed and rider had been sore wounded. And he exulted in his heart, and he reviled Rustem with his lips, but in his soul he was filled with wonder at the Pehliva, and his heart went out to him.

Now when Zal and Rudabeh beheld the Pehliva and that he was wounded, they rent the air with their cries, for never yet was he returned unto them vanquished, neither had any man done hurt unto the elephant-limbed. And they wailed sore in their distress, and Rustem joined his lamentations unto theirs. Then they pondered how they should act, and Zal bethought him of the Simurgh that had been his nurse, and the feather that she had given him from her breast that he might call upon her in the day of his need. So he brought it and cast it into the fire as she had commanded, and straightway a sound of rushing wings filled the air and the sky was darkened, and the bird of God stood before Zal. And she spake and said unto him-

"O my son, what is come about that thou callest upon thy nurse that shielded thee?"

Then Zal told her all, and how Rustem was nigh to die of his wounds, and how Rakush too was sick unto death. Then the Simurgh said-

"Bring me before them."

And when she had seen them, she passed her wings over their hurts and forthwith they were whole. Then she spake unto Rustem and questioned him wherefore he sought to combat the son of the Shah, and Rustem told her. Then she said-

"Seek yet again to turn Isfendiyar unto thyself; yet if he listen not unto thy voice, I will reveal unto thee the secrets of Fate. For it is written that whosoever sheddeth the blood of Isfendiyar, he also shall perish; and while he liveth he shall not know joy, and in the life to come he shall suffer pains. But if this fate dismay thee not, go forth with me and I will teach thee this night how thou shalt close the mouth of thine enemy."

Then the Simurgh showed unto Rustem the way he should follow, and Rustem rode after her, and they halted not until they were come unto the sea-coast. And the Simurgh led him into a garden wherein grew a tamarisk, tall and strong, and the roots thereof were in the ground, but the branches pierced even unto the sky. Then the bird of God bade Rustem break from the tree a branch that was long and slender, and fashion it into an arrow, and she said-

"Only through his eyes can Isfendiyar be wounded. If, therefore, thou wouldst slay him, direct this arrow unto his forehead, and verily it shall not miss its aim."

Then she exhorted him once more that he bring this matter to a good end, and she led him on the path of return unto Zaboulistan, and when he was come there she blessed him and departed from out his sight.

Now when the morning was come, Rustem came unto the camp of Isfendiyar, and he was mounted upon Rakush his steed. And Isfendiyar slumbered, for he thought that of a surety Rustem was perished of his wounds. Then Rustem lifted up his voice, and cried-

"O man, eager to fight, wherefore slumberest thou when Rustem standeth before thee?"

Now Isfendiyar, when he heard his voice and saw that it was truly Rustem that stood before him, was amazed, and he said unto his nobles-

"This is the deed of Zal the sorcerer."

But unto Rustem he cried, "Make ready for combat; for this day thou shalt not escape my might. May thy name perish from off the earth."

Then Rustem spake, saying-

"I am not come forth to battle, but to treaty. Turn aside thine heart from evil, and root out this enmity. Make not, I pray thee, thy soul to be a dwelling-place for Deevs. And suffer that I recall unto thee the deeds I have done for Iran, and the list thereof is long. And feast this day within my house, and let us ride forth together unto the courts of the Shah, that I may make my peace with Gushtasp thy father."

But Isfendiyar was angered at these words, and he said-

"Wilt thou never cease from speaking? Thou exhortest me to quit the paths of God, for I do wrong when I obey not the voice of my father. Choose, therefore, betwixt chains and the combat."

When Isfendiyar had so spoken, Rustem knew that his speech was of no avail. So he sighed and made ready for combat; and he took forth the arrow that was given to him of the Simurgh, and he let it fly towards his enemy. And it pierced the eye of the young King, and he fell upon the mane of his steed, and his blood reddened the field of battle. Then Rustem said unto him-

"The bitter harvest thou hast sown hath borne fruit."

Now Isfendiyar swooned in his agony and fell upon the ground. And there came out to him his brother and Bahman, his son; and they wailed when they beheld how his plight was evil. But when he was come unto himself he called after Rustem, and the Pehliva got him down from Rakush and came unto where he lay, and knelt beside him. And Isfendiyar said-

"My life ebbeth unto the close, wherefore I would confide unto thee my wishes. And thou shalt behold how greatly I honour thee, for it is not thou that hast brought me unto death, but Gushtasp, my father; and verily the curse of the prophet shall fall upon his head, for thou wert but the instrument of Fate. And listen now unto the words that I shall speak, for it is not given unto me to say many- I desire that thou take unto thyself Bahman, my son, and that thou rear him in the land of Zaboulistan, and that thou teach him the arts of war and of the banquet. And when the hour of Gushtasp shall be come, I charge thee that thou put Bahman in his place, and aid him with thy counsels that he may be upright in the sight of men."

And Rustem sware unto him that it should be done at his desire. Then Isfendiyar made him ready to depart, and he spake words of comfort unto his son, and he sent greetings unto his mother and to his wives that were in Iran. And he made them say unto his father that hence-forward he need not fear him beside the throne; and he cursed the name of Gushtasp, and he said that the Shah had done that which was worthy of his black soul. And he bade them speak before the throne and say-

"We shall meet again before the judge, and we shall speak, and listen to His decree."

Then he said unto Rustem, "Thou hast done this deed by the arts of magic."

And Rustem said, "It is true, for thou wouldst not listen unto my voice, and I could not bend my spirit unto chains."

And Isfendiyar said, "I am not angered against thee; thou hast done that thou couldst not alter, for it was written in the stars, and surely that which is written in the stars is accomplished."

Then Rustem said, "God is my witness that I strove to turn thee from thy resolve."

And Isfendiyar said, "It is known unto me." And when he had thus spoken he sighed, and the sun of that King was set. And there was great lamentation for him in the army, and Rustem, too, bewailed the hero that was fallen, and he prayed God for his soul. And he said-

"May thine enemies reap that which they have sown."

Then Rustem made ready for Isfendiyar a coffin of iron, and he caused

it to be lined with silken stuffs, and he laid therein the body of the young King. And it was placed upon the back of a dromedary and forty others followed in its wake, and all the army of Isfendiyar came after them, clad in robes of mourning. And Bashuntan marched at the head of the train, and he led the horse of Isfendiyar, and its saddle was reversed, and its mane and its tail were shorn. And from its sides hung the armour of the young King. And weeping resounded through the ranks, and with sorrow did the army return unto Iran.

But Rustem remained in Zaboulistan, and he kept beside him Bahman, the son of Isfendiyar.

Now when Gushtasp learned the tidings of woe, he was bowed down to the earth with sorrow, and remorse came upon him and he strewed dust upon his head and he humbled himself before God. And men came before him and reproached him with that which he had done unto Isfendiyar, and he knew not how he should answer them. And Bashuntan came in and saluted him not, but upbraided him with his vile deeds. And he said-

"Neither the Simurgh, nor Rustem, nor Zal have made an end of Isfendiyar, but only thou, for thou alone hast caused him to perish."

And for the space of one year men ceased not to lament for Isfendiyar, and for many years were tears shed for that arrow. And men cried continually, "The glory of Iran hath been laid low, and it is at the hands of her Shah that it hath been done."

But Bahman grew up in the courts of Rustem, and the Pehliva guarded him like to a son.

THE DEATH OF RUSTEM

*H*ow shall a man escape from that which is written; How shall he flee from his destiny?

There stood a slave in the house of Zal, and she was fair to see, so that the heart of the aged man went out to her. And there was born to her a son, goodly of mien, like unto Saum the hero, and Zal named him Shugdad. Then he consulted the Mubids concerning him, and they searched the stars for his destiny, and they read therein that he would do much evil in the house of his father, and lay low the race of Saum, the son of Neriman. Now Zal, when he heard this, was sore afflicted, and he prayed unto God that He would avert this fate from his head. And he reared him tenderly, and when he was come unto man's estate he sent him forth into Cabul. And the King of Cabul rejoiced in the sight of the hero, and he kept him beside him and gave unto him his daughter to wife.

Now the King of Cabul paid tribute unto Rustem, and it was a grievance to him to do so, and since he had taken Shugdad as his son he deemed that it was fitting that he should be relieved of this burden. And he spake thereof unto Shugdad, and said how Rustem ceased not to demand it.

And Shugdad said, "This man is foolish. What mattereth it whether he be my brother or a stranger, let us consider how we may ensnare him."

So Shugdad and the King of Cabul passed a night pondering how they should bring Rustem unto destruction. And Shugdad said-

"Call together thy nobles unto a feast, and when thou shalt have drunk wine, speak insults unto me, and I will be angered and ride forth unto Zaboulistan and make plaint of thee before Rustem, and assuredly he will come forth to avenge me. And while I am gone, cause a deep pit to be dug on the road that Rustem must pass, a pit that will swallow him and Rakush his steed, and line the sides thereof with sharp spears, and swords, and lances. And when it is done, cover it with earth and let no man know thereof, nay, whisper it not even unto the moon."

And the King said, "Thy device is good," and he made a great feast and called thereto his warriors, and he spake words of insult unto Shugdad, and he reproached him, and said that he was not of the race of Saum, but son unto a slave. And he said that Rudabeh would refuse to him the name of brother unto Rustem. And he spake lightly also of Rustem. Then Shugdad uprose as though he were angered, and vowed that he would ride unto Zaboulistan and call forth Rustem to avenge the words that the King had spoken.

Now when Shugdad was come unto the courts of Zal, and had told unto Rustem the words that the King of Cabul had spoken, he was beside himself with anger, and he said-

"I will slake my vengeance for this speech."

Then he chose out an army and made ready to go into Cabul. But Shugdad said-

"Wherefore dost thou take forth so large an army? Surely Cabul shall be obedient when it but looketh upon thy face. Yet this army will cause the King to think that thou holdest him an enemy worthy of regard."

Then Rustem said, "That which thou sayest, it is wise," and he disbanded the army, and took with him but few men and rode with them to Cabul.

In the mean season the King of Cabul had done that which Shugdad had counselled, and the pits that had been dug were concealed with cunning. Now when Rustem came nigh to the city, Shugdad sent a messenger before him unto the King of Cabul, saying-

"Rustem cometh against thee, it behoveth thee to ask pardon for thy words."

And the King came forth, and his tongue was filled with honey, but his heart was filled with poison. And he bowed himself in the dust before Rustem, and he asked his forgiveness for the words that he had spoken, and he said-

"Consider not the words of thy servant that he did speak when his head was troubled with wine."

FERDOWSI

And Rustem forgave the King, and consented to be his guest. Then a great banquet was made, and while they feasted the King told unto Rustem how his forests were filled with wild asses and with rams, and he invited him to hunt therein ere he should return unto Zaboulistan. And these words were joy unto the ears of Rustem, and he consented unto the desires of the King. So the next day the King made ready a great hunt, and he led it unto the spot where the pits were hidden. And Shugdad ran beside the horse of Rustem, and showed unto him the path. But Rakush, when he smelt the soil that had been newly turned, reared him in air, and refused to go onwards. Then Rustem commanded him to go forward, but Rakush would not listen to his voice. And Rustem was angry when he beheld that Rakush was afraid. But Rakush sprang back yet again. Then Rustem took a whip and struck him, and before this day he had never raised his hand against his steed. So Rakush was grieved in his soul, and he did that which Rustem desired, and he sprang forward and fell into the pit. And the sharp spears entered his body and tore it, and they pierced also the flesh of Rustem, and steed and rider were impaled upon the irons that had been hidden by the King. But Rustem put forth all his strength, and raised himself. Yet when he had done it he was weary, and fell down beside the pit. And he swooned in his agony.

Now when Rustem was come unto himself, he saw Shugdad, and he beheld in his face the joy felt of this evil man at this adventure. Then he knew that it was his brother that was his foe. So he said unto him-

"It is thou who hast done this deed."

And Shugdad said, "Thou hast caused many to perish by the sword; it is meet that thou shouldst perish by it thyself."

Now while they yet spake, the King of Cabul came nigh unto the spot. And when he beheld Rustem, that weltered in his blood, he feigned a great sorrow, and he cried-

"O hero of renown, what thing hath befallen thee?

I will send forth my physicians, that they heal thee."

And Rustem said, "O man of wile, the time of physicians is gone by, and there is none that can heal me, save only death, that cometh to all men in their turn."

Then he said unto Shugdad, "Give unto me my bow, and place before me two arrows, and refuse not unto me this last request. For I would have them beside me lest a lion go by ere I am dead, and devour me for his prey."

And Shugdad gave unto Rustem his bow; but when he had done so he was afraid, and he ran unto a plane tree that stood near by. And the tree was old and hollow, and Shugdad hid himself in its trunk. But Rustem beheld him where he was hid, though the dimness of death was come over his eyes. So he raised him from the ground in his agony, and he took his bow and bent it with force, and he shot an arrow and fixed Shugdad unto the tree wherein he was hid. And the aim was just, and pierced even unto the heart of this evil man, so that he died. And Rustem, when he saw it, smiled, and said-

"Thanks be unto God, the Merciful, whom all my days I have sought to serve, that He hath granted unto me to avenge myself upon this wretch while the life is yet in me, and ere two nights have passed over this vengeance."

But when he had so spoken the breath went out of him, and the hero who had borne high his head was vanished from this world.

Now a warrior of the train of Rustem rode with all speed unto Zaboulistan, and told unto Zal the tidings of sorrow. And Zal was dismayed thereat, and his grief was boundless, and he cried continually after his son, and he heaped curses upon Shugdad, that had uprooted this royal tree. And he said-

"Wherefore have I been suffered to see this day? Wherefore have I not died before Rustem, my son? Wherefore am I left alone to mourn his memory?"

Now while he lamented thus, Feramorz, the son of Rustem, gathered together an army to avenge his father. And he went into Cabul, and he laid low all the men he found therein, and he slew the King and all his house, and he changed the land into a desert. And when he had done so, he sought out the body of Rustem, and of Rakush his steed, and he did unto them all honour, and they were borne in sorrow unto Zaboulistan. And Zal caused a noble tomb to be built for Rustem, his son, and he laid him therein, and there was placed beside him also Rakush, the steed that had served him unto the end.

And the wailing throughout the land because of the death of Rustem was such as the world hath not known the like. And Zal was crushed with sorrow, and Rudabeh was distraught with grief. And for many moons were no sounds save those of wailing heard in the courts of Seistan. And Rudabeh refused to take comfort, and she cried without ceasing-

"He is gone before us, but we shall follow. Let us rest our hopes in God."

And she gave unto the poor of her treasures, and daily she prayed unto Ormuzd, saying-

"O Thou who reignest above, to whom alone pertaineth honour and glory, purify the soul of Rustem from all sin, and grant that he rejoice in the fruits that he hath sown on earth, and give him a place beside Thee."

And now may the blessing of God rest upon all men. I have told unto them the Epic of Kings, and the Epic of Kings is come to a close, and the tale of their deeds is ended.

THE END

Copyright © 2020 by ALICIA EDITIONS
Credits: CANVA, Wikimedia Commons
Mohammad Ebrahim- Fritware tile with polychrome underglaze colours -
London, British Museum.
Shahnameh, Iran, XVIe
All rights reserved.
No part of this book may be reproduced in any form or by any electronic or mechanical means, including information storage and retrieval systems, without written permission from the author, except for the use of brief quotations in a book review.

www.ingramcontent.com/pod-product-compliance
Lightning Source LLC
LaVergne TN
LVHW092011090526
838202LV00002B/90